PRAISE FO

"Rich world-building and a great quest, with great characters. Kids will love it!"
—KEVIN SYLVESTER, author of *Apartment 713*, *The Almost Epic Squad*, and the MiNRS series

"Nguyễn whisks the reader away on a fantastical adventure both thrilling and smart. Immigration, friendship, loyalty, magic—what's not to love?"
—HIROMI GOTO, critically acclaimed author of *Chorus of Mushrooms*, *Half World*, and *Shadow Life*

"Nguyễn's debut, *No Place Like Home*, is full of action and adventure in a vividly imaginative setting, but the story's true heart comes from the protagonist's search for something bigger—the longing to find her place in the world. . . . Lan's wish for her life to be something else, something better, is a yearning so palpably drawn, and as a child of immigrants, I felt myself relating to *No Place Like Home* on so many levels. An adventure story as comforting as a warm bowl of phở."
—ANGELA AHN, author of *Double O Stephen and the Ghostly Realm*, *Peter Lee's Notes from the Field*, and *Krista Kim-Bap*

"Told with heart, authenticity, and just the right touch of humour, Lan's struggles ring true to anyone who's had to make the unfamiliar, familiar. A cross between *The NeverEnding Story* and *The Wizard of Oz*, overlaid with a Vietnamese viewpoint, *No Place Like Home* is the perfect read for lovers of fantasy, 'magic, adventure, and for all of those who've yearned to belong, and for a place to call home."
—NATASHA DEEN, author of *The Signs and Wonders of Tuna Rashad*

"A fresh, contemporary take on a classic fantasy adventure."
—Cary Fagan, author of *Water, Water*; *King Mouse*;
and the award-winning *Mr. Zinger's Hat*

"*No Place Like Home* is a powerful reminder that fiction sparks young readers' imaginations, challenges their perspectives, and allows them to be heroes of their own stories. An absolute must-read for middle grade readers!"
—Ann Y. K. Choi, acclaimed author of *Kay's Lucky Coin Variety*

"Linh S. Nguyễn's *No Place Like Home* pulls readers into its pages and straight into worlds filled with magic, risk, and courage. This quest is not just a search for or a return to home, but a journey to understanding all of its real and imagined forms. Nguyễn conjures an elemental magic in this brilliant debut, each page so full of hope, so full of heart."
—Gillian Sze, author of *You Are My Favorite Color* and *My Love for You Is Always*

No Place Like Home

Operation No-More-Desert, etc.

No Place Like Home

Linh S. Nguyễn

HarperCollins Publishers Ltd

No Place Like Home
Copyright © 2023 by Linh San Nguyễn.
All rights reserved.

Published by HarperCollins Publishers Ltd

First edition

No part of this book may be used or reproduced in any manner whatsoever without the prior written permission of the publisher, except in the case of brief quotations embodied in reviews.

HarperCollins books may be purchased for educational, business or sales promotional use through our Special Markets Department.

HarperCollins Publishers Ltd
Bay Adelaide Centre, East Tower
22 Adelaide Street West, 41st Floor
Toronto, Ontario, Canada
M5H 4E3

www.harpercollins.ca

Library and Archives Canada Cataloguing in Publication
Title: No place like home / Linh S. Nguyen.
Names: Nguyen, Linh S., author.
Identifiers: Canadiana (print) 20220405298 | Canadiana (ebook) 20220405301 |
ISBN 9781443466202 (softcover) |
ISBN 9781443466219 (EPUB)
Classification: LCC PS8627.G89 N6 2023 | DDC jC813/.6—dc23

Printed and bound in the United States of America
23 24 25 26 27 LBC 5 4 3 2 1

For Nicky, Mark, and Tim, my teachers who defined risk.
For my family, who defined home.

A STORY OUT OF PLACE

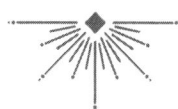

On the morning of the annual book fair, Lan dragged her feet to class. She dragged them up the stairs of the basement where she lived with her dad, past the bright yellow dandelions blooming on the neighbouring lawns, and along the wide pavements to her school's decorated fence. She did not glance up, for she had memorized every step of the way. Besides, Lan was busy moping. Who could blame her? The annual book fair was reason enough to mope, even if it happened to be a beautiful May dawn.

In fact, the sun breaking through spring rains only made things worse. It reminded Lan that summer danced around the corner, which would've been good fun if she'd had any plans in store. Instead, a decidedly non-vacation awaited. No cottage. No trip abroad. Not even a glimpse of her faraway family back in Việt Nam.

"Do you listen to anything I say?"

Lan jumped at the voice and banged her elbow on the half-open double doors of Cordella Elementary.

A tall kid held it ajar for her, his big brown eyes inches away. He shook his head. Lan took several paces back, clutching her throbbing funny bone.

"I didn't see you," she said, gesturing awkwardly at the door she'd walked into. "Don't take it personally, Manav."

Manav sighed. He was the only kid in Lan's sixth-grade class who wore button-down shirts and dress pants on a regular day, but no one questioned it. Being the fastest hundred-metre track runner had its perks. Manav waited for Lan to pass before following her up to their lockers.

"I was asking if you know what you want from the book fair at lunch," he said. "That is, if you haven't read every book on the shelves already."

"Ha," said Lan humourlessly. "What I want isn't the problem."

"What's that supposed to mean?"

"It means stuff at the fair costs money, Manav. Not that I'd expect you to know," said Lan with a sniff, glancing over his polished shoes and ironed jacket. She was pretty sure her own shirt had cost four bucks from Chinatown. The touristy maple leaf print was starting to peel. Manav looked offended.

"Just because my parents work hard—" he began.

"Oh please, save it." She slammed her locker shut with a bang, banishing the reflected version of herself scowling in the dollar-store mirror. Her long black hair, unkempt, shielded her round face and wide eyes. Lan grabbed her bag and turned away from Manav's miffed expression—but not before she caught two girls in their class whispering, tossing their blond curls as they turned from her.

"Why do you always look like you're half zombie?" whispered her seatmate, Segen, as Lan slid behind her own desk. Her gaze lingered on the retreating backs of the whispering girls. "You sure you're alive in there?"

"Last I checked," said Lan, glumly. "At least a zombie apocalypse would make for something new around here."

Instead, she had to sit in class and listen to their teacher, Ms. McCrimmon, talk up the book fair as if Lan didn't want to go with all her heart. All those new releases! But she would have to wait to get them at the library, or stumble across one on a neighbour's lawn, or borrow from some kid who was already through with their copy. As if she wasn't enough of a loser in every part of her social life at this school.

"I'd have thought you'd be excited about today," Segen continued. "Don't you like to read? I mean, you must, right? It's all you ever do."

"I can't get anything at the fair anyway," said Lan.

She remembered stepping into the school library for last year's fair, months after she had joined Cordella Elementary. Of course Lan loved the usual stacks of old books, their corners dog-eared and browned pages stained with thumbprints. Each mark seemed to change the story a tiny bit. New books, though, that was something else. Those covers shone, boastful. The pages were crisp. Reading a new book felt like it was meant just for her, and Lan hadn't had much for herself lately, ever since she and her dad had moved to Toronto across the world from Hà Nội, the only home she'd ever known.

It was where her mother remained with their big family and Lan's baby brother, Khôi. Their move to Canada kept getting delayed for some work reason. That was as much as Lan could understand. All she knew was that one day, her family had shrunk. An ocean expanded between the rest of her family and Lan and her dad. Her parents had told her, "Rồi sẽ qua nhanh," but when a year passed, she stopped believing they would be reunited soon.

When she'd seen the books on display at the fair last May, Lan had wanted one so badly it almost made the homesickness disappear. But she knew better than to ask her dad. It didn't matter what his reason was or how sad he looked when he refused her. After a year, Lan couldn't bear to hear the word *no* any longer. The books were her favourite part about her new school, but she'd save herself the disappointment this year by not going to the fair at all.

Without the refuge of the library to look forward to at lunch, morning crawled by. Through open windows, birds chirped and sunlight drifted into the warm room. The blue of the sky was so unlike the pale grey of Hà Nội, but there was something lovely about that grey. Lan wondered what her mother was doing back in their old flat, and whether her brother had stopped his teething. Leaving him had been the hardest part. He was too little to be separated from their mom and home, but they'd thought *she* could handle it. Lan wanted to prove them right, but most times, it felt easier to pretend she was elsewhere altogether.

Someone coughed loudly. Lan's head snapped back to the board, where Ms. McCrimmon was talking about the order of operations. Lan had learned this stuff ages ago. Her mom had a habit of assigning extra homework to make sure she was ahead. It was hard to pay attention. Segen's pencil tapped incessantly by her side. A glance at the clock showed a half hour to lunch break. Then she could sidle off on her own.

But as the lesson drew to an end twenty minutes before the bell, Ms. McCrimmon switched off the projector and waved her arms like a conductor, looking oddly chipper for a Friday. Her curls bounced, which either meant something very good was about to happen or quite the opposite . . .

"Look alive!" she said. "What do you say we call it a morning and put aside those math problems? Let's take lunch early and go to the book fair as a class!"

"Are you kidding me?"

Lan's groan was hardly audible above the cheers and scraping of chairs as her classmates stowed their books and rushed to form a line out the door. She should've guessed by that eager look that Ms. McCrimmon would make the fair a bonding activity! So much for Lan's plan to stay away. Could anything go right? Before she could protest, Lan was shepherded downstairs and through the library doors, where a twelve-foot gold-and-silver balloon arch had been set up for the occasion, swaying ever so slightly in the open window's breeze.

"It's a little much, isn't it?" said Lan, grimacing at the spectacle. Her school could be so extravagant sometimes.

"I think it's sweet," said Segen, and she hopped off to join her friends by the stationery display.

Lan didn't move. She stood alone beneath the arch as her classmates dispersed, feeling the exact thing she'd dreaded: a deep, familiar longing in the pit of her belly. Gleaming new releases winked at her from the shelves, teasing. She wanted them all. Tentatively, Lan took a book off the display and turned it around. The price was marked in bold, and the first digit alone made her shove it back in a rush. She glanced at the clock above the librarian's desk. Fifteen minutes to the lunch bell, when she could leave—but was she supposed to look at the pens for that long? Perhaps a glance around wouldn't hurt any more than it did already, Lan decided. She slipped behind the nearest case.

The rest of her class faded into background noise. Lan walked, pausing at captivating titles. Well-known words whispered when she passed. Old characters waved. She saw familiar names and ran her hand along the neatly stacked spines, sighing contentedly. Libraries never failed to put Lan at ease. They struck that special balance between comfort and excitement that no other place managed to.

No matter how much had changed in her life since the move, she could at least return to the stories she loved best.

Lan's hand snagged on a strange book jutting out.

She doubled back and pulled it from the shelf. The plain cover was dark red with a single puffy dandelion shape printed in gold leaf. The book was heavier than most in the kids' section. It must have been mis-shelved, for no colourful image marked the front, and not even a title or author name was embossed on the hardcover. It looked like an old adult book, though the pages were crisp as could be, untouched as though waiting for her. Lan ran her fingers along the sharp white edges then opened the book to the first chapter. The cream-coloured page was blotted with a brown stain, smelling faintly of chocolate. *So much for brand new*, thought Lan, unimpressed. But as her eyes scanned the elegant font, her palms began to tingle. Words leapt at her—*price, quest, witch, king*, and the names *Annabelle* and *Marlow*. Lan began to read.

IN WHICH A GIRL TAKES FATE INTO HER OWN HANDS

"Once upon a time in Silva, the land of lost and found, a powerful king named his price of admission."

"Tell me what it would take," Annabelle said. She leaned forward in her chair.

"Why?" her grandmother asked, tilting her head back to stare at the girl. "Planning to take on the king?"

"I just might."

The old woman smiled and ran a hand through her greying hair. She lowered her voice conspiratorially.

"For that, you'll need a heart," she said.

"I have one," Annabelle declared.

"But do you have proof? Easy to claim without proof."

"It beats. I can feel it."

"Many things beat, Annabelle, what makes you say it's a heart? Can you prove how much it holds, how much it bleeds?"

"I can get proof," said Annabelle. "Tell me what else."

"Courage," said her grandmother, "in large supply."

"Is that all?"

"Not quite, but the last bit is easy: a good story."

"Proof of a heart, courage in large supply, and a good story," Annabelle repeated. "I can get them all. I'll go to Asta and find this wizard king, Nebulo. He has to restore Sol to how it was before his curse ruined us. It's the least he can do."

"Careful, love. If it was that easy, we'd have sent one of our own ages ago."

"Everyone is needed in Sol, except me," said Annabelle. "It has to be me."

The lady took a drink from the goblet before her, eyes closed and lips cracked. Her forehead was creased, but she did not protest. Annabelle looked beside her at Marlow, the fourteen-year-old nicknamed "golden boy" of the Border Academy. His blond hair fell over green eyes that held her steely gaze. Their features were complete opposites. Marlow's light hair and built frame contrasted her sharp edges, deep brown hair, and eyes sunken into a bony face. His gaze was guarded, but their five-year friendship founded on secrets meant she could recognize his slightest frown. Marlow was worried, but he would go anywhere Annabelle asked. She knew that much.

"Lady Marya," he said to the old woman.

She brushed aside the title. "None of that Silvan nonsense. Call me by my name, Marlow. That shows proper respect in my homeland of Sol."

"Marya," Marlow tried again. "Do you know anyone who has crossed the desert and made the journey on foot to Asta, let alone gained audience with the king?"

"Not without a powerful witch. Few of those around these parts nowadays."

"Where have they gone?"

"Fled the southern coast to Maare, I expect, or bartered their way to Asta years ago when the desert dried up our land. What's left of our witches in Sol have their hands full keeping everyone alive."

"Nothing's going to change if we don't do something about it though, right?" said Annabelle. "Shouldn't we take a risk? You always said our people are warriors."

"So we are," said Marya. "You most of all. How I'd love to bid you to go on your own quest, but you must remember why you live within these high walls and not under the open skies of home. The world has shifted with the careless magic of the Silvan king. The Border Academy keeps you safer, stronger than you would be in Sol."

"Only because nothing ever happens in the middle of a desert," said Annabelle. "Am I expected to stay here forever? I haven't been home in five years."

"A warrior understands patience, Annabelle. It will take time for us to rebuild."

Marya pushed her chair back, wooden legs scraping the stone floor. She grasped her granddaughter's hands and stood, tall and muscular despite her weathered face. She had come in her Solian armour, soft leather fitted over her brown skin, unlike the tough pads that everyone at the Border Academy wore. Annabelle hated how they made her slow and heavy in a fight. All that whacking and blundering around was ridiculous. Fighting was not so different from dancing: smooth and graceful. That's what her grandma had taught her, before Annabelle was sent away.

"I will bring Daisy your love," said Marya, cupping Annabelle's cheek in goodbye. The ride back to Sol cost half a day, and the sun was already high.

"You can tell her I'll see her soon enough," said Annabelle.

Annabelle's sister had been two years old when the Silvan king's spell turned their coast into sweltering sands. Daisy couldn't remember much from the times before, but Annabelle still saw the leaping turtles cresting the ocean's waves of her homeland each time she closed her eyes. There'd been so many colours in Sol, a hundred shades of blue and green in the water alone. The smell of salt in the air would've been enough to lift her spirits now, but there was none of that at the Border Academy. In the heart of the enchanted desert, only dust and hunger reigned.

Annabelle's stomach twisted when she tried to recall Daisy's little face, her large eager eyes slipping from memory. She let out a gasp as her grandmother's uneven nails dug into her wrist.

"Don't do anything foolish, Annabelle," said Marya. "Stories only go so far. Remember why we sent you here. You'll come home when the coast is restored."

Marya stood and drew her cloak up to cover her mouth. Marlow rose and offered his arm to walk her to the stables. Her grandmother took it, Annabelle suspected, to be polite. As if Marya, the greatest fighter of her generation, needed an escort. Marlow, as usual, was drawing longing stares from Academy recruits wherever he walked, his golden hair catching the sun. Annabelle trailed them, steps behind. Her mind raced. Her dark eyes focused as if sizing up an opponent before a fight. Her hand moved subconsciously to the black stone blade on her hip. Marlow glanced over his shoulder and shot her a look of warning—but it was too late. Her grandmother should have stayed quiet if she'd wanted Annabelle to stay put.

For now that Annabelle could see a path beyond the dreary halls of the Border Academy back to her family in Sol, she had to try. She would cross the desert, make her way to Asta, and give that stupid king they called Nebulo the items he wanted for his "price of admission"—what a pretentious idea anyway! What kind of ruler charged his people to repair mistakes that he himself had made?

She could change that, thought Annabelle. She would ask him to return the Solian lands to how they were before, when generations of her people lived on the southwestern coast undisturbed. All she needed was proof of a heart, courage in large supply, a good story—and perhaps a witch.

A BARGAIN STRUCK

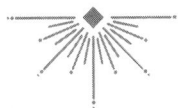

The loud buzzing of the lunch bell jolted Lan back to the library stacks. She gasped and nearly dropped the book. There were no other copies like it on the shelf. She turned it over again in her hands, rifling through the pages quickly and catching glimpses of characters like the tree guardians, the Cognitor, and King Nebulo. Lan frowned. The story seemed like a classic fantasy quest, which probably involved many trials on a long journey and eventually a happily ever after for Annabelle, Marlow, and Sol.

But Lan couldn't bring herself to put the book down. She was filled with the strangest feeling that it was important. She might never find it again if she walked away now. Pins and needles lit up the tips of her fingers. She stood frozen.

There was only one thing to do. Lan stuffed the tome in her bag before she could think twice. A furtive glance around her showed no one in sight. A few of her classmates lingered by the library counter, but most had taken off for lunch. Lan's heart pounded, too insistent to ignore. She'd never done anything as outright shameful as stealing, but just as she considered changing her mind and returning it, Manav stepped into view. His arms were crossed, ready for an argument. Something about his righteous glare made Lan set her jaw, prepared to defend herself.

"Seriously, Lan?" he said. "You're straight up gonna steal a book now?"

"No clue what you're talking about. Why are you following me anyway?"

"I wasn't *following* you. I actually thought I'd be nice and remind you that track tryouts are in ten days, but instead you decide to commit theft right before my eyes."

"I'm not stealing!" Lan protested, knowing that had been exactly her intention. "Maybe I wanted to carry it around, or make a note of the title, or shelve it in the proper place because it doesn't even belong in this section!"

Lan waved at the sign above them, which read Biographies, 9–12. Manav rubbed his forehead. What now? Would he demand the book back, march her to the counter, and rat her out to the librarian? Lan's hand tightened around the smooth spine. For a split second, she thought about making a run for it—but Manav's next words were so unexpected her mouth dropped.

"If you want it that badly, I'll get it for you."

"You'll do what?"

"Give it here. I'll get it. My parents gave me a fifty. I've got change leftover."

Lan stared. Manav's earnest eyes told her he meant it. Her father would certainly not approve. He'd taught her better than to behave this way, but just once, did he have to know? Just once, was it okay to accept a gift she so desperately wanted, even if it had been offered out of pity?

"You don't have to . . ." Lan began.

"Of course I know that," said Manav, "and I didn't say it'd come without a price."

"I won't be able to pay you back. Forget it."

"Who said anything about money? There's plenty of other ways to pay."

"What do you want?" Lan asked warily.

Manav eased the book out of her hands and turned it over.

"Weird," he murmured, examining the gold dandelion print on the otherwise blank red cover. "Did you take it out of its sleeve? Make it easier to steal?"

"I wasn't stealing!" said Lan automatically. "I found it like that."

But now that he mentioned it, Lan thought, it made sense. Someone must've removed the shiny shell that all hardcover books came wrapped in. Perhaps that was why it looked so out of place. Covers made books inviting. Without them, the plain weighty tomes were almost foreboding.

"What do you want for the book?" Lan repeated. "I don't have much."

Manav looked up and smiled. "Sure you do. Like I said, I stayed behind to remind you about track tryouts, ten days from today. I've seen you run. I'll get you the book, but I want you to come out."

"You're kidding," Lan laughed. "Try out for track and field? No way."

Manav looked confused.

"Why not? You'd totally make the team."

Lan stared at him. She could not tell if he meant it, but even so, this was middle school! There were lines you had to be *very* sure about crossing, and trying out for track was one of them. Lan's scene was the library. If she made a fool of herself on the sports field, she would never live it down—especially not in front of the snickering kids who kept trying to rhyme her name with weird words.

"That's a popular-person sport," said Lan, "and in case you haven't noticed, I definitely don't qualify."

"What's that got to do with anything?" said Manav, frowning. "For the record, people talk to you! You just don't talk back."

"That's exactly what a popular kid would say."

"You're unbelievable," Manav said with a groan, "but, like it or not, that's the deal."

"I'll just embarrass myself."

"No, you won't. I live two doors down from you, and I've seen you run to school when you're late, which is actually super often. You sprint faster than me biking! We're up against tough competition at provincials this year, and the team could really use you."

Lan hesitated. Manav could be pompous and ignorant about some things, but he was never malicious. Besides, track and field was his life. He wouldn't go to the trouble of setting her up for nothing, would he?

"Even if I did try out," said Lan, "I wouldn't be able to join the team. Your meets are so far away. My dad wouldn't agree to the fees, not to mention your fancy uniforms and early practices. It'll mess up our schedule, and he's busy enough these days."

"Have you even tried to ask?"

"Yes," said Lan at once. She had asked too many times. In September, she'd wanted to run with the cross-country team, but her dad found it hard to keep tabs on her whereabouts. He worked such long hours at the superstore across town. It was far easier to know that she'd be at school and home at the same time every day.

"We'll figure that out later," said Manav, looking unconcerned. "The book's yours, but Monday after next, you show the team what you can do. Deal?"

He held out his palm to shake. Lan stared at the story clutched in his other hand. There were certainly easier ways to get hold of books, but would she find another one like this? Lan wanted to know how Annabelle would escape and cross the great desert, whether Marlow would prove as loyal as he appeared, and where they'd find a witch to help them get to Asta with the magical items for the king. Besides, if Lan had learned anything from fantasy novels, she knew she could not let a mysterious book pass her by. That was just foolish.

"Throw in a chocolate bar, and you've got yourself a deal," said Lan at last. She took Manav's hand and shook before he could respond. "No take-backs."

"Hey, that wasn't fair. *I'm* the one getting you the book!" said Manav, but Lan could tell he wasn't truly upset. "Fine, I'll bring you chocolate, but only when I see you on the field! Make sure you show up."

"I'll be there," Lan said. It was a sweet deal. She wondered if she might soon regret her promise, but at least she had a good story to look forward to on the weekend.

They walked to the counter. Lan couldn't remember the last book she'd bought, let alone a hardcover, and barely noticed the librarian's puzzled expression when he scanned it through. He turned it over several times before using another book's sleeve for the barcode. Then it was back in her hands—and truly hers! Manav said something that Lan did not catch. All she could think of was how she couldn't wait to dive in.

WHAT LONGING DOES

Lan turned down the driveway of the red house on the corner of Langdon Street after a tedious hour of history. It left a strange taste in her mouth. All these "explorers" were overrated, she decided, or straight-up villainous. Taking over people's homes was far from heroic.

Thinking of home made Lan's heart ache for the bustling streets of her own familiar town, the lakes scattered throughout the city, and the branches of red flowers bent over the wide boulevards. At least Canada's bitter cold had let up. The snow had been cute for a few days last December, but by April, it was sickening. Unprepared for the chill, Lan had stayed inside most of her first year in Toronto, buried under blankets, escaping into whatever story she could scrounge up. Now she tightly clutched the book fair book, ramming her shoulder against the door to wedge it open, eager to start reading the moment she stepped inside their basement flat.

Homework discarded on the coffee table, Lan hopped on the tattered couch and picked up where she'd left off in the library stacks. No matter how many fantasies she ploughed through, sword fights and spells never got stale when compared to her less-than-thrilling routine—and reading about other people's quests made her hope that her own adventure might be just around the block, waiting for her to step into the right shoes or find the right wardrobe . . . however many she'd tried.

"You know, it's not a bad thing if you want to cry," said Marlow.

Annabelle glared at him, his elbow propped on the fence post, somehow making their drab Academy uniform look good. It was easy to see why her bunkmates stared each time he moved. It made Annabelle want to constantly roll her eyes.

"Marlow, I'm fine."

"I know you've been thinking about making a break for it forever. It's okay to reconsider though. What your grandmother said—that's enough to scare anyone off."

"Don't be daft," said Annabelle. "I'm more sure than ever."

"We could wait—"

"For supplies to dwindle? Those fancy folks in Asta don't care about us here on the outskirts. We're getting less every shipment."

"All right, I get it. You're right. As usual."

"You don't have to come."

"Come on, Annabelle, you know that was never an option."

"I'm not kidding. Everyone loves you. You've got prospects here."

"Of joining the elite border guard? Or rising through the ranks to bully the kids as a certified Border Academy trainer?"

"You'd never bully anyone. In fact, I daresay you're a shockingly good teacher for someone so cocky."

"A genuine compliment from you? You must be missing me already. No need to beg, Belle. I already told you, I'm coming with you."

Annabelle had to laugh. Even now, Marlow spoke with a

sureness born of more talent than anyone should be allowed—talent, and a lack of familiarity with loss. Escaping under darkness from the Border Academy? No problem. Crossing the enchanted desert with whatever rations they could steal? Bring it on. It almost made her believe that her wild plan was possible, that there was a future where she could return to the Solian coast where she belonged, instead of living in this old training camp where meeting Marlow had been the one good thing.

Tucked in, with the fluorescent lights bright, Lan read deeply as Marlow and Annabelle plotted their escape route, and as they planned to leave under the cover of a new moon. The latch on the upstairs screen door creaked, but only when her dad came in, bags of groceries in hand, did Lan glance up.

Lan's father was a man aged solely by hardship. His youth shone through the moment you got to know him, in his thick, mostly black hair, unlined face, and muscles from his karate days. Lan knew people didn't usually see those traits when they glanced at him scanning items behind the counter of the superstore where he worked as a cashier. She herself had noticed his creased eyebrows and stooped frame much more since those long winter days. But back in Việt Nam, he had been laid-back and confident on his electric blue motorbike. The minute he stepped inside the flat, he shrugged out of his navy T-shirt, along with the nametag that read Ben rather than his real name, Bình. It meant peace. He smiled when he saw Lan.

"How was school?" He did not wait for an answer before unloading food into the freezer. "Did you eat?"

"Not hungry," Lan lied, not wanting to admit she was sick of microwave pasta.

Their diet now consisted of whatever her dad picked up from

the sales racks, which hardly compared to their meals in Việt Nam. They'd been spoiled in a family of great cooks and voracious eaters. Lan's mom had been especially skilled at whipping up any dish. Lan folded the top of her page over to mark her spot as the fridge door thudded shut.

"Tối nay ăn nem nhé," said her dad. "Got it on sale."

"Nem?" said Lan, surprised. Spring rolls were her favourite food, but she had not eaten them since leaving her mom in Hà Nội. "I thought you couldn't find them here."

"Well, they won't be your mother's," he said, "nhưng vẫn ăn được."

Lan put the book down and walked to where her dad was waving a Styrofoam package of frozen nem. She poked at them. They looked nothing like the colourful, delicate rolls her mom made.

Her father headed to the shower, calling over his shoulder, "Con cho vào lò đi nhé. Bố đi tắm đã."

Lan nodded. She unwrapped the packaging and placed the frosty rolls on the oven tray. Staring at the dull white clumps side by side, she felt an unexpected wave of anger. She knew her dad had only wanted to make her happy, but nem wasn't meant to look like that. It was supposed to be deep-fried in vegetable oil, freshly wrapped by fingers dipped in water, rice paper soaked in beer. Even now, she remembered the tuck, crease, and roll over a wooden cutting board. Her mother had taught her years ago, not long before they found themselves separated. Lan had been a natural, but in this house— too many foreign ingredients and too little counter space.

Sudden tears rose in her. Lan slammed the oven door shut, banishing the copycat rolls from view. She sank into a hard chair, taken aback by her own bitterness.

When they'd first moved, Lan had even liked the change—the sprawling parks, big hills to roll down, full libraries every few blocks, and the peaceful stillness on summer nights when the sun did not set 'til past bedtime. Her friends in Hà Nội envied her. Everyone had told her Canada was full of opportunity, whatever that meant, and Lan believed them. She couldn't pinpoint exactly when things changed. Perhaps it was Mother's Day that first year (an entirely new concept) when she realized the challenge of celebrating special occasions eight thousand miles apart. Or maybe when her hair grew out, and Lan could not do any of her favourite braids by herself.

The sound of water running in the bathroom stopped. Lan coughed and hastily wiped her face so her dad would not see her confused weeping over random spring rolls. It would only make him sad.

Briiing!

From the table behind her, the phone sounded, startling Lan out of her sniffles. Seeing the name on the screen, she took one more breath, forced her face into a smile, and picked up the call. A second later, her mom was peering at her, pixelated.

"What's wrong?" she said at once, squinting at Lan's face. "Sao trông buồn thế? Something at school?"

Her mother's pixie bob haircut and similarly round face took up most of the video screen, but Lan could see the potted plant with the giant leaves in their sixteenth-floor apartment peeking out from behind her. The window was open. It looked sunny, a hot May morning. Lan spoke with her mom often, but tonight, her throat constricted at the glimpse of her former home.

"Nothing new," Lan began. She cleared her throat. "Well, I might be trying out for the track team in a week. That's new, I guess, and a bit scary."

"What team is that?"

"It's like a competitive running club. Well, I'd be running at least. There are other parts like long jump or shotput."

"Running is good. You're a fast runner."

"I am?"

"Don't you remember beating all those neighbourhood kids in the foot races on our street?"

"Those haven't happened in forever."

"Still, it's part of you. What's joining this team gonna take?"

Before Lan could answer, her father entered the room, towel in hand, and stepped into the frame. He gestured animatedly at the nem cooking in the oven. Her mother laughed. Lan slid behind him and took a sip of water, but the morose feeling in her throat refused to leave her.

She found herself longing for her old ocean-themed bedroom, their chaotic family reunions, and of course, all the food, fresh from the market and seaside! What she would do for a fresh pomegranate from her grandparents' garden! Tropical fruits were so much tastier. Lan could not remember ever feeling hungry before this year, but then everything she knew had vanished. Her parents had barely given her two weeks' warning! They had said some nebulous thing about better choices and bluer skies, but not for the first time, Lan wondered why it had been so important to leave.

With a reminder to eat their greens, Lan's mother excused herself to run to work. Her father grabbed two pairs of chopsticks, tossed leftover rice in the microwave, and pulled the spring rolls out of the oven. They were still soggy, but Lan's stomach rumbled. They sat down to eat.

"Nem thế nào?" he asked.

Lan dipped her roll into the cheap, too-salty fish sauce and took a bite. It lacked the crispness that she loved. Still, the flavours surprisingly held true.

"Not bad," she answered, taking another roll.

Her father beamed and leaned back in his chair, his eyes already droopy.

"No rude customers today," he told her, nodding. "Thế là được rồi. A good day."

They ate in a tired silence, broken up by the odd comment about food or groceries. Her dad had driven Lan to school every day on his motorbike in the "before times" (as she'd taken to calling them). They'd had time to talk, take detours to narrow alleyways to peruse hidden knock-off jewellery stores, even make an impulse buy once in a while. Now Bình looked so worn that Lan hardly shared much about her day, not that anything exciting ever happened.

"What's this about a track team?" her father asked unexpectedly. Lan looked up in surprise. "You telling your mom but not me?"

"Oh, just something I thought I'd try out for," said Lan. She began to describe the different events and, once she started talking, found that she could not stop. "Manav's the fastest kid in school. If he's saying I've got a shot . . ."

Lan avoided all mention of the strange book, innocently tossed on the coffee table. She grew more eager with every word. What if she *could* actually make the team and compete? Everyone was jealous of the kids who left midway through class to race at schools all over the city. They wouldn't care then that her English sounded weird, or that she wore mismatched clothes and preferred spending lunches alone in the school library. Not that it really mattered, but that kind of popularity boost could change everything!

"We'll talk about it if it comes, okay?" said her dad, frowning. Lan could tell he was struggling to pay attention. "Shouldn't you be focusing on your schoolwork?"

"That's all I ever do!" Lan protested.

"Not true," he countered, brandishing a soggy spring roll at her. "You read all those storybooks. They make your brain distracted."

"Of course you'd be upset that I *read too much!*"

"I'm agreeing that it would be good for you to make friends, Lan."

"Well, I wouldn't be joining to make friends anyway," said Lan stubbornly. "It'd be to do something cool for once and make the other kids jealous!"

"That's not a very nice thing to think."

"You know what would be nice? If I wasn't stuck in this basement every day!"

Lan's father sighed and put down his chopsticks. "How much did you say this track team costs?"

"I don't know," said Lan, still annoyed. "Probably doesn't cost a whole lot, but everyone's got nice uniforms, too, for the practices and meets at other schools."

"Maybe you can simply practise with the team at your school, not bother with the fancy clothes and field trips. If you want to run, then just run."

"Ugh, no, Dad! What would be the point of that?" Why had she even bothered to bring it up? She had known all along he would not understand.

But her father had already moved on to a different topic, brushing aside her longing like it meant nothing. He floated the idea of a walk to IKEA, not to buy anything but to browse. It was their favourite pastime in Toronto, putting together a dream home from the curated displays—but even if he didn't change his mind the next day, Lan's heart was not in it. Her appetite was gone, and her mind started drifting to Silva, where Annabelle and Marlow were setting off across the sands. Eager to return to their far-more-interesting quest, Lan cleaned up the dishes quickly and bid her dad a stiff one-word goodnight. She left him settled on the sofa with a china cup of boiled water by his side, chatting with his old friends back home.

In her room, Lan changed into her snowflake-print pyjamas, scooted under her covers, and switched on her night light. It had been an odd up-and-down day, but now she had somewhere else to go, somewhere safe from random bursts of homesickness for a life left behind. With a shake to clear her loose thoughts, Lan opened the book, her finger absentmindedly tracing the characters' path on the roughly drawn map on the first page. They'd started at the Border Academy, marked with ominous looking Xs in a rectangular camp, and were traipsing across the enchanted desert to the snaky river on the other side. As she sank into the story, her father's voice and clacking laptop keys soon faded out of hearing.

They had been walking across the sand for days, their boots dipping into the dunes so that each step forward felt at once like a step back. Annabelle's head pounded from dehydration, and her throat was parched. Her blade weighed heavily on her hip, and the straps of her leather bag cut into her shoulders, leaving red indents on her skin. Her white shirt had soaked through with sweat. It had not stopped her shoulders from blistering. She took the water Marlow offered. Ignoring his concerned look, she savoured every drop, even though it was warm from the sun.

"My burns are starting to peel," she said. "Look at my hands." She waved her hands in Marlow's face. "I must've been out of my mind to think we could do this."

"Don't be silly. It's the best idea you've come up with. Think about the story you'll have to tell your children. Annabelle of Sol, Saviour of the Coast."

"Nice ring to it," Annabelle said. She tried to laugh. It came out like a wheeze.

Cradled within the quest, Lan's gloominess subsided, though she could not shake the loneliness that remained. Even on a perilous mission through the desert, Marlow and Annabelle had each other, not to mention a noble cause to guide them. How great it would be to know exactly what you wanted, then go out and do it! Lan envied them. People in books always had their paths so clearly mapped out. Fighting dragons was one thing, but not knowing—well, much of anything really, that was even harder.

Lan had grown so sick of her same old routine in Toronto she'd begun to check her mailbox daily, hoping for a letter that would whisk her away. But she wasn't daring like Annabelle or a skilled fighter like Marlow. No matter how much she wished otherwise, Lan knew in her heart's heart that she was a plain girl with overgrown hair and an embarrassing amount of acne for an eleven-year-old. She had a family that loved her, even if some of them were annoying and others were very far away. Interesting things didn't happen to people like her. She'd read enough to know. Heroes were beautiful, brave, and ready to avenge their forsaken homelands. Lan was simply lost. Where could she go? What could she do?

Even so, there had to be more, Lan thought as she flipped through the novel, pausing to take in the vivid descriptions of the magical world. Beyond the terrifying desert lay the promise of enchanted forests, a thriving city, and a wizard who could grant wishes. So much was out there. There had to be more than this basement and more than this waiting. There just had to be.

A SUMMER STORM

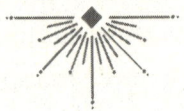

Shortly before midnight, Lan's eyes grew heavy and began to droop. Pins and needles ran through her hands and feet. Her father had turned out the lights some time ago, calling at her to do the same. Lan ignored him, just as she ignored the clouds steadily darkening the sky and the insistent ringing of their neighbour's wind chimes. Her head stayed bowed toward her book, only half awake. Marlow and Annabelle had reached the end of the desert and collapsed by a river. While Marlow snuck around to get firewood, Annabelle single-handedly fought off a troop of ferocious tree guardians on the banks. Lan was rapidly growing to like her.

Lan flipped the book on its pages, wedged open on the blanket beside her, and leaned over to check her clock. 11:59 blinked at her. She did not have school the next day, but she was also not a morning person. She would pay for it if she didn't sleep now. Besides, maybe her dad had been serious, and they could wander IKEA in the afternoon. Now that her anger had subsided somewhat, it could be fun to see those decorated rooms and try out the hanging pods, perfect for reading. Lan switched her lamp off, and the room turned pitch-black.

For a second, silence hung in the air, expectant.
A low whistling began to sound.
What was that noise?
Lan frowned.
It grew louder.

Then, all at once, the howling of the wind overcame her senses, so fierce her breath caught. Lan gasped and sat up in her bed. It roared like an animal raging at her window, begging to be let in. Lan was no stranger to rough weather. In Hà Nội, monsoons came down so thick it was impossible to see five feet ahead—but this one felt different, teeming with undecipherable energy. Her skin tingled. Her breathing grew shallow. What was happening? Surely, it was only a summer storm. She resisted calling her dad for a silly reason at this late hour.

Don't be dramatic, Lan. Go to sleep!

But it was impossible. Lan tried to reach for the light again but to her terror found that the room was starting to tilt. Her bed began rocking like a boat on wild seas. She heard objects jostling on her nightstand, picture frames fallen. She could not see a thing. Had the storm somehow breached their walls? She desperately grabbed around her for something stable to hold, but even her blankets were wrestling out of her grip. The bottom of her stomach dropped as if she was going over the edge of a rollercoaster. The book, still propped open, thudded on the floor—too late, she cried out.

"Bố ơi!"

The words were torn from Lan's throat, vanishing at once into the noise of the wind. Where was her father? Was he sleeping peacefully or also caught up in the storm?

Suddenly, Lan was airborne before she could gasp. She fought to stay upright as the winds tossed her upward. She squeezed her eyes shut and shielded her head, bracing to hit the low ceiling or the walls of her bedroom, but she felt nothing. The musty basement smell was gone, replaced by the heavy air of a fast-approaching thunderstorm. It sucked her in its centre, holding on so tightly she could not cry out. Within seconds, she could no longer tell which way was up. Tentatively, Lan forced her eyes open the tiniest crack. It was no use. In the dimness, she could see nothing but unidentifiable debris, hear only whooshing, a low buzzing, and crackling—was that lightning?

After struggling in vain for a full minute, Lan was too drained to move. She fell still and let the storm carry her, half-conscious. The winds calmed. She tumbled through the air like a rag doll and landed—astonishingly, on her feet—at the edge of a riverbank.

Heaving, Lan had time to register a yellow field and two shocked faces before her legs buckled. She teetered backwards and fell into a stream behind her.

Submerged, she inhaled a breath of cold water and choked on it, frantically crying. She felt herself sinking with each panicked kick.

Her feet hit the sandy riverbed, and Lan blacked out.

When she woke, Lan's head was throbbing. She fought to open her eyes, but the blinding light made her shut them quickly. She lay on what seemed like grass and struggled to catch her breath. She was drenched and shivering despite the sun on her skin. After several minutes, her senses began to return. Lan heard two voices, a boy's and girl's.

"She's gotta be. Not a very good one, obviously."

"Maybe she can help, at least point the way."

"She's not some tour guide. You think she just dropped in to greet us? I told you I'm not lost."

"Well, *I'm* telling you, we're not doing so hot right now."

The girl snorted, and they both laughed. Lan had no trouble understanding them, but their words were tinged with unidentifiable accents. The girl's was lilting and rhythmic as waves rolling in from the sea. The boy's voice was hard at the edges, sharp like mountain peaks. Their conversation triggered something in Lan's brain, but she could not remember it at the moment. She could not remember or make sense of much at all. The most she could manage was a pathetic whimper as she rolled onto her side and tried to pry herself up.

"Whoa, hang on, take it easy," said the boy. Lan felt his steadying hands on her shoulders.

"I can stand," Lan said without thinking. Her head spun, but who knew who these people were? She was determined to not appear weak.

"Sure, go on and get up then," came the girl's lofty voice. "Why don't you get the fire going while you're at it? Whip up a few eggs and toast?"

"Don't be rude . . ." the boy said to her.

Lan managed to crawl to her knees. Then she swayed, leaned over, and promptly threw up. The girl sighed, loudly. Even in her sodden state, Lan felt a twinge of irritation. Did she think Lan was vomiting on purpose?

"You know, you really shouldn't teleport if you don't know what you're doing."

Apparently, she did. Wait—*what had she said?*

"Teleport?" said Lan. "What are you saying? I don't know how to teleport!"

"Do you usually just talk or do you think first when you're not magic-sick?"

"Chill out for a second, will you?" That was the boy. "She looks bad."

"She'll be fine. The witches at the learning grounds back in my home did this all the time and recovered no problem. Some of them were smaller than she is."

Lan heard their words but only took in pieces. *Witch? Magic-sick? Teleport?* She struggled again to her knees, shuffling away from the pool of vomit. What was wrong with her vision? Bright spots blurred her surroundings. Dimly, Lan noticed she still wore her snowflake pyjamas, now sopping wet. She fought to stay alert as waves of nausea rolled over her. *No,* Lan thought, she refused to puke again. Slowly, the world began to right itself. Lifting her head, she peered at the two figures standing.

The girl, her oval face framed by waves of dark brown hair, had her hands on her hips. Unlike the boy beside her, she was not white-skinned, but Lan could not place her background. Her rich brown skin was patchy, peeling from what Lan assumed were recent sunburns. Her eyebrows knitted in a frown, and a fresh scratch ran down her cheek. Clad in a loose white top, black pants, and sturdy boots, she was intimidating, athletically built, yet clearly exhausted—and young. She couldn't have been much older than Lan and might have even fit into her class if she didn't look so worn out.

A long dagger in a beaded leather sheath dangled from her belt. Lan didn't doubt for an instant this girl knew how to use it. Her hooded amber eyes, rimmed with dark circles, stared haughtily. Lan was used to judgy looks from her classmates, but this one made her quail. Perhaps the weapon added that to that effect. Armed or not, Lan did not want to cross her.

The blond boy next to her stood squinting at the sun, looking so handsome Lan was certain he would turn every head if he walked down her middle-school hallway. He seemed apologetic. His light skin glowed red under the heat, but it did not for a second detract from his assuredness. He reached out to help Lan up. She took his hand without thinking. Shakily, she got to her feet. The boy stood a head taller than her, was strongly built, and looked older than the girl, but not by much. His eyes shone green in the light. He, too, wore a white top and black pants but had neither shoes nor blade. Lan realized that he was wet. He must've jumped in the river to save her. The thought made her cheeks flush red.

"First time teleporting?" he said. "I hear it's rough."

Lan stared at him, blinking densely. Finally, his words sunk in, and she replied, "Sorry, I have no idea what you're talking about. Am I dreaming?"

The two kids exchanged a confused look. Then the girl spoke carefully. "Well, from our view, it seemed like you tumbled through a blip in the sky and fell into the river."

"I suppose it did feel that way to me too," said Lan, looking around the empty fields and shockingly purple sky. "Is my father here? Did the storm get him too?"

"Uh, no," said the boy. "Did you mean to bring him?"

"I didn't mean to do anything—hang on, do you think *I* caused that freak cyclone that dumped me into the river?"

"Cyclone?" he said. "That's a flashy way to travel. I'm a fan."

"No, I'm telling you," said Lan, "I didn't *do* anything! I should find my father. If he's here, he'll be as lost as I am."

"We didn't see anyone else. And if it wasn't you, who summoned that magic?" said the girl, looking bewildered. She snuck a glance at the oddly violet sky. "We definitely didn't. I don't meddle with that stuff."

"What stuff? You mean, nature?" said Lan. "I did nothing! Why would I try to drown myself *on purpose* in such an ungraceful way?"

"Training accident?" The boy shrugged.

"You shouldn't be playing around," said the girl. "Magic storms are no joke."

"Well, sorry I have a hard time believing *I* can now summon storms out of nowhere!" said Lan. "That would've been nice to know while I was bored out of my mind in Toronto! How do you figure I did that exactly?"

"Well, I should think it's obvious, isn't it?" said the boy slowly. "You're a witch."

A HERO'S TEST

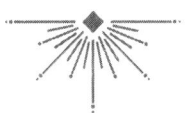

An average eleven-year-old might've stammered at this claim, talked themself out of it, and asked for the nearest exit as fast as possible. Lan was average in many ways, but the moment the boy's words hit her, she leapt up, amazed, all reason forgotten.

"Did you just tell me I'm a witch?" she whispered.

The girl rolled her eyes.

"Told you she'd be fine," she said to her companion.

"No, seriously," Lan said, wide-eyed. She stepped closer, wringing her hands. "Please, say it again, because if you did, I have actually been waiting my whole life to hear that."

"Well, as far as I know, only witches are able to teleport," said the boy. He sounded uncertain and looked to his companion for help. She frowned. "I don't know any other word for what you did, dropping in from out of nowhere like that."

"Does that mean you're witches too? Are we in a witch land?"

"Uh, I guess you could say that?"

"*Yes!*"

The boy was definitely staring at her weirdly now. Even in her elation, Lan squirmed. How was it fair for someone to be *that* good-looking? Maybe he'd turn out to be a jerk, so she wouldn't have to think about how he looked at her.

"We're not witches though," he continued, gesturing at himself and the girl. "I mean, I suppose we could learn a bit of magic if we tried, but—"

"Learning a couple spells wouldn't make us witches," the girl cut in, addressing Lan directly. "Witches have to create. They don't just copy spells, so don't get excited. You're barely one either. Where I'm from, you don't mess around with magic before you know what you're doing, and you clearly don't. You're being irresponsible. It's how people royally mess up, like the stupid Silvan King Nebulo did with the great desert spell that destroyed everything."

"Okay, no need to get all huffy," said Lan. What was this girl's problem? "Sorry for being excited, but where *I'm* from, it's a big deal to be told—hold up, did you say '*desert spell*'?"

A second late, her words sunk into Lan's slowly recovering brain. In an instant, the pieces clicked into place like clockwork. Lan fell silent and gazed around her.

She stood in a field of bright yellow, stretching miles into rolling hills dotted with shrubbery. A closer look showed millions of small flowers, some unknown and some plain dandelions, all blooming like sunlight. Birds twittered, flitting too high and too fast to observe. No one else was near. She glanced up at the sky, which looked clear blue at first sight, but lavender expanded across it like a sunset at midday. Lan turned to look behind her. Down a slope a dozen paces away trickled the river that she had fallen into. On the far side of the bank, a smattering of pines blocked her view. She could not see beyond the trees but the land rose upward. On the ground before her, two leather bags had been tossed beside a woodpile and makeshift firepit, the stones blackened with soot.

"Where am I?" Lan whispered, but she suspected she already knew the answer.

"Now she asks," said the girl, rolling her eyes. "You're in the western valley."

"And you're Annabelle," said Lan, turning to face her shocked expression. How had she not realized sooner? This was too much, Lan thought, her head spinning. She had somehow, apparently by magic, transported *into her book*, to Silva.

The boy, who was obviously Marlow, looked confused. But at the mention of her name, Annabelle backed away. Lan stepped closer. That was a mistake. Annabelle's hand jumped to her blade. Marlow hastily moved between them.

"I don't know what you think you're up to, but by all means, show yourself out," said Annabelle. "I'm not a fan of careless witches on the best of days."

"I'm not trying to hurt you," said Lan, struggling to find the right words as questions raced through her brain. How was she supposed to explain herself? "I don't know how I got here, but I'm not from Silva. My world doesn't have magic at all."

"First off, all worlds have magic," said Annabelle. "Magic lives in people, not worlds. Secondly, how do you know my—"

"That's not entirely true," Marlow interrupted. "Some worlds have more magical residue. That's what makes the magic in Silva so strong, even if it comes from people."

"You're saying you came from one of these lesser-magic worlds?" said Annabelle to Lan, who had not understood a word Marlow said. "Are you a runaway?"

Annabelle stared at Lan for the first time with interest, but her hand still rested on the knife at her hip. Between them, Marlow remained with his arms outstretched.

"Well, not exactly. I—" Lan took a deep breath. "I'm not sure how to say this nicely, but you're both—well, you're sort of characters in my book."

Dead silence met her words. Even Marlow seemed dubious. *Oh well,* thought Lan, *too late to backtrack.*

"I can prove it," Lan said quickly. "I know why you're here, Annabelle. You want to find that wizard-king Nebulo in the capital, Asta, and give him his 'price of admission' to return Sol to how it was before the enchanted desert wiped out the coast. You both ran away from the Border Academy and just made it across the desert."

"How could you possibly know that?" Annabelle whispered. Marlow drew a shaky breath. "Are you tracking us?"

"No, I told you, I read it in a book I found at my school's fair."

"How does this book end?"

"I haven't finished it yet."

"What? Why not?"

"Why? Even I can't read that fast. That's not important. Point is—"

"Not important? You're telling me you read about me in a book and the ending's not important?"

"Not what I meant. You twisted my words."

"Stop, both of you," Marlow cut in. "What's your name?"

"Lan."

"Let's say you're telling the truth, Lan. It's not unheard of that people cross between worlds—not usually by accident though. You're telling us you didn't know about your magic at all? That's actually impressive."

"Or super careless," Annabelle repeated. "Like I said."

"I don't know . . . We're talking advanced stuff," said Marlow. "How many people do you know who have crossed worlds? Even in Sol, that's gotta be rare. She's strong, to even make it across in one piece."

Lan drew herself up at his words. It wasn't everyday that she got to hear she was a strong witch, though her head felt like it might explode from the news. Marlow's brow was furrowed in thought, but Annabelle's expression had begun to harden. Lan took an involuntary step back.

"I don't like this," said Annabelle. "I think you should leave now."

"Leave?" Lan protested. "Even if I knew how to, I—"

"Just do what you did to get here."

"But—"

All at once, the weight of Lan's unusual situation hit her.

She was in Silva. Marlow had said she was a witch (with powers to be determined!). Wasn't this turn of events precisely what she'd been longing for?

Of course, she had to wonder: Why this story? Why now? Had the storm taken anyone besides her? Likely not. After all, it had been *her* book. It had called to her at the fair. Well, no one else was around, but surely the fact that she'd read it meant something! However, if her father *was* safely in his bed, what would he think when he woke up and found her missing? Would her family worry, or did time work differently between worlds? Perhaps she would return to find no time had passed at all.

That thought comforted her. Lan had read so many fantastical stories that she could confidently consider herself an expert in such matters. Usually, time did not pass in these kinds of tales. Well, usually, the kids were all orphans. They didn't have to reassure their worried parents. But why should Lan be denied an adventure just because she wasn't? The more she thought about it, the harder it became to deny an incontrovertible fact: Lan did not want to leave this world. Not yet.

At the very least, she had to test out her magic powers and see if she truly was a witch! A few days wouldn't hurt. Anyhow, she needed time to figure out how to get home. Why not linger while she was at it? Lan nodded absently to herself, then looked at the other two, resolute.

"I don't want to go back right away," Lan declared. "Can't I stay with you?"

"No! We don't need some half witch hanging around on an all-important quest," said Annabelle. "Don't you have anything better to do?"

"Not really. Everyone at school's got big plans for their summer, but I'll be stuck inside doing the same boring *nothing* every day if I go back! I won't be in your way... too much. Though if you've got any food to share, I wouldn't mind a bite."

"We barely have enough to feed ourselves!"

"Well, wouldn't a witch be able to help with that?"

"What are you going on about?"

"Your grandmother," said Lan, suddenly remembering. "She told you so herself. No one's ever gotten to Asta without a witch."

"I'm not gonna get used to your weird knowledge," said Annabelle, rubbing her temples like she was warding off a headache. "What's your point?"

"I know I'm not much, but let me hang around a few days. Maybe *I* could help!"

"You found out you were a witch ten minutes ago when we told you!" Annabelle said. "That doesn't count. You don't know any magic."

"That's why I said I'll learn! And I'll be careful if that's what you're worried about. Marlow said I was strong. I summoned a storm to carry me into another world without even meaning to! Or at least, I survived it."

"She could be right, Annabelle," said Marlow slowly. "Having a strong witch around *would* be really handy right now."

"Who exactly is supposed to teach her?"

"I can teach myself," said Lan. "I taught myself to juggle last year."

"In any case, if she's stuck with us now, we can't let her starve," Marlow pointed out.

"I've eaten bad food all year. It can't be worse," Lan offered.

Annabelle paused. She looked at Marlow, and something passed between them. Then she turned back to Lan, hands on her hips, suddenly businesslike. Lan felt a chill rush down her spine.

"Let's be honest. You just want to play the hero, don't you?" said Annabelle. "I've met the type. Well, if you're so eager, I know something you could do that might actually help."

"What's that?" said Lan cautiously.

"Get us past those tree guardians on the other side of the river. If you manage that, you're welcome to stay with us as long as you like. If we can, we'll also help you on your way when you feel like going back."

Silence hung in the air. Lan's limbs felt heavy. Playing with spells on a sunny riverbank was one thing, but fighting scary magical creatures? That was a whole other game. Lan's eyes lingered on the scratch on Annabelle's cheek. Across the river, the pines swayed innocently in the gentle breeze. There was no sign of the ominous wooden beings that had attacked Annabelle and Marlow in the last chapter of the story, nothing but dandelion-strewn fields.

"What's wrong?" said Annabelle. "Too scared to actually do something useful with your power? Did you think quests were all about fooling around by the fire? Thought you could stay without giving anything back?"

"Well, it's just that I don't know much about fighting . . ." Lan began.

"You don't have to," said Marlow. He seemed uncomfortable with Annabelle's taunts but did not stop her. "We can handle ourselves in a skirmish, but a spell or two to clear our path would help tons."

"I thought you fought them off already?" said Lan.

"I did yesterday, but they surrounded us when we tried to cross the river at dawn," said Annabelle. "There's too many."

"Have you thought of fire?"

"And burn down the whole forest?"

"All right, I get it," said Lan.

She looked from Annabelle's stubborn face to Marlow's guarded expression, then up to the skies stained purple. A flock of birds—at least she thought they were birds—flew across in a spiral formation, dark silhouettes dotting the clouds. Lan hesitated, but the truth was she had known from the moment Annabelle asked that she had to say yes. Hadn't her parents taught her to always help people if she could? If they did miss her, she would explain once she got back. They would understand. A few days wouldn't matter, and what kind of coward would she be if she backed down now?

"I—I'll see what I can do," Lan said. She had to try. "I will stay with you a bit longer and magic us through those pines. Then I'll work on getting myself home, and I would really appreciate it if you could help me."

"Deal," said Annabelle.

Lan tried to smile but couldn't stop the butterflies taking flight in her belly. She was striking a lot of bargains lately. Speaking of which, she would have to make sure she was home a week from Monday, exactly ten days, to make the track tryouts and keep her word to Manav, on the off chance that time in Toronto was still passing without her.

"What are we working with here?" said Annabelle. "Can you do *any* magic yet?"

"Um, other than the storm?"

"Yes, other than the accidental storm that we're not even sure was yours."

"Whose else could it be?"

"Maybe a powerful witch wanted you in Silva," said Marlow, shrugging. "Or the book was an abandoned portal from years ago that you tumbled into by chance."

"I doubt that," murmured Annabelle. "Look at the sky. Everything I know about magic says it happens on purpose. More likely she teleported and hit her head real hard."

"Hey..."

"Well, are you going to show us what you can do or what?" said Annabelle, crossing her arms.

"Now?" said Lan.

"You could wait a few days until our food runs out."

"Stop it, Belle," said Marlow. He turned to Lan. "No pressure."

"Well, a bit of pressure," countered Annabelle. "You volunteered, remember?"

Lan gulped. How to start? *Think.* What had happened earlier? She'd been moping, longing to be elsewhere. She'd been missing her home in Việt Nam. And then—

A fizzling noise sounded. Lan glanced down. A sad-looking dandelion sprouted between her feet. It drooped and then aged swiftly into a fluffy ball, ripe for wishing. Seconds later, the seeds blew off in the gentle breeze, leaving the barren stem in the dirt.

"I think I did that!" said Lan in wonder. She stared at her tingling palms. The magic had given her a rush of energy better than the feeling of coming off a good run. It made her want to do more.

"It's a start," Marlow said kindly.

Annabelle groaned louder. "It's literally a dandelion, in a field full of dandelions! Now we have to feed some amateur witch with delusions of grandeur!"

Annabelle walked away and knelt by the firepit, poking in their bags for food. She straightened up and pointed a carrot at Lan.

"Three days," she said. "Then you get yourself home. Somehow. We'll find our own way around."

PRACTICE MAKES . . . POTATOES?

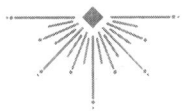

The moment Annabelle walked away, Lan sank to her knees on the grass, exhausted and very hungry. Whenever Lan had imagined a grand adventure back in her world, she'd pictured herself full of energy and miraculously gifted in all skills quest-related, but now she couldn't have defended herself if she tried. Her father's spring rolls from last night seemed far away.

"You should take it easy," Marlow said quietly. He knelt beside Lan.

"I don't have time to take it easy. You heard her. I'm in a strange magical land with powers that I have to figure out in three days! *Your* quest depends on it! Then I have to figure out how to get myself home, and make sure my parents don't worry, and go to track tryouts in ten days, because I promised this guy so he'd buy me the book, which was a really good deal now that I think about it . . ."

"All right, slow down. You don't *have to* do anything."

"No, I'm sick of sitting around!" The weeds around Lan appeared to shoot up a couple inches at her words. "That's all I've done since we came to Canada. I want to see what I can do with *magical powers!*"

"Not gonna lie, you sound a little delirious," said Marlow. "Anyway, your powers aren't going to work well if you're still sick from the whole world-crossing adventure. Come get some food. You can sleep it off and start doing your magic thing tomorrow."

"Magic thing?" Lan repeated, miffed. She had only just found out she was a witch, but she felt protective of her vague powers already.

Marlow helped her up. He offered her his arm as she hobbled to join Annabelle. Lan stole a glance at his easygoing expression, his wet hair falling over his light eyes, and realized she knew little about him. Her book had focused on Annabelle. Marlow had grown up in the Border Academy, which served as an orphanage and training camp. He had risen through his classes with unrivalled skill, winning the admiration of every person that mattered (and the hearts of more than a few). And then, he had left them all.

"You followed her," said Lan. They reached the roughly constructed stone pit where Annabelle was tending to baby flames snaking their way up a log. Marlow helped her to the ground. "Why?"

Annabelle paused, her hands still over the paper-wrapped packs of food she had pulled from their bags. Marlow gave Lan a curious look.

"You cut to the chase, huh?" he said. "Greet every stranger that way?"

Lan looked at her feet. She had chattered non-stop as a little kid. Her family had made fun of her firing off a million questions a minute, but the move to Toronto had turned her taciturn, especially among her peers. It was hard to join in when her English words came out warped and mismatched.

"Hey, it's not a bad thing," said Marlow. "Hard questions beat dull ones."

"The book mostly talked about Annabelle," she tried to explain.

Annabelle laughed. Lan blinked, surprised as the girl's whole face lit up, changed. She still seemed peaky, cheekbones high and hollow, but years younger.

"You hear that?" said Annabelle to Marlow. "You're my sidekick! The Border Academy's *golden boy* reduced to a valet. Bet you wished you'd stayed now."

"Come off it," said Marlow. He sat between them. "Have you looked around?"

The sun had risen high above them, streaking the sky in warm light. The lavender colour had darkened, not quite like sunset anymore but something else entirely. The billowing clouds looked stained from the purple.

"What is that?" Lan asked.

"Residue," said Annabelle uneasily. "It makes magic run, in every world but ours more than most. I remember on the bluffs back home, the sky used to fill with a hundred colours on a good day."

"I was actually talking about the scenery," said Marlow mildly. "These hills, the river . . . Did you see those fluffy things poking around at dawn? I've never seen more than sand and sand."

Lan couldn't help notice he'd neglected to answer her earlier question. An hour into meeting someone was too soon to push, she decided. Instead, she asked, "Was it so bad at the Border Academy? What were you training for anyway?"

"Patrol in the northern ranges, coast guard, some stay on as trainers," he said. "They liked me, so I guess I didn't have it so bad. I never knew anything else. It can be rough for some. They work us pretty hard."

"You would've had your pick of assignment though," said Annabelle. "All that talent squandered for a nice view."

"*Talent* is generous. I'd say at least half was charm," said Marlow with a wink.

"Whatever." Annabelle rolled her eyes, smiling. "I'm not complaining. You charmed your way into all the supplies for our trip."

"You bet I did. Some hero you are, getting your lackey to do all the work."

When Annabelle laughed this time, Lan couldn't help joining in. With the tart taste of apple in her mouth and warm fire to dry her, her fatigue was wearing off. She breathed in the dandelion-scented air. Her head clearing, Lan began to feel a pulse around them, like a heartbeat underlying this world. She stretched out her hands and felt invisible forces jump to them like magnets. She tried to grab hold but they eluded her, dancing out of reach. If she squinted closely, she could see hints of soft colours trailing the air.

"You feel it?" said Marlow, glancing sideways at her.

"Is that the residue stuff?"

"Yep. Leftover magic seeps out of any cast spell. That's why it's called residue. You know the whole energy-creates-more-energy idea? The more spells, the stronger the residue, the better the magic, and so on."

"My world hasn't got any of that," said Lan.

"It must have some," said Marlow. "Maybe not as much as Silva, but even here, it varies. Asta's always buzzing, but the sky didn't look like this when we got to the valley. This purple—that's the magic that brought you here."

"I made the sky purple?" Lan whispered.

"Careful," said Annabelle, an edge creeping back into her voice. Lan heard fear. "With magic, it's easy to get carried away, especially starting out."

"I'll start small," said Lan. She eagerly got to her knees. "Tell me what to do."

"I told you," said Annabelle. "I don't do that magic stuff."

"Some people are naturally more in tune with residue," Marlow explained. "It's never come easily to Annabelle or me. Never had a teacher to draw it out either. The middle of the desert isn't where anyone goes if they've got a choice, so we didn't have many witches flying around."

"*I* am perfectly fine as I am," Annabelle muttered.

"All right," said Lan. "But you wanted food, right? I'll start there."

Lan took a breath and reached in front of her, above a patch of flowers and grass. She hadn't a clue how to begin. Everything she had done so far had simply spilled out, but Lan felt that unseen energy pooling around her hands, begging to be played with.

Mouth-watering dishes jumped to mind when she thought of food: smoked bún chả doused with fish sauce on the streets of her hometown, sweet-and-sour bún riêu with deep-fried tofu at the corner of her aunt's house on Lạc Trung. But Lan could barely list the ingredients that went into them. A refreshing bubble tea would be welcome, but she had a feeling even that might be hard the on first try. Tree guardians or not, Annabelle would definitely banish her if Lan drowned them in milk tea or made it rain tapioca. She'd be completely lost in this world without help. Even fresh fruit, like a handful of ruby-like pomegranate seeds, left her lost as to where to start. As Lan ran through the options silently, her mother's voice came to her from a muggy balcony in Hà Nội two years back: *Potatoes are the easiest things to grow.*

That would do. Lan pictured a tuber rooting in the dirt, the plant breaking through the surface, leaves unfurling. She couldn't help but feel silly. What if they were mistaken, and she wasn't a witch after all? What if someone else had caused the storm and the dandelion was a fluke? Then, to Lan's shock, dark leaves rose from the ground, followed by stems. Lan brushed aside the layer of dirt to find the vines entwining half a dozen purple potatoes. She cupped them in her hands in awe.

"Told you she was strong," Marlow said. Lan glowed.

Annabelle leaned over and plucked one off the roots, her face clouded. She turned it around her palms like she had never seen a potato before.

"It's, uh—a potato," Lan said, just to make sure.

"I know what a potato is," Annabelle said with an eye roll. But when she looked up, Lan caught a hint of gratitude in her brown eyes.

"Told you I could help."

But Lan's confidence did not last the afternoon. No matter how she tried, she could not produce a single other sprig. Her mother had been right. Nothing grew like potatoes. Marlow soon got tired of watching her sprout plant after plant in the dirt around them and sprawled on the ground for a nap, a spare shirt tossed over his face. A wooden bow lay within arm's reach, his quiver of arrows full. Annabelle kicked dust over their fire to quell it but kept an eye on Lan, who felt like she was being supervised.

"You don't have to babysit me," Lan said after a frustrating half hour in silence. She looked up, her hands dirty. They felt heavy, even when holding nothing.

"I'm not gonna let you mess around alone. Who knows what could happen!"

Lan sighed. What was it gonna take for Annabelle to loosen up? "I told you I want to help."

"Last time someone nice wanted to help us, our coast got turned to sand."

"What?"

"You didn't get to the backstory part of your book yet? The reason why that cursed desert exists in the first place?"

"It was an accident. A spell by the Silvan king gone overboard."

"*Accident* is generous," said Annabelle disdainfully. She leaned in. "Do you want the full story?"

Lan paused, then nodded.

"It's not a happy one," Annabelle began. "In my grandma's warrior days, the ice giants invaded from the northern range—near Mireille, where Marlow's from. He was one of the kids orphaned before Nebulo decided he'd stop the attacks himself. Powerful magic has always run in the royal Silvan bloodline, and they've got all sorts of amplifiers hidden away to strengthen their spells.

"Anyway, Nebulo decided to play hero and work this massive curse. He blasted enough heat to shut the giants in their caves for good . . . scorched half the country in the process. Most of the troops along the border made it back to Asta on camel. They were still sending rescue units in the early days. The rest fled to the coast, took the last boats out. But we didn't want to leave. Sol is our homeland."

Her eyes seemed to grow darker as she spoke, her back hunched and frail frame carved out by grief. The bitterness in her voice made Lan want to pull away, but curiosity pushed her forward.

"Isn't it good to not have giants attacking anymore though?" Lan ventured.

"A lot of people thought so," said Annabelle. "King Nebulo is very popular in Asta. The folks there think he did the right thing. That's why no one bothered to look closer. But in Sol, we were doing fine holding the giants off on our own. Besides, they only started coming so far south because Silva was messing around with their northern lands to begin with. That's what my grandma told me. They were nosy about the ice giants' weather magic, wanted to have some for themselves. The whole line of Astan royals will take over anyone's home if it means bettering their own."

Lan kept quiet. She had read something to that effect, but it felt different to hear the story from Annabelle herself. The book had told of how she'd been enrolled at the Border Academy at seven years old. The orphanage turned training camp still got shipments of aid from the capital, unlike the independent people of Sol, who had thrived off the coast for centuries until the dry spell.

Few parents had chosen to send their children away, but within boarding school grounds, Annabelle could keep up a semblance of her education. She got to fight. She was properly fed and clothed. Her family had sent her there to survive while Sol trudged along, all but forgotten, a proud warrior nation scraping remains to stay alive.

"I know you read about me or whatever," Annabelle continued, "but where I'm from in Sol, our people know that reading tells you only so much. Some things, you have to live through, and that matters more."

"Well, you'd be surprised—"

"I don't care if you can recite facts," Annabelle ploughed on, her voice growing louder with every word. "When Nebulo created that desert, we got wiped off the map. We lost hundreds. You didn't feel how horrible it was to never see my sister again. My grandmother can rarely spare time for the journey on camel. No one's attempted to cross that desert without magic, but Marlow and I did. We have one shot. Then my sister can grow up in a real home, and I'll never have to look at the Academy gates again. I can't let anything get in the way."

"I get it," said Lan.

Annabelle raised an eyebrow.

Lan steeled herself, then continued. "I get it's not the same, but if it means anything, I haven't seen my mom in more than a year, and I've got a baby brother far away too. He'd be around three now, and I don't know when *I'll* see them again. It's not because of some magical desert—more like a couple oceans. I'm just saying I know how you feel."

Lan's voice choked on the last words. She had never spoken about her family to anyone in Toronto, and yet the words came as easily as her tears.

"By choice?" Annabelle asked quietly. Her hard gaze almost softened.

"As much as yours," said Lan, wiping her eyes with her damp snowflake-printed pyjama sleeve. "I didn't choose anything. It seemed important to my parents though. They said we'd have better chances in our future, whatever that means. I was so excited at first, but it got lonely real fast."

"I'm sorry." Annabelle paused, looking down. "I guess we're both missing home a whole lot."

Lan nodded. She pulled her knees in close to her chest and wrapped her arms around them.

"You know what my grandma used to tell Daisy and me?" murmured Annabelle. She looked distant, lost in memory, and Lan waited. "When I was little, she told us our people were descended from giant stone crabs. We have the same tough skin. After time, we'd slip in and out of our shells to live on land, but our existence was always tied to the ocean. Stone crabs are sacred in Sol, but no one's seen any since the spell. They've left the coast."

"That doesn't mean they won't return," said Lan softly. "My people are supposed to be descended from a dragon and a fairy. Everyone knows the tale of Lạc Long Quân and Âu Cơ, but just because we haven't seen them, it doesn't mean they're gone."

Lan did not know if what she said helped in the slightest, but Annabelle gave a her a grateful smile. Lan returned it, trying to ignore the pinch of jealousy she felt in listening to the other girl talk. Sol was her home. Annabelle had a way forward and the guts to get there. Hà Nội was Lan's home, but she didn't even know if she wanted to return for good and live with her big family now. She had a feeling things might never go back to how they were before. Could it be enough for her mom and brother to join them in Toronto, in a more sunlit room that they could decorate together? Lan decided she didn't have to think about it yet. She was in Silva. She understood that much, and briefly, it meant she could forget about everything that hurt.

"I'll be careful," Lan promised. "My parents would want me to help if I can."

Annabelle didn't say anything for so long that Lan assumed she was being ignored again. She turned back to the heaps of purple potatoes.

"Thanks for the potatoes," said Annabelle finally.

"Plenty more where they came from," said Lan, "if nothing else."

"Maybe not, but they'll keep us fed. We were running low."

"I know I can do more . . ."

Lan's hands tingled as if in response. She tried again. Maybe she could summon a carrot this time, or a rutabaga. Something pulsed in the ground.

"Have you managed more than potatoes?" said Marlow groggily, getting up.

"Almost," said Lan, examining the plant. "I think this one's a yam."

PAINT-SPLATTERED SKIES

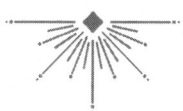

When Lan opened her eyes the next morning, it was dawn. Her back ached from resting on the ground, but falling asleep by the fire's glow had been surprisingly easy. The sight of the sun rising over a lavender sky drew Lan awake at once. She flexed her palms, testing the air for beats of magic. They pulsed in response, stronger and steadier than the day before. Lan looked around. Marlow was nearby, firing perfect shots at a knot in a tree fifty metres away. Annabelle was fiddling with something by the river.

"She's setting a trap for fish," Marlow explained, catching sight of Lan awake. "Apparently, they learn to do that pretty young on the coast."

He shouldered his bow and tossed Lan a bread bun. She caught it.

"You look better," she said without thinking. It was true. His sunburns were healing quickly.

"Really?" He raised an eyebrow. "I feel like crap. Almost like I walked across a cursed desert or something."

"Wish I could shoot that well after walking across a desert."

"You know, I could really get used to your steady stream of compliments to start my every morning. Here I was feeling off my game."

"Don't get used to it," said Lan, ignoring the rising heat in her cheeks. No wonder Annabelle was constantly rolling her eyes.

Marlow laughed and returned to his shooting. He was so at ease in motion. Nothing seemed to faze him. Lan tried to not stare. She wasn't in a magical valley to get her head turned by some boy, however smooth a talker he was. Marlow joked around with everyone, and Lan had her own magic to practise.

The residue in the empty valley became easier to notice as the hours dragged on. Lan chewed on her stale bread, focused on the magic pooling around her hands: bubbles of vibrating energy that she could play with and draw from. Soon, they sharpened enough for Lan to grasp and see faint colours in. She managed to summon a clump of mushrooms from the ground that they devoured for lunch with Annabelle's freshly caught fish. The smoky smell reminded Lan of her family dinners by the seaside back home.

Surely, her parents would be proud if they saw how much she was learning here, Lan thought. She had so much to tell them! The more her dad crossed her mind, the more Lan convinced herself that he was sleeping soundly in his bed, ready to welcome her home when she returned. She would figure out how to later, but so far, Marlow was right. Energy created energy, which meant every spell was easier than the last. By sundown, Lan had covered the ground in morning glory, kohlrabi, and lettuce heads that the rabbits in the valley delighted in. The riverbank was looking less like a dandelion field and more like her mother's dream vegetable patch with every passing minute. The sky exploded with colour. Magic was addictive.

In fact, the hardest part was keeping her promise of restraint to Annabelle and not trying something wild, like raising an army of the living dead to march them past the pines. Even though her muscles ached, Lan had a feeling she could do more than grow produce.

She would have to before the three days were up, unless Annabelle planned on making salad and launching it at the tree guardians. Lan's fear of the snarling beasts hadn't left her, but she also felt bolder than she could ever remember.

Perhaps getting home wouldn't even be too hard when she put her mind to it, Lan thought, but she had no desire to try just yet. Silva was full of wonders. She took in the oddly shaped fish that swam past her feet, the cawing of birds (some very large) that never flew close, and later that night, the darkened sky sprinkled with foreign constellations. Like Marlow, Annabelle looked better after a rest. She lost the dark rims under her eyes. The scratch on her cheek began to scab over. As they regained their strength, Marlow and Annabelle began to discuss the items they needed to bring to Asta.

"A good story is easy," said Annabelle. "We'll have it just by getting to Asta. You're good at spinning tales, Marlow. You can handle that one."

"Are you saying I'm good at making things up?" said Marlow.

"I'm saying that somehow, people always believe you."

"One of my many talents."

"We'll definitely need courage in large supply when we cross the Weathering Woods," said Annabelle, ignoring him. "Though how we harness it to bring to the king, I'm not sure . . ."

"Seems like it'd call for magic," said Marlow. "Proof of a heart too—I've got a feeling we'll need a witch for that."

Marlow snuck a not-so-subtle glance at Lan, who accidentally showered herself in a cloud of marigolds at his gaze. Annabelle frowned and brushed a stray one off her lap.

"Lan's got to get back to her dad as soon as we're past the pines," said Annabelle.

"I also have track tryouts in nine days," Lan agreed. "If time really is passing in my world, I shouldn't be late. I made a promise, and my family will be full-blown panicking by then!"

Her father would already be worried if he had woken to find her gone, Lan thought guiltily, but she could explain away one week with a good cause. Surely, he'd have to forgive her. Marlow looked like he was going to say something else but bit his tongue. Instead, his hands gathered the gold flowers on the ground and began to weave them into a surprisingly shapely flower crown.

"In any case," he said, "I think you could stand to step up your training a notch. We can't get past anything by growing mushrooms. No offence."

"I was actually thinking the same thing," said Lan.

"Is that wise?" said Annabelle. "I mean, witches take years to train before they step outside the learning grounds in Sol."

"This was your idea," Lan reminded her.

"I know, but I didn't *really* think—"

"How did you picture us getting across exactly?" said Marlow. "With an armful of vegetables?"

Annabelle hesitated, then said, "Be careful. I'm staying out of it."

"I know what I'm doing," said Marlow. He got to his feet and gently laid the finished flower crown on Lan's head. She blinked. It perched perfectly on her head, even when she shifted. Annabelle raised an eyebrow.

"Complements your hair," said Marlow. "I'll be right back."

Lan watched curiously as he slid down to the riverbank and returned with two large sticks. He shoved one in her hands.

"Up you get," he said, pulling her to her feet. "Show me what you got."

"I thought you said I didn't have to fight," said Lan, not moving.

"No, but you can learn the basics. Tree guardians are nasty. You should know how to swat one away if it's clawing at your face."

Lan looked at her stick. It was about half her height and felt foreign in her hands. Back home, she'd spent hours pretending to be in battle with her coat-hanger bow and chopstick wand. She even had a foam sword to wave around in Hà Nội, much to her bà nội's disapproval. Somehow, this stick felt way scarier.

"You're not giving me instructions?"

"You'll have to step closer," he prompted.

"What if I hurt you?"

"You're not gonna hurt me."

"You sure about that?" said Lan. She lifted the stick and charged with a yell, sending her flower crown flying.

Marlow stepped smoothly aside as she ran straight past him and skidded to a halt.

"Pretty sure, yeah," he said, smirking. "Try to be a little less obvious next time."

Lan swung again. Marlow dodged, then raised his stick to meet hers, calling out comments with every move.

"Parry, duck, watch your back leg, *lighter swings*, you're tiring yourself out."

"She's got spirit," said Annabelle grudgingly when Lan paused for a drink. She hadn't left her spot by the empty firepit but sat watching with her arms crossed. The sun blazed high above them.

"Try it again," said Marlow. "Don't be scared to use your magic."

"Are you sure?" said Annabelle, biting her lip.

"What's she gonna hurt me with? Potatoes?"

Lan puffed indignantly, and a bushel of leeks sprouted at his feet. Marlow sidestepped them smoothly and swung. Lan ducked. Where was that residue when she needed it? She felt nothing at her fingertips, not without the quiet concentration she usually had. She tried to imagine Marlow's stick flying away. Nothing happened. His next blow caught her in the stomach. She fell on her butt.

"You good?"

Lan took his outstretched hand and pulled herself up.

"Again," she said.

This time, when Marlow swung, she dodged and focused on the weight in her hands. A pulse responded, but before she could decide what she wanted to do with it, Marlow's stick tapped her lightly on the head. Lan sighed.

"You need to be quicker," shouted Annabelle. "I can practically see you thinking. Even when you're starting out, the moves are just one part. You only need to master a few good ones, but you can't forget to listen to your gut."

"I don't know what my gut's telling me."

"You're not even listening."

"And how do you suggest I do that?"

Annabelle shrugged. "You have to trust your body."

"That's very unhelpful," said Lan.

She nodded at Marlow to go again. *Okay, gut, anytime now.* She could do this, Lan told herself. She'd promised to help Annabelle. She had learned so much already!

Parry. Parry. Step, and—Lan felt a buzzing in the air. Her fingertips tingled. She fumbled to hold on to the pulse. A rush of energy coursed through her, and she used it to summon a strong gale. She remembered to duck from Marlow's next swing, but—

Inches from her chest, his stick wobbled and fell limply to the ground.

"Nice!"

Lan jumped in the air and whooped, all thoughts of conjuring rutabagas forgotten. This magic was so much cooler! If she could bring this power back to Toronto, Lan thought, she could do anything. She'd never feel lost again.

Marlow worked Lan hard until late afternoon. Annabelle left to practise by herself partway through. Lan took it as a sign that she trusted them to not destroy the valley. That was progress, she decided. Each time they paused for a drink, she stole glances at Annabelle on top of the slope. The girl moved like a dancer, her hair pulled back in a high ballerina bun. She had whittled herself a small spear and was alternating between the new weapon and her familiar dagger. When Lan asked to see the blade, she saw it was not made of metal but black stone, about the length of her forearm. The handle was rock, carved and painted in shades of ocean blue.

"My grandmother's," Annabelle explained. "The only thing I carried with me from home. She was a bit of a legend in Sol."

Lan handed the blade back at once. It felt wrong in her hands and so sharp she feared it would slip and cut her. Her magic somehow seemed more predictable, though she knew Annabelle would disagree. Even if Lan could now consistently disarm Marlow before he got too close, her gestures felt stiff and slow compared to the grace with which Annabelle moved.

"Why wasn't she popular like you at the Border Academy?" Lan asked when she and Marlow finally called it a day. They rolled up their pants and waded into the river. He bent over Annabelle's trap, prodding it. Two glassy-eyed fish stared glumly back.

"Annabelle? If I had to guess, a lack of smoothness and misfortune at not being a boy," Marlow joked.

"Well, you don't move like her."

Marlow looked offended. "You do realize I'm going easy on you?"

Lan rolled her eyes.

"I meant your style's different. You're more—I dunno—technical?"

"Annabelle comes from a long line of warriors," said Marlow. "She grew up with a knife in her hand. The mix of Academy training makes her unique."

"Then why are you the so-called golden boy with all the *prospects*?"

Lan half expected another lighthearted reply, but Marlow paused as if deciding whether he wanted to answer honestly. His hands fumbled over the twine of the trap, where the fish were growing agitated.

"I've never known anything but the Academy," he said finally, standing up. "Brought in when I was one, maybe two. I caught on quickly that the right words got me what I needed. Not Annabelle. She spent good years at home. Knows what she wants but won't compromise a smidge of herself to get it."

"And you would?"

"I do what I have to. That's why she keeps me around."

He said it like a joke, but Lan wondered how much he meant it. She tried to picture Annabelle wheedling her way to extra servings at mealtimes or an extra hour of sleep. The thought was laughable, but so was Marlow's ability to breeze through any situation, light on his feet as if daring anything to touch him. Lan wanted to ask more, but he seemed eager to move away from the subject. He lifted the trap out of the water, fish squirming inside.

"I actually have no idea what to do. Our training trips never reached the sea."

Lan tried to hide her discomfort. Her mother was a brilliant cook, and everything back home was fresh, but Lan had always avoided looking at the animals before they were to be eaten. She liked to think of herself as a baker—cookies, banana bread, and the occasional chocolate cake. Seafood was beyond her. Before she had to stammer an answer, she saw Annabelle striding down the hill toward them.

"Sol's sake, Marlow, just clean them in the river," she said.

Marlow passed Annabelle the trap. She took over, her hands moving skilfully over the scales. It reminded Lan of the stories her mom had often told of her childhood on the farms just beyond the limits of Hà Nội. She had grown up knowing how to gather the right plants from nearby ponds and raise her own ducks. Lan had loved playing by the marshy water by her grandparents' house, but market stalls had taken up most of the area in recent years. Again, she wondered what her mom would think of her being by this riverbank. Annabelle would certainly impress her.

"You're learning quickly," Annabelle said as she worked.

"Oh," said Lan, surprised. "Thank you?"

"The tree guardians are small. If you can knock a branch out of Marlow's grip, you can blow them back to clear a path. They won't stand and wait for you though."

It was the first time they had spoken about the crossing. Lan peered at the other side of the banks. She'd caught no glimpse of the elusive creatures across the river and wasn't sure she wanted to. The book had described them as wooden beings with razor-sharp claws, no bigger than a housecat but with the ferocity to match. Knowing any more about them would probably make her lose her nerve, Lan thought.

"What do they want with us?" she asked.

"It's not personal," said Annabelle. "In the stories my grandma told, tree spirits created guardians out of their own bark to keep intruders away. Apparently, pines are particularly hostile. I think it depends on the type of tree."

Lan shivered. She had one more day to practise, and then they'd cross. Afterward, she would figure out how to get home.

Before her, the grove of pines betrayed nothing. Lan could not even tell how far the trees spanned. Marlow and Annabelle hadn't made it to treeline last time. Maybe with Lan, they would dash through in minutes—or the woods would grow thicker, trapping them all.

Together, they walked back to the fire, picking their way through the mess of a vegetable patch Lan had grown. The sun sank low over distant dunes where Marlow and Annabelle had trudged earlier that week. The valley's sunset, stained from Lan's spells, took on more colours. They made a stunning paint-splattered blend of pale oranges, blues, and violets. The dark purple from the first day—the original, strongest spell—had faded, leaving no sign of the mysterious storm. Lan might've been in Silva all along.

Her arms ached, but Lan tried her best to help with dinner, sprouting dill and lime to season the fish like she remembered from her days in Việt Nam. Her mother would have scolded her to no end if Lan did not pitch in like she'd been taught. The result was not the exact same, yet dinner that night still tasted better than any meal she'd had in a year. Lan had to smile when she looked at Annabelle chewing with her eyes closed to savour every bite, the same way Lan's grandfather did. On her left, Marlow had wolfed down his share. He was leaning on their bags, focused on weaving a fresh crown of mint leaves and scallions. He smiled when he caught Lan staring, and for a second, the air around her almost smelled like home.

THE TREE GUARDIANS

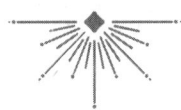

On the day of their planned venture across the river, Lan woke with the sun. She was not usually an early riser. Living underground in Toronto meant that she had no sunlight to wake her in the mornings, but that wasn't a problem on a field. Blinking, she stretched her fingers wide. After three days of steady practice, the air around them teemed with residue. The familiar touch of magic calmed her. Slowly, she rose. Annabelle was washing by the river. Marlow nibbled on a bean bun that Lan had managed to conjure the previous night.

"No, thanks," said Lan when he held one out to her.

"You should eat," he said. "Treat it like any other morning."

"I'd rather get it over with."

"Be careful around wishing."

"Thanks, Marlow, that's comforting."

"Leave her be," said Annabelle, coming up the slope. She squeezed her wet braid. "Everyone's different before game days. If you don't want to eat, we might as well go."

Lan nodded. Waiting was always worse. Marlow had offered to push their crossing back a couple days, but Lan was determined.

If they didn't go soon, her fear would outweigh any progress she made. Besides, she needed to get back to Toronto before long. With one of Annabelle's elastics, Lan tied her hair in a messy ponytail.

"Hang on," said Annabelle, looking at Lan's bare feet. "I have spare sandals."

She dug through her leather pack and pulled out a pair of gladiator sandals and a set of what Lan assumed was Border Academy uniform: black pants, loose shirt. Unlike Marlow and Annabelle's white tops, this one was crimson red.

"Southern troop colours," said Annabelle in response to Lan's questioning look. "My uniform for the longer trips out."

Lan took the clothes and ducked behind a shrub to slip out of her much-stained snowflake pyjamas. She rolled them into a tight ball and tucked them in Annabelle's bag. The shoes fit her perfectly. An odd feeling caught in her throat as she smoothed the loose red shirt over her waistline. A stranger would now see three Border Academy runaways at first glance. The thought made her feel weird.

"Look at you, making our Academy uniform look good," said Marlow. He stared as Lan stepped out from behind the bush.

Annabelle shot him a glare. Lan did her best to not meet his gaze.

"Come here," said Annabelle, her eyes appraising.

Lan approached, dropping the bag with her pyjamas at her feet. Annabelle spun her around and retied the shirt straps at the back of her neck. Then she pulled off the elastic and twisted Lan's hair in a thick braid.

"Important to keep your view clear in a fight," she said. "One more thing." Annabelle thrust her makeshift spear into Lan's hands. She took it. Her gut was doing backflips in double time. Was this how her classmates felt before tests? Lan had never cared for school enough to get nervous, but the worst that could happen there was one bad report card. The worst that could happen here . . . well, she didn't know, and she couldn't think about that.

Marlow and Annabelle shouldered their bags. Sadness welled up in Lan as she watched Marlow kick dirt over their firepit, scaring the lurking rabbits. She would never see this valley again. Her ragged vegetable patch had begun to feel homey.

"Stop looking so squeamish," said Annabelle. "If everything goes to plan, we'll pass untouched."

"I know."

Marlow took the lead, bow and quiver slung across his back. Lan could not understand how he looked so relaxed. His blond hair caught the sunlight, bringing back the butterflies she'd felt around him from the first day. *Focus*, she reminded herself.

Behind Lan, Annabelle walked with her hand on her dagger. She was running through their plan again. With the other two defending both sides, Lan could focus her magic to clear their way forward. It sounded simple. They'd soon be on their merry way.

"We want as little ruckus as possible. Just get to the other side of the trees."

They stepped into the river. The water seeped uncomfortably into Lan's sandals. She clutched the spear and tried to calm her nerves. Her attempts at deep breaths came out in angry huffs. Annabelle raised an eyebrow at her, followed by a tight-lipped *settle down* glare.

Marlow reached the opposite side and hopped on cautiously. The treeline stood a dozen feet away, but the rocky riverbank provided no shortage of crevices. He crouched, waiting. Nothing moved. Slowly, he reached back to help Lan up the bank. The moment she grabbed his hand—

"Marlow!"

Marlow pulled back and drew his bow in one swift move. Lan slipped, halfway out of the water. She screamed. He knocked away the creature bounding at his back.

"Get up!" he shouted at her.

Lan saw Annabelle launching herself onto the bank where a dozen wooden creatures growled. Lan scrambled up after her, cutting her knee on a rock.

Great start, she thought with rising panic.

She came up so quickly she nearly ran into Marlow, with his back to the river. They stood, encircled. Lan's eyes widened. After days of picturing them (or more accurately, trying to not picture them), the tree guardians had emerged on cue, almost exactly as her book as described yet at once so much more frightening.

They were walking logs, covered in a bark-like texture, with gnarly twigs curled menacingly like claws and angry knots for eyes. They hissed, moving on four legs like feral cats, more sinuously than Lan had imagined. The one that Marlow had hit was oozing something like sap from its side, revealing a green underbelly like the inside of a young plant.

Lan stood, stunned. Her limbs felt frozen. What had she been thinking, wishing for a quest? This was terrifying! She was no hero. Annabelle had known that from the start. Lan should've listened and tried to get home while she still could!

The largest creature stood in front her. It seemed to be the leader. Harsh sounds came from its throat as though barking commands. Lan could not understand them, but she guessed they meant something to the effect of *back off or die*! Disarming Marlow in practice suddenly seemed miles away from sending a moving being flying twenty feet in the air. It was too late to think about that, she reminded herself. She had a job to uphold.

"Your move," Annabelle prompted, dagger spinning in her hand. Lan shoved away her doubt. She reached out her left palm, feeling for pools of magical residue around her. They drifted toward her like soap bubbles in the wind. She quelled her rising fear. They had to pass. Marlow and Annabelle were counting on her.

A gust of wind rushed forth from her hands. The snarling tree guardian before her screeched. It tumbled through the air, blown back to the treeline. Lan barely heard Marlow's and Annabelle's cheers. They were cut off. The remaining creatures did not wait. In sync, they attacked. The last trace of Lan's hesitation disappeared.

"Run!" Marlow yelled.

The morning air erupted in high-pitched squeals. Annabelle charged past Lan, swinging. Her blade collided. Before the first creature hit the ground, another jumped at her face. Annabelle dodged, hitting it square in the chest. Lan heard a whistling noise. She spun on instinct and smacked away the tree guardian leaping at her head. Marlow was using his bow to strike the creatures too close to fire at. Lan gathered every ounce of energy and sent a gale racing over the ones clutching at his legs. They tumbled head over heels. Marlow regained his footing. He grabbed Lan's hand. They hurried to catch up with Annabelle in the trees.

Instantly, another dozen had them surrounded, clawing from all sides. Lan broke through their ranks with every bit of energy she could muster. Arrows soared past her, hitting targets circling the edge of the fight. The creatures prowling the nearest branches scattered. She forced an opening, her magic cleaving through the air and sending everything flying in its path. They ran.

This plan had been way too optimistic! Lan raced over pine cones and fallen logs, aware of Marlow keeping pace by her side. Had he and Annabelle truly believed they could make it out unscathed? Or had they only been reassuring her? She'd been foolish enough to believe it. Steps ahead, Annabelle was bleeding from a long scratch down her neck, her movements slowing. Lan winced glancing at it. So far, she had repelled every blow coming at her, but she could not protect the other two. The creatures kept coming. The trees grew denser. Lan knew she would be lost the moment she stopped running.

"Just push forward!" said Marlow.

Lan could hear them fighting, steps behind. Her shirt was damp with sweat. She fought the urge to look back and help. Like they'd rehearsed, she focused on clearing the path out. Blow by blow, Lan's jumbled thoughts faded into the background, replaced by something like adrenalin. Dimly, she registered the spear in her hand growing heavy with that weighty feel of residue. She used it to direct her spells. It answered with bursts of magic. Was this what Annabelle meant by gut instinct? Her moves grew lighter, smoother with each swing. Lan noticed the air glowing in an orange haze.

At last she saw sunlight ahead. They had almost made it out!

She charged, Marlow right behind. They burst into the clearing.

"Annabelle!"

A few paces behind, Annabelle struggled to shake two tree guardians clawing at her legs. Marlow fired. One fell, staining the ground with sap. The other lunged for her chest and knocked Annabelle backwards into the dirt.

Fear gripped Lan. She sent a gust roaring. The creature did not let go but rolled, claws sunk into Annabelle's shirt, taking her with it. Lan heard a cry. The spell missed.

"Shoot!" Lan cried at Marlow. He had nocked an arrow, aimed, but did not move.

A second later, Annabelle broke free with a hard elbow to the tree guardian's nose. It shook its head vigorously. Marlow loosed his arrow before it could give chase. Annabelle stumbled to her feet. He ran forward and caught her as she fell.

"I'm fine!"

Lan was not convinced. Her white shirt was stained red.

Marlow dropped his bow and helped her sit. She rested her head on his shoulder. Lan sunk to her knees beside them, her whole body shaking.

"I couldn't get a clear shot," Marlow said. "You had it though."

"I know."

PROOF OF A HEART

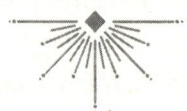

Marlow did his best to staunch the blood flowing from the cuts in Annabelle's side. Arms around her, they passed through the grassy fields clear of the pines and slowed when the terrain gave way to a cliffside of boulders leading out of the western valley.

"I'm not climbing tonight," Annabelle said, gazing up at the rocky hill. Her face had a sickly sheen to it.

"Of course you aren't, don't be ridiculous," said Marlow.

Lan did not want to think about what it must've taken for Annabelle to admit that. She wished she could heal the wounds with a wave of her hand but she would probably make it worse. And Annabelle would never agree to it.

They made camp at the base of the slope. Lan ducked behind a boulder for privacy, partly to relieve herself but more to freak out for a moment alone. She shoved away the thoughts of her parents and what they might think if they saw her now. Her father, protective as he was, would order her back home at once. If she knew how to return, she'd surely be tempted to go. Lan had had quite enough of an adventure.

But even as she thought it, Lan knew she couldn't leave Annabelle as injured as she was, and Marlow to support her on his own. At some point on the afternoon road, they had silently agreed that Lan could spare one more day. She was far more needed in Silva, even if she could do nothing to speed up Annabelle's recovery. She'd see how they were faring after an evening's rest, Lan decided, and then she really ought to try getting back.

After a few breaths, Lan gathered her courage and returned to the fire. Marlow had struck a match and was blowing on the kindling to encourage the flames. Lan itched to help them along but did not dare try in case she lost control and set the valley ablaze. Annabelle had already changed and fallen asleep. To Lan's relief, she didn't look bad cleaned up with a fresh shirt. Marlow glanced at her every few seconds. His hair was damp with sweat, but Lan was amazed by how unharmed he appeared. It was near dusk, and she could barely keep her eyes open.

"Get some rest," said Marlow. "You did good today."

Lan smiled wanly. He was roasting the last of their potatoes that she had conjured the previous night. The smell made her stomach grumble. She was too restless to lie still on the gravelly ground. Her magic had weakened since leaving the woods. She missed the riverbank, the snuffling rabbits peeking out of the tall grass and the yellow dandelions dotting her jungle of vegetables. There would be no more flower crowns here.

Lan pulled her dirty pyjamas out of Annabelle's bag and tried to fashion bedding. She lowered herself on it tentatively. Perhaps because she could feel every pebble on her back, her eyes remained wide open. She stared at the sky and watched a dozen colours pass before her—reds, purples, blues, and golds—and automatically reached her hands out. Energy sluggishly returned to her palms. The longer she looked upward, the stronger the pulse grew. Soon magic no longer thrummed only in her hands but in her whole body pressed on the earth. She grasped the wooden spear beside her and felt the residue course through the stick like it was an extension of her arm.

"You should hold onto that while you're here," said Marlow, watching her.

"It's stronger for some reason, the residue," said Lan. She reached over and grabbed a potato from the fire, and then another.

"That's odd," said Marlow. "I doubt anyone's doing more magic around here."

"What about objects? Do they hold residue?" asked Lan.

"Of course," he said. "Some people use wands, jewellery. Animals too. A lot of witches keep pets to help their magic."

"Like black cats?"

"Black cats?"

"It's a superstition, where I'm from. People think black cats belong to witches."

Marlow shrugged. "Never heard of it, but could be. Believing probably makes it more true."

The sky had darkened while they talked. She'd never bothered to glance up much in Toronto or Hà Nội. There hadn't been much to look at after nightfall. In Silva, the blanket of stars stunned her—some a barest glimmer far away and others close enough to kiss the top of the valley. It seemed an infinite walk from where they lay, and Lan's legs were groaning already. She had never walked so much in her life.

Lan did not remember falling asleep, but when she woke, it was far past dawn. The sun sat directly above, golden in a clear blue sky free of visible residue. Annabelle was up. She looked pale but determined to move.

"Are you sure you can make the climb?" Marlow was saying.

"I'm not spending one more night on this barren cliffside."

"Well, it's past noon. You practically slept a full day."

Lan pushed herself up, brushing grit and pebbles off her arms. They made little indents in her skin. She reached for a water pouch.

"Careful," said Annabelle. "We're low already."

"Actually," said Lan, "I really should be getting back. If he isn't still in his bed, my father will be quite worried by now. Besides, I did make a promise to Manav first."

"Who?" asked Marlow.

"This guy from school. Sort of a friend? He got me this book."

"Okay, and how exactly do you plan on returning home?" said Marlow. His voice was strangely quiet.

"I can start by trying to summon a storm," Lan suggested half-heartedly.

"Seems like you've got yourself sorted," said Annabelle. "Thanks for the assist back there, and wait until we're out of range before calling up a storm, please."

"Well, if you do have any tips, I would appreciate—"

"This isn't right," Marlow cut in.

Annabelle paused. His tone was so uncharacteristically hard that Lan looked up.

"What are you talking about?" she asked.

"Don't you see?" he replied. "We need you."

"Marlow . . ." said Annabelle warily.

"Think about it," he continued, ignoring her. "Marya told us that to seek audience with Nebulo, we need proof of a heart, courage in large supply, and a good story. She also said we'd need a witch. A day after we get here, Lan appears via mystery storm, through a portal that led straight to *us*. Isn't that a bit too *fateful* to be coincidental?"

Lan shifted uncomfortably. Her head was beginning to hurt again.

"My grandma didn't say we *need* a witch exactly . . ." said Annabelle.

"We couldn't have made it past the pines without Lan," said Marlow. "What if she's meant to be the witch we need throughout our whole quest?"

They stared at her. Lan took a step back. She did not know how to react.

"Didn't you say you always wanted to be a witch?" Marlow pressed, addressing Lan directly. "Isn't that why you stayed?"

"Yes, I do," Lan answered without thinking.

"But Sol is nothing to you," said Annabelle. "We'll take it from here. I said I'd help you get back if you needed though—whatever bit we can do. You did get us past those pines."

"You don't know magic," Lan began.

"Everyone knows that for a spell to work, you have to want it," Marlow interjected. "Do you? Are you really going to leave us now? Chances like this one aren't for nothing. You might never make it beyond your world ever again."

"Don't say that!" Lan said, her voice rising. His words brought on a wave of fear. The thought of leaving Silva, of going back to her world and reading about Annabelle and Marlow's quest as if she'd never been with them, hurt more than any wound.

They were staring at her now. Annabelle's mouth hung open in surprise, but Marlow's expression had cooled to a sympathetic stillness. Lan struggled to grasp at her jumbled thoughts.

"Ever since we came to Toronto, all I've wanted to do was leave. Everything's so confusing, and school doesn't help. The only good part is all the books I get to read. At least I can understand other people's stories, not like the whole messy move that took over my life. Your journey makes sense, Annabelle! Nothing makes more sense than a quest! But even if I wanted to, how could I stay? I've never been picked for anything. That book was probably waiting for an orphan or a third child of some poor peasants. I've got a nice family, so I have to get back."

Lan didn't realize she was crying until her cheeks were already wet. Annabelle still stood open-mouthed, eyes wide. Marlow looked like he wanted to give her a hug. Lan's chest felt achingly tight, as though a hand was wringing out her heart, stretching it in too many directions. Her family in Hà Nội, her father and promise to Manav left behind in Toronto, and Marlow and Annabelle ahead of a great challenge in Silva—where did Lan fit in? She dropped onto her knees, suddenly bone-tired and overcome. What was she supposed to do? Then her palms touched the dirt.

All around them, the bleak landscape suddenly transformed. Scraggly weeds grew into thick plants. They bloomed and deepened in colour to a bright, bold crimson. *Poppies.* Lan recognized them at once from the pins people wore on Remembrance Day at Cordella Elementary. Like an ocean wave, the sea of red flowers blossomed in a wide circle around her, stretching to Marlow and Annabelle, who took a quick hop backwards. Lan gasped, her fingers brushing the soft stems. At the same time, the tightness in her chest began to loosen.

"What's happening?" she whispered.

No one spoke. Then after a long moment, Annabelle let out a shaky breath.

"Is this what I think it is?" she said.

"I told you," said Marlow in awe. "Flowers born of tears. What else could it be?"

"What do you mean?" said Lan.

"This is it," said Marlow excitedly. "The first thing we need for Nebulo's price of admission: proof of a heart. This is the closest we've gotten! We do need her, Annabelle!"

Lan sat reeling amid the poppies. The book that she had found, the storm that had brought just her, and now these flowers she'd summoned . . . Could Marlow be right? Did they truly need her if their quest was to succeed? Gently, she scooped up a handful of the poppies surrounding them, *her* poppies. How beautiful they were! They felt so light in her hands, and Lan somehow knew they would not wilt as long as she kept them close.

"You can't leave just yet," said Annabelle, agreeing with Marlow at last.

"But home—" stammered Lan. "I'll be late for track tryouts, and I promised."

"We need answers first," said Marlow. "Everything you said—you can make your place here. You already have! Please, we need you."

He leaned in as he spoke, and Lan felt the fluttering in her stomach whenever he drew close. She knew Annabelle was too proud to beg, but Marlow didn't hesitate. No one back in her world had ever looked at her like she was irreplaceable.

"How do we get answers?" said Lan. "I need to know if my dad is okay."

Annabelle chewed her lip in thought. They waited for a long moment.

"My grandmother did tell me stories . . ." Annabelle murmured. "An all-knowing being built from a magical orchard's power centuries back . . . A creature in the cornfields. If we sought it out—yes, that might work."

"What kind of creature are we talking about?" said Lan. She'd had enough of tree guardians for a lifetime.

"One with answers. They shouldn't be far," said Annabelle absentmindedly. She ignored Lan's questioning stare. "Just over the valley's edge, on our way to Asta. You can hang around another day or two, right?"

"Are you going to tell me why?"

"Because I have an idea."

THE CORNFIELDS

Two minutes into climbing up the valley's edge, Lan tripped and fell, almost landing on the spear she'd been using as a walking stick. Her face glowed with embarrassment. Sleep had not restored her throbbing feet, but at least her magic felt steady, thought Lan. How did teleporting work exactly? Could she whisk them straight to the top of the hill?

"Should we slow down?" called Annabelle.

"Of course not, I'm fine," said Lan with a nervous laugh. Annabelle raised an eyebrow but said nothing.

Annabelle hadn't given them much to go on, but the hope of finding real answers, of having someone to tell her what to do, kept Lan moving. She limped her way along, tripping over stones and fearing for her ankles with every step. As they moved northeast, she was relieved to find the ground more packed. Dirt and boulders provided better grip. They were soon clambering up on all fours. Her hands and knees were quickly bruised. She leaned heavily on her stick to push herself along. Mid-afternoon, they paused, sitting beneath a rocky overhang for shade until the heat abated. They continued their climb, Marlow leading and Annabelle at the rear.

Occasionally, he hung back to offer Lan a hand in support or point out a wobbly rock.

Lan was sweating through her clothes. She could see Marlow was as well. His white shirt stuck to his skin. Every couple minutes, he wiped his forehead with the back of his hand. Lan tried to keep pace without letting on that each step made her legs burn. Annabelle's sandals no longer felt like a perfect fit. Straps scraped at her feet, which were swelling with blisters. No one talked about these dull parts when they recounted their daring exploits, Lan thought bitterly.

The sun sank into the hills. Lan kept her eyes on the road, looking up only when Marlow called out or stood to wait. Occasionally, she glanced behind at Annabelle, her dark hair standing out against the grey slope. She was keeping up well. Her cuts must not have been too deep, Lan thought, reassured. When she peered all the way down to the bottom of the slope, the distance they'd climbed astounded her.

They crested the hill before sundown. Marlow reached the summit as the light was fading and stopped on a patch of sand surrounded by rock walls. Lan heard him whistle as he looked over the side. He helped her up the last boulders, then turned to help Annabelle. Lan panted in relief. Her jellified legs were ready to buckle. She limped past Marlow and peered over the valley's edge.

Acres of gold cornfields spread before them, stalks ranging as far as the eye could see. They emanated an intangible magical glow. No buildings stood in sight. A hazy green forest stretched in the distance, thankfully not pines. Lan couldn't see a river, but the land was so vibrant that water must be close. She took her first long gulp from the water pouch since midday. Annabelle and Marlow came up behind her, staring in awe.

"That's it," said Annabelle. "Those are the enchanted cornfields from the stories the witches spoke of in Sol. They said something lives inside. Something with answers."

"Is that all you know?" said Lan. "What if it's dangerous?"

"We've faced plenty of danger," said Marlow easily. He had relaxed visibly since Lan had decided to stay longer. "Hey, you want to magic us more water?"

"I'm not sure I can," said Lan. "Bit tired tonight."

"Is something wrong?"

"A lot is different now that we're far away."

Marlow held her gaze for another second but did not push. She did not want to admit it out loud, but Lan was starting to understand what Annabelle meant about the unpredictability of magic, how hard it was to get right. She had begun to count on the steadiness of the residue by the riverbank. Now, on the road, it shifted constantly. It depended not only on her environment but also her own energy and concentration. So many new factors had entered into play.

Not to mention Lan hadn't read past the chapter on tree guardians in her novel. Far from their familiar river, she felt blind to this world. She could remember the large forest drawn on the map at the start of the book and the towers of the capital city, Asta; they were impossible to miss. This indistinct area between the river and the woods was mysterious and harder to recall.

With no more firewood, Lan shivered in the night air. Marlow always slept like a charm, but she could hear Annabelle huffing. The sandy spot was softer than the previous night's bedding. Unfortunately, the sand wound its way into the most awkward places on her body. Marlow and Annabelle must be used it, Lan thought. She didn't envy them.

The difficult day should've meant an easy sleep, but Lan couldn't stop her mind from racing. The task of getting past the tree guardians, however daunting, had given her something to focus on. Now her thoughts drifted back in earnest to the basement apartment on Langdon Street. Had her father noticed Lan's absence or had time stilled since the midnight storm? With any luck, she could find out tomorrow.

A hundred questions danced around Lan's head until her eyes fell shut: How had that book gotten on her school shelf? How did it end? Would the ending change because of her choice to stay? Now that Lan too was embedded in the story, Annabelle's initial fixation on the conclusion made perfect sense. When she had picked up the book, Lan had assumed a happily ever after. Even if one was assured for the other two (and it certainly wasn't), where would that leave Lan? How would she get home? Even when she did—Marlow's words from the valley haunted her. Now that she knew a world of magic existed, could she ever be happy in her old life again?

When Annabelle shook Lan awake, the sun was shining high. She blinked and stumbled to her feet, taking in the oddly gold sky.

"You slept in," said Annabelle, handing her a piece of dried fish. "Make it last."

The food only made Lan's hunger grow. She could hear a chorus of their rumbling stomachs as they made their way down the slope. Lan's head began to throb.

"We need water," said Annabelle. "I feel it too."

In a few hours, they reached the edge of the fields. The cobs shone in the sunlight. Radiant green stalks rose far above their heads, providing some relief of shade. They saw no one nearby.

Lan's hunger had overcome the pain in her legs. Her vision was beginning to blur. She forgot the ache of her blisters, the hum of magic she had felt as they approached, and even the mystery of the creature they sought. Without hesitation, she dropped her spear and plunged her hand through the leaves. She plucked an ear, peeled back the husk, and bit in. The sweet juice filled her mouth. The cob was still underripe and very raw, but she scarcely noticed. Within minutes, she had devoured the whole thing and grabbed another, the others right beside her. They ate ravenously. Discarded cobs, clumps of corn hair, and husks littered the ground at their feet.

Lan noticed the crows first. She had been about to reach for another cob when she caught sight of the large black bird staring at her from the top of the plant. Its eyes glinted, obsidian black. It had been silent in watch. The creature cocked its head as it regarded her with a stare too intelligent to ignore. She took a step back and noticed at least a dozen more perched on nearby stalks. In the same moment, Lan suddenly became conscious again of the powerful buzz of magical residue running around the field. It felt different from anything she had sensed in the valley. These weren't pastel-coloured pockets of energy. The air thrummed around them, radiating a deep gold hue.

Lan cleared her throat nervously. Marlow was still eating. Annabelle looked up and saw the birds at once. Her hand jumped to her dagger, but she did not draw it.

"Hey, look up," she said to Marlow.

Marlow stopped chewing midway through a cob. He saw the crows and took a step back. The half-eaten cob dropped from his hands. He inched closer to Lan.

"It's normal to see birds around a cornfield, right?" he said.

"They're staring at us strangely," said Lan. "You don't feel that magic?"

"Nothing unusual, no."

Lan dropped her cob and picked up her spear. It vibrated in her hands.

"Hold up," said Annabelle, squinting at the cornrows. The plants were packed densely, making an impenetrable wall. "There's no way forward."

"Let's move along the stalks until we can find an opening," said Marlow.

The three stepped back several paces and walked south, scanning for a way in. The fields stretched as far as they could see in either direction. The crows followed them, hopping along the tops of the stalks. They stayed quiet but alert.

"There!" said Marlow at last. He pointed to a spot where several plants were missing. A clear path lay beyond it, inviting.

"Something feels off," said Annabelle.

"What choice do we have?" said Lan. "We came this way for answers, right?"

Lan was trembling—from anticipation, fear, or something else entirely? It was hard to tell. Currents of magical energy washed over her, stronger every second.

"Do we run for it?" said Marlow. He looked to Annabelle.

"Let's get close first. Don't draw your bow. We don't want to alarm them."

Cautiously, they inched toward the opening. It was narrow, wide enough to approach comfortably but in single file. A path led straight for several rows but ended abruptly in a wall of more cornstalks. The nearest crows were feet away, watching for their next move.

"If that's a dead end, we'll just turn back," said Lan.

"I'm not worried about it being a dead end. I'm worried about it being a trap."

"We're a little low on options," Marlow pointed out.

"On my count, move forward," said Annabelle, frowning. "No sudden moves."

"I can go first," said Marlow.

Lan's body quivered. She fought to contain her trepidation. Annabelle moved back to take the rear. With her hand grasping the hilt of her dagger, she counted down . . . *Three. Two. One.* Marlow stepped through the opening.

As though a fuse had ignited, the wind began to howl. The cornstalks swayed.

"Move!" cried Annabelle.

Before Lan could figure out whether she meant ahead or back, Marlow bolted forward. They had no choice but to follow. The bird nearest them let out a shriek. The crows rose in a black cloud, at least a dozen strong. They dived, claws outstretched, and cawed menacingly in Lan's face. Her feeble spells missed, the magic refusing to respond to her call. As Marlow approached the wall of stalks ahead, he hesitated. The path split, one way leading left and the other right.

"Don't split up," he yelled, grabbing both their hands. But a second later, he was forced to draw back and shield his face from the pecking that ensued. They reached the corner and turned, standing backs to each other.

"It's a maze!" shouted Annabelle. She swiped at the descending birds. "You have to move! I'll draw them the other way."

"Lan, run! Go left. I'm right behind you!" said Marlow, yelling to be heard over the roaring wind. He drew and shot at a skinny crow hovering above them, screeching.

Covering her head with one hand, Lan ran. The cornstalks seemed to leap out of their neat lines to bar her path, their leaves whipping in her face. She abandoned her failing attempts at fighting back. Within minutes, Marlow's and Annabelle's voices and the screams of the crows were drowned out. All she could hear was the pounding of her footsteps on the dirt as she ran as fast as she could, jumping over loose roots in the way.

Wild winds swept the fields, reminding Lan of the strange storm that had brought her to Silva. She couldn't leave now, Lan thought, not without warning in the middle of nowhere! Fragile stalks snapped as she shoved them aside. The farther she ran, the fewer crows followed. Finally, feeling like her heart was ready to burst, she slowed and began to consider and adjust her route. Marlow had told her he'd follow, but Lan's last glimpse of Annabelle was of her running the opposite way. Lan had no clue where that would've led her, but she tried to turn back toward where they'd split.

Without warning, the stalks thinned and Lan broke into a clearing in the midst of the plants, no larger than the size of her tiny bedroom back in Toronto. She had not come out on the other side of the field—cornstalks surrounded her still—but where she stood, nothing grew and the wind stopped blowing so suddenly that the silence was deafening. She halted abruptly and fell to her knees in shock at the change in the air. The ground was dirt. Marlow and Annabelle were nowhere in sight . . . *but she was not alone.*

THE COGNITOR

In front of Lan, their back turned, stood a single tall figure in a cloak. At her gasp, they turned to face her, and she realized they were not human at all. Her mouth dropped.

What she first took for multicoloured skin, Lan realized with a closer look, was objects blended in the form of an adult human body—clocks, buttons, cloths of different textures, metal scraps, and pages of crumpled paper filled with words—shifting slowly like a galaxy in orbit. They wore a cloak made of fur and foliage. Two black marble eyes stared serenely out of a smooth head. Heavy magic vibrated in the clearing, but the golden beats of energy were not floating aimlessly for Lan to grasp. They came directly from the being, who was no misshapen robot but a seamless creation full of life.

"Lan!" said the figure. They raised their arms in welcome, as if greeting an old friend. Their voice was deep, husky, and echoing even in the open air. "You've come a long way. It has been a while since I've had a visitor of such . . . interesting . . . cause."

Lan jumped to her feet and grabbed her spear from the ground. "You know me?"

"Ah, ah—careful now, you only get one."

"Huh?"

"One question, dearest. I'll take that as a practice round. Do lower your weapon. It spoils the mood, don't you agree?"

"You're the all-knowing being," said Lan, clueing in at last.

"Folks call me the Cognitor. At least the ones who seek me do."

"Well, my friends and I—they should be here any second—we've got some pretty big questions."

"It is my fate to oblige. I am built to provide answers after all."

Lan did not miss the hint of resentment in their voice, even as the creature bowed. She hesitated for a second, then sank to her knees in the dirt. The fight seeped from her body. She was exhausted. Her blisters had burst. She felt ill-prepared to converse with an all-knowing being. All she could do was look. There were so many wondrous parts to the creature that she did not know what to focus on.

"Isn't that better?" said the Cognitor, politely ignoring her gaze. "Tea?"

Lan gaped. Had she misheard?

"It wouldn't be proper to host a guest without tea! It's been so long since I've had good company. Chai? Green? Chamomile? I can whip up some sugar if you please."

"No, thank you," said Lan, feeling rather confused. Then, realizing how thirsty she was, "I mean, green, please."

"Coming right up!"

The Cognitor reached inside their cloak and set out a cast iron kettle, tea bags, and china cups. Lan tried to peek at where the objects were coming from—thin air, seriously deep pockets, or the body itself—but she could not tell. Within seconds of placing everything on the ground, water boiled with a loud whistle.

"How—I mean, never mind."

"Self-boiling kettles, one of Asta's many wonderful inventions," they said with a wink. "Magic wears off with time, but then, I have my own magic too. It's very confined, of course. I can only perform little tricks in my field to welcome my guests."

"You always stay here," said Lan, careful to not waste her only question on tea.

"Goodness, yes," said the Cognitor. "Can you imagine an all-knowing being with the freedom to roam? Even I would say that's extravagant, wouldn't you agree?"

"I suppose so," said Lan, but she thought of her basement. How lonely it must be! No wonder the Cognitor seemed excited for company.

"It's not so bad with my ravens around." They gave her a sad-eyed smile.

"I don't think I could stop myself from wandering off if I were you," replied Lan.

"I did do that once, after a particularly nasty encounter with a visitor. I decided I'd had enough and ventured right to the edge of that slope you came down. My magic vanished when I stepped beyond the fields. So did my ravens. But the knowledge— All that cursed knowledge remained. There's no other life for me. I had to return."

"But that's awfully sad. I hope you find another way one day."

"If only my all-knowingness were to disappear, then I could live like anyone else, free of guilt in good conscience. The chances of that—well, my wisdom is as old as the source of Silva's magic itself. I've known nothing else."

Lan watched the Cognitor's long fingers handle the kettle. They passed her a cup of steaming tea and watched with a smile as she took her first sip. It tasted just like her mother's best jasmine. Her muscles began to relax.

"Now, Lan of Another World, what brings you to my fields?"

Lan opened her mouth but did not speak. How was she supposed to pick one question to ask an all-knowing being? Should she ask about her father? Whether he was safe and if time was passing in her home world? Or who had sent the authorless book at the fair? She thought about Annabelle's quest. Was she meant to accompany them as a witch like Marlow suspected? If so, how could she master her magic? Had she really manifested proof of a heart? How was she to return home?

"You have to tell me if there are rules first," Lan said slowly. "Like the genie, you know, no wishing for more wishes or bringing back the dead kind of thing."

"Smart girl." The Cognitor chuckled. "I suppose there is only one rule in my fields: not even I can tell you what is to come."

Lan nodded. She had expected as much, but before she could speak, the stalks rustled. Marlow burst through the entrance Lan had come through. He tripped over her.

"Marlow of Mireille," said the Cognitor in a pleasant tone.

Marlow drew up short, his eyes wide. Suddenly, the stalks opposite them were shoved aside. Annabelle appeared. Her face gleamed with sweat and her hair was fly-away. Fresh scratches covered her face and arms. She was panting but looked otherwise unharmed. Lan jumped up.

"This cursed country!" said Annabelle. "Can't we go anywhere in Silva without something attacking us?"

Then she turned and saw the Cognitor. They stood silent, tall and imposing, head tilted like a curious observer. Annabelle's eyes widened, taking in the colourful form. Then she looked at Lan's teacup, knocked over on the dirt at her feet.

"What is this supposed to be, tea time?" said Annabelle.

"Well"—Lan gestured at the Cognitor—"we were talking over tea, yes."

"Annabelle of Sol," they said cheerily. "You're as bright as your name. Can I interest you in some cushions? Fresh scones? Tea?"

Before she could answer, the being held out a platter of baked treats and hot tea, smiling in welcome. Lan's cup refilled. Marlow's eyes widened. Annabelle frowned.

"How do I know this is safe?" she said.

"I—um, already drank it," said Lan.

"Lan, you can't go around drinking strange drinks!"

"I was thirsty! Why would an all-knowing being want to poison you anyway?"

"Oh," said Annabelle. She did not lower her guard. "That's supposed to be you."

The Cognitor nodded happily. Annabelle refused to budge. She glared at the cup offered. Marlow hesitated only a second before drinking. Lan sheepishly took a biscuit.

"It's soothing," said Marlow, shrugging, grabbing his second dessert.

"You are wise to be cautious," said the Cognitor to Annabelle, "but I mean no harm. I exist only as a compilation of knowledge, accessible to those who ask. It's a dreadfully boring life, don't you agree?"

"It'd be cool if your maze hadn't tried to kill us!"

"This maze and its guardians, the ravens, alert me—a first line of defence, if you will. My apologies, they do tend to get overexcited from time to time. I did rein them in. Like me, they grow weary of a confined existence. When the old rulers of Silva brought me into being with their magic eons back, they understood the danger of such knowledge and hid me in these fields, where I've remained for everyone's good. My powers are kept secret—makes for an awful life—but rumours do fly. I don't mind the odd whisper. It livens things up to get visitors! Some travel across oceans in search, armed with bodyguards and cartographers. They plot out paths in the maze for days. Sadly, so many ask the silliest things when they reach me, but not you!"

The Cognitor looked at them and beamed, their arms wide open again. "More tea?" they offered.

Slowly, Annabelle brought her cup to her lips and drank.

"Apparently we're allowed one question," Lan filled the other two in.

"One each," said the Cognitor. "Full answers guaranteed. You have my word."

"But nothing about the future."

"A waste of a question. Even I couldn't tell you that."

"Well, you have the hardest questions, right?" said Annabelle, turning to Lan. "Shouldn't you go first?"

"Um, I could use a minute to think," said Lan, shrinking back.

"I suppose *we* should deliberate our questions, shouldn't we? Strategize?" said Annabelle to Marlow. "There's so much we don't know about the road ahead."

Marlow frowned. Then he slowly shook his head. "I don't think so, Belle," he said quietly. "One question for each of us—I know what you want to ask. Do it. It should be personal. We'll figure out the rest."

Annabelle did not protest. Instead, her face filled with relief as if she'd been waiting for his permission all along.

"Then I want to know how Sol is faring," she said without hesitation. She sat on her knees like a child waiting for storytime. "Is my family well?"

"This answer is easiest to show," said the Cognitor, raising their arms.

The air before them shimmered. A hologram appeared. Annabelle gasped.

"You can see into Sol!" she said. "All our outer communications channels have failed since the curse. It messed with the residue so badly, magic's barely functioned."

"A powerful blocking spell can have that effect, yes," said the Cognitor. "I may be able to look in on Sol, but even I cannot make contact."

Lan stared at the picture before her. The curse's impact was clear at first glance. They had a bird's-eye view of what Lan assumed was the city centre. The ground was smooth brown earth, unpaved. The buildings were arranged in a circular formation around a carved metal firepit, a communal hearth. A fine layer of sand dusted the village like powdered sugar on a gingerbread house. It looked like a windy day. Faded banners whipped in the ocean breeze, carrying swirls of sand along with them. A closer look showed that the houses were squat like seaside cottages, built of stone and no taller than two stories. All were distinctly decorated with unique patterns of seashells and paint on the wooden doors. The scene zoomed in enough for Lan to catch glimpses of people dressed in colourful garb, long hair braided, bent over nets and prayers.

"I haven't seen home in five years," Annabelle whispered. Her expression was at once wonderstruck and pained, her eyes unblinking as she stared at the scene. "It hasn't changed a bit."

Tears streamed down Annabelle's face. Lan tentatively reached over and squeezed her hand. Annabelle did not pull away.

"Is this . . . the main area of Sol?" Lan asked. She had only lived in big cities. The scene looked too small to be a downtown.

"Oh, yes, I suppose so," said Annabelle, sniffling. She perked up at the chance to play tour guide and pointed at the image when she spoke. "All our homes are arranged in pods, like that one. Usually, you stay near your family pod, but you can build or expand into new blocks with chosen family too. They all connect. This circle is in the middle, the largest gathering place in Sol where all the important decisions happen. Our leader's home is far left, with the fish on the door, but you can also see the buildings used as learning grounds. The shops are scattered all over. They used to trade for spells, though probably not now that magic is so rare in Sol. Mostly people make what they need out of their homes."

"They're tiny for schools or offices," said Lan, gazing at the stone structures.

"All the buildings are small, because we're usually outside."

"It looks beautiful," said Marlow.

He was right. Despite the drab colour palette, every detail in the village looked crafted with care. In the silence, Lan could almost hear the sound of waves lapping on the shore close by, smell the salty ocean air so similar to the coastline where Lan had spent her own childhood. The sky in Sol was clear blue.

"You should see it in motion," Annabelle said. "That's what I loved most. Sol had the most skilled witches in Silva, not like those casual magicians in Asta. Our witches kept everything linked. We had enchanted waterways to get between blocks and air channels to float packages to people across town. It was always loud. Now it's empty."

"Not quite," the Cognitor said gently. They gestured at the image.

Lan leaned closer and saw an older woman enter the frame, a cluster of young children around her. They stopped in the centre by the firepit, an open cauldron so big that the shortest child equalled it in height. The woman stepped forward, facing the hearth. Her hair was silver, pulled up in a ballerina bun like Annabelle's. She wore a long sleeveless dress and loose belt. Knives hung on both her hips. She beckoned a girl forth.

"Gran?" Annabelle whispered as if in disbelief.

"You asked to see your family," the Cognitor said. "Marya and your sister are in their usual spot, training."

"That's Daisy?"

"I imagine she looks a bit bigger now."

The little girl who had stepped forward wore a knee-length pink dress cinched at the waist. Her brown hair reached her lower back. She was skinny, too skinny. All the kids were. Lan could not see her face well, but her expression was determined.

"She's training to be a fighter like Gran, like me!" said Annabelle.

The Cognitor said nothing.

Annabelle's grandmother nodded at Daisy, who lifted her hands and squinted in concentration. Lan remembered the girl was only six years old. She watched, fascinated, as Daisy shoved her arms forward, like she was pushing an invisible object . . . Instantly, flames erupted from the hearth. The kids watching cheered, jumping in the air. Daisy beamed, showing a gap in her front teeth. Then, as quickly as it had appeared, the scene dissolved into thin air.

Silence followed. With bated breath, they waited for Annabelle to speak.

"She's learning magic," said Annabelle finally, her face blank. "She's a witch."

"One of few able to draw such power from so little residue," said the Cognitor. "Her talent is widely recognized in Sol already."

"But my grandmother wasn't a witch," said Annabelle. "She was a warrior."

"You've been away from Sol a long time, child. You forget that she was both."

Marlow raised his eyebrows. Annabelle's mouth fell open, silent. Lan could see her struggling to reconcile the Cognitor's reminder with what she knew of her grandma.

"Witches have always played a part in Sol's survival, Annabelle, from centuries back and still today," continued the Cognitor. "Your fear is well-founded, but those like Marya wove magic seamlessly into their lives. She never relied on it or used it without need—a rare balance. The key to her success on the battlefield and beyond."

"Those times she visited . . . she never told me that Daisy was training."

"She must have had her reasons."

Annabelle drew her eyes away from where the vision had been and looked at Marlow and Lan. The fearless warrior was gone. She had never before seemed like a lost child far from home. Lan's heart twisted to see her fierceness so worn out. This quest meant everything to her, and she had to succeed.

Lan's mind was made up. She needed to know what role she held in Annabelle's journey, whether she was meant to stay and help, or if it was even in her power to . . .

When the Cognitor turned to her for their next question, Lan was ready.

BIGGER PURPOSE

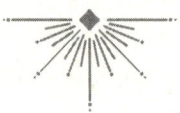

"How did I come to be in Silva and why?" said Lan. She knew she was cheating with a double question, but the two were too closely linked in her mind, and the Cognitor seemed to let it slide.

"An interesting query indeed," said the Cognitor, their hands together in thought. A slow smile spread to their lips. "How to begin? It has been a long time since I've had the pleasure of providing such a rich answer . . . I suppose we should start with the orchard, shouldn't we? The origin of Silva's portals. My origin too—there's a fun fact for you. Yes, Asta's orchard can do pretty much anything. It has been the source of much strife and is the seat of the Silvan crown's power. Let me tell you a story."

Lan expected to see the same hologram-type vision that had pulled up the scene from Sol like a television broadcast. Instead, a lavender haze descended on the clearing and enveloped them. Lan could no longer see the others, but vague shapes shifted in the mist, taking the form of books, shelves, doors, and rows upon rows of trees. She squinted. Then a booming voice filled Lan's head. It was the Cognitor, amplified. As they spoke, the images in the magical fog moved to illustrate their speech.

"Centuries ago, a parcel of seeds was delivered to Asta in the dead of the night. From them grew an orchard so powerful that Silva was flooded with magical residue for anyone to use, not only the kings and witch clans. Around the planting of these trees, witches across the land noted that worlds thinned between the covers of books. At least, the borders did. Those hazy tears in the fabric of reality were easy to pry open if you knew how. They could be preserved, pressed between pages like dried flowers in spring.

"With the help of the orchard's magic to amplify their power, truly skilled witches passed through worlds often, discarding half-opened portals on shelves of every universe. As a result, casual crossings still take place. One minute, a fellow might be sipping on his afternoon tea, and the next, he'll tumble headlong down a rabbit hole, unsure of how he got there. Accidents happen, but intention—few witches know the spells involved in summoning a new door altogether. Fewer still know how to balance multiple worlds in only one life and move through portals at will.

"Even the ones who understand this power struggle to maintain it, for portals are built with a healthy dose of Hope and Longing, the supply of which is impossible to control. You, Lan, have an unusually large amount of both, and you made use of it when you reached out and pried open a door to a land willing to greet you. Silva has always prided itself on its open borders, and Asta is home to stragglers from all worlds who have chosen to stay. In short, you are here because you asked."

At these words, Lan saw a shadowy version of herself in the fog reaching for a bookshelf, her face tilted, undefined. She had time to recognize her Chinatown shirt before the mist cleared and the cornfield reappeared with Marlow, Annabelle, and the Cognitor watching her. She stared blankly back.

"Wasn't that beautiful?" said the Cognitor proudly. "One of the best answers I've ever given, if I do say so myself! *I* quite enjoyed it."

But somehow, Lan was more confused than before she'd asked her question.

"Just to be clear," she said slowly, "there's no *bigger reason* for me being here?"

The Cognitor's face fell.

"How did you get that from the answer I gave?" they said indignantly. "That was not what you asked!"

"You said in that loud booming voice that I opened a portal because I wanted to, with Hope and Longing bound in a book or whatever," said Lan. "I thought someone might've brought me here to help Annabelle, but there's no one else and no big purpose!"

"You're in Silva, Lan," said the Cognitor. "You entered the portal when it opened—only a willing witch could've done so. You are here. What you do now is up to you, and that can be as big as you choose."

Lan looked to Marlow and Annabelle, still puzzled. Did this mean she was supposed to stay and help on their quest?

"But the book—" she began. "Annabelle's story will change because I'm here."

"All books change the minute they touch a reader, child. That is nothing new."

"But what I *should*—"

"You asked for a door to open, and it opened to a place that could use your help, simple as that. If you feel that you have more to offer in this world, then do so. If not—"

Lan held her breath.

"—I trust you will return home when you decide your adventure is through."

"It's up to you, Lan," Marlow said. His voice grounded her, and finally, the Cognitor's words began to make sense. "You can stay with us. The poppies are proof of *your* heart. Go home when we know Sol is safe again. Don't you want to see the end?"

"But the road ahead . . ." Lan hesitated. What dangers would the journey bring? "My parents . . ."

"What you seek is daunting indeed," said the Cognitor gently. "Convincing the king will be no easy task. Even with his price of admission, seeking an audience means a long wait. Nebulo values his popularity. No matter the consequences for the coast, the desert's creation was well supported in Asta. He will not reverse the spell at any cost to himself. Not to mention a journey straight through the Weathering Woods and down the main road to the capital will take weeks on foot, longer if you run into trouble, of which the forest has plenty. I'm growing fond of you lot. I suggest you don't run into trouble."

"And how exactly do we do that?" said Lan.

"I'm afraid that will be up to you."

Lan shivered at the Cognitor's words. She did not think they were exaggerating about the forest's dangers, if they even could exaggerate at all. More questions fluttered on the tip of her tongue, but the Cognitor turned to Marlow. Her time was up.

"I believe we have one more question," they said.

Marlow did not say anything for a long moment. He was looking at Lan in a way that made her warm, his head cocked to the side and green eyes bright. Her heart began to pound. She hadn't the slightest clue what Marlow was considering, but when he spoke, each word was chosen with care.

"How is Lan's family doing, especially her father, now that she is here?"

Lan stared in shock.

"Marlow, you didn't have to . . ."

"Just listen."

For the third time, the Cognitor waved their arms, and an image appeared. Lan's father, Bình, was sleeping soundly in their basement apartment back on Langdon Street. At once, Lan recognized the flowered bed sheets they'd brought over from Việt Nam. His mouth was slightly parted, his expression serene. The digital clock on his nightstand displayed the same date as the night she had left. Lan's eyes welled with tears of relief. He was okay! Time had not passed, at least not in the way it had in Silva. Her dad had no reason to worry. She would be back by the time he woke.

"He's not missing me! Everything's all right!"

"Wow, your magic reaches other worlds," Annabelle murmured.

"A limited glimpse, but your father seems well from what I can tell, Lan," said the Cognitor. They waved again, and the vision changed.

It was morning, and Lan's mother was rousing her baby brother in their sixteenth-floor apartment in Hà Nội. The sight made Lan cry in earnest. She watched as a fan whirred beside the bed. Lan could not hear any sound. The scene was not as sharp as Sol's had been, but she caught the sad look in her mom's eyes as she spoke unheard words, her feet dangling off the mattress. She was wearing her house slippers and the light cotton indoor clothes they often got in bulk from the street markets. Her brother smiled, batting his eyes awake. Lan lost track of how long she stared.

"We should go." Annabelle's quiet voice pulled Lan out of her thoughts.

Lan glanced up. The sun had crossed half the sky while they sat. Late afternoon light spilled onto the cornfields. The thought of leaving the clearing behind saddened her, but Annabelle was right. They rose.

"Before you go," said the Cognitor, "I too have a question for you."

"For us?" said Lan. The familiar anxiety of school tests filled her with dread. "Um—I'm not an all-knowing being."

"No, you are far better than that. Better than many. Some seekers spend days in the maze searching. Some never reach me at all. My question is this: How did all three of you find your way so quickly to the centre of this maze, where I reside?"

They looked at each other, confused. Then Marlow spoke. "I followed Lan. I told her I would. I looked for her footsteps and where she pushed the leaves aside."

"I turned back to find Annabelle," said Lan.

"I drew half your ravens the other way," said Annabelle. "Then I went back—best I could, anyway—to find them both."

"You see," the Cognitor said with a wink, "the bonds that link you are your greatest strength. Remember that on the road, will you?"

"You already knew our answers," Lan realized. "You just wanted us to see it too."

"After all I have seen and known, my greatest belief is that true wisdom comes from the heart. It's the best I can give you as a send-off, since these cakes will disappear the moment you leave my clearing. Oh, I do hate to say goodbye."

Lan couldn't ignore the sorrow with which they spoke. *What a dreadfully sad life*, she thought. She hadn't lived nearly as long as this being, but she knew too well what it felt like to be stuck in one place alone. She wished she could do something more, but all she could manage was to say, "Thank you for your answers, Cognitor."

"My birds will show you out," said the Cognitor. They gazed up at three ravens circling above. "You put up quite a fight, but they won't hurt you now. They simply got—well, a bit enthusiastic."

"Um, sorry about the ones we killed," said Marlow awkwardly.

"Oh, they'll be good as new by nightfall," said the Cognitor, "being my immortal guardians and all." Marlow looked simultaneously annoyed and relieved.

Together, they walked to the path that Annabelle had come through, where the birds hovered. Lan glanced once more at the Cognitor, who was waving at them, looking forlorn. The cornstalks closed to shield the clearing from view.

"Safe journeys!" the Cognitor called. Their last words hung in the air. "Until we meet again!"

INTO THE WOODS

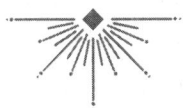

The sun had set by the time they reached the edge of the field. Lan almost sobbed with relief when she took the sandals off her aching feet. They set their bags down under the cover of the plants and settled in for the night. Annabelle began to eat and fill their bags with corn ears. The other two followed her lead. Several times, she looked as if she was about to speak but changed her mind. Finally, when she disappeared behind the stalks for a moment alone, Lan turned to Marlow.

"You didn't have to ask that for me. You said it yourself. We each got one question. You could've asked something you really wanted to know."

"Who said I didn't?"

"Please, you're gonna tell me my family matters enough to you to spend your only question to an *all-knowing being* on it?"

"Maybe they do. You would've never stayed if you weren't sure they were safe."

Lan stared. Marlow tossed the bags at their feet and slid to the ground, his back pressed against the stalks. She lowered herself beside him. They sat facing the Weathering Woods, which appeared as a looming shadow in the distance. In the light of the waxing moon, Marlow's eyes were dark. Lan couldn't see the green in them that was clear in daylight. When he looked at her again, she held his gaze instead of staring down at her feet.

"Aren't you curious about where you came from?" she whispered.

"When I was little, I was," said Marlow, "but not anymore."

"So what? You're happy to follow Annabelle around forever?"

"Nothing in my life matters the way it does to you," he said bluntly. An edge entered his voice for the first time. Lan waited.

"I know that my past is dead—unlike Annabelle's, unlike yours," he continued, his voice barely louder a breath. "I don't long for anything left behind."

Lan hesitated. Then she answered, "Who cares what we long for anyway? It'll never go back to being the same for me, no matter where I live."

Marlow paused. "Annabelle told me how you got separated from your home too," he said. "I doubt it's gone for good though. You're still holding on so tight. But what do I know?"

His head was tilted toward her, his voice low. In the silence that hung between them, Lan wanted to tell him everything at once: how her parents had told her two weeks before their flight, the expression on her bà nội's face when she found out, and the way her old classmates had piled on her in a giant group hug in the schoolyard. But her throat constricted and no words came out. Instead, tears spilled hot and fast down her face.

"Hey, maybe I should've checked before asking," Marlow said. He looked like he wanted to reach for her but stopped himself. "I'm sorry if you didn't want to hear."

"You asked the right question," said Lan, sniffling. "I feel better knowing my dad isn't worried sick about me missing . . . But—"

"But what?"

"Do you really think that I could help? That Annabelle wants me around? I mean, I can't even build us a nice fire right now or make a hot bowl of noodles appear."

"Both of those things would be great, I won't lie," said Marlow. "But it's not like I wanted you to stick around for noodles. We're gonna need your magic when we cross through the Weathering Woods. Annabelle knows that. You've helped so much already."

"You keep saying that—"

"—because it's true. Besides, don't you want to see what you can do if you really put your mind to it? Especially in a place teeming with magic like Asta!"

"Yes, I do. You were right that I'd miss it. There's so much more to learn."

"So you'll stay?"

"Until the forest at least. I don't feel good leaving you two to walk in there alone. Why's it called the Weathering Woods anyway?"

"We didn't learn much about it at the Academy, but apparently the forest is the oldest part of the country. The magic is different. I don't know how exactly, but it's less polished than Asta's quick-to-use spells. The creatures and people that live there don't follow the same traditions as those in the capital. The name's what us outsiders call it."

"Think there'll be more tree guardians?"

"Nothing we can't handle."

He had turned back into his easygoing self, confident and unfazed. Lan stayed with a thousand thoughts racing through her head. They sat in silence. Without thinking, she leaned her head on Marlow's shoulder and felt tension loosen its grip on her tired body. He wrapped his arm around her.

Leaves rustled in the night air. Slowly, their lull made her eyes grow heavy. Lan began to drift into sleep. She faintly heard Annabelle return at some point and felt her cozy up on Marlow's other side. She must've said something funny, because Marlow laughed softly. It was the last thing Lan remembered before her dreams took over.

Lan was walking with her dad on a busy Toronto street. It looked like Roncesvalles, where they liked to browse the independent shops, occasionally even enjoy a scoop of the best ice cream in the city. Red streetcars ambled by. Pedestrians rushed to catch them. It was summertime. Lan wore jean shorts and a shirt her old friends had given her when she moved away last year. They turned into a shop with a colourful cartoon logo of a girl on a scooter.

The bell on the door rang. Lan recognized the inside as a toy store that they visited often, or at least as often as they made the long trip by bus, subway, and then streetcar over to this neighbourhood. The floor was carpeted. Kids flipped through the spinning sticker displays and chased each other with stuffed dinosaurs. Lan wasn't sure what she was looking for, but she had a feeling she'd know when she saw it.

And she did. At the back of the shop hung the costumes for dress-up, neatly arranged on coat hangers. Lan caught sight of them and strode confidently in their direction. She glanced over the princess outfit but quickly decided it would be too cumbersome. The pirate one would do nicely.

"I'll have to move quickly," she explained to her dad. "They'll be waiting, and the dress will only slow me down."

"Ai?" he said, puzzled.

"Marlow and Annabelle, of course. I told you."

"Ah, your book people," he said. "I thought we came to buy presents for your mom and brother."

"But they're in Hà Nội," Lan said. "Marlow and Annabelle are right here, and I promised I'd get back to them straight away."

"Don't you remember?" said her dad. "They will be flying in this weekend. That's why we got the new place."

Lan wracked her brain but could not conjure an image of what this new Toronto house looked like—nevertheless, her dad must be right. She abandoned the pirate outfit and helped him pick out a ladybug-patterned music box set to her mother's favourite waltz. Her brother would like their spinning dance. Lan still felt dazed when they stepped back onto the busy street. She'd have to let Marlow and Annabelle know she couldn't make it the rest of the way after all. Hopefully, they would not need her.

When she woke the next morning, Lan had no recollection of the dream.

Lan was sorely reminded of her bruises when she opened her eyes. Her stomach was uneasy. The green corn was catching up to her. Her hair felt grimy, and there were definitely zits forming on her chin. She glanced at the other two. Marlow was getting to his feet beside her, slinging his bow over his shoulder. Annabelle was fighting her tangle of hair into a high bun. Lan got up, her back stiff from the weird sleeping position.

Her new blisters had swollen to the size of grapes, but they had a bigger problem. Their water pouches were dry. Lan could feel Marlow's and Annabelle's fear as they packed up, the memory of the desert weighing on their minds. They needed to find water fast. Lan spread out her right hand, trying to draw out particles of moisture in the air but felt nothing. The Cognitor's magic overrode it all. The farther away they travelled, the more light pulses returned to Lan's fingers, but they were still too weak to work with.

By the time they reached the forest, the sun was blazing and their throats were parched. Lan's steps faltered. Their last skirmish with the tree guardians replayed in her mind. That had been a relatively small grove of pines—but a whole forest? She gripped her spear tightly. They wouldn't stand a chance if these trees wanted them gone, and they would never make it around with no water. Ahead of her, Marlow stopped, no longer as poised as the night before. He hesitated as though having the same doubts.

"This forest is huge," said Annabelle before either of them spoke. "We have to risk it. It'll take months going around. Even the Cognitor said it was the quickest way."

Marlow didn't answer. Lan couldn't read his expression. Though she wanted to turn and run, Annabelle was right. They still hadn't found any sign of a stream. They had to carry on. Marlow took a step forward. Holding their breaths, they tread carefully past the first tall birches. No tree guardians made a move—but a wave of magical energy hit Lan so hard that she stumbled, winded. It felt like walking into a wall.

"Are you okay?" said Marlow, stopping.

"I—you seriously don't feel that?"

"I feel something," said Annabelle, her lips pursed. "Icky all over."

"It's . . ." Lan paused to find the words. "Dark green and *heavy*, like a blanket. I feel like I'm being smothered in moss."

"Do you want to turn around?" asked Marlow.

Lan almost said yes, but one look at Annabelle's desperate, determined face stopped her. Lan shook her head. She had agreed to come, and seeking another way now would be enough trouble to discourage them all, if they didn't die of thirst first.

"Let's just get through as fast as we can," said Lan.

They kept going, their steps tentative. Sweat trickled down the back of her neck. Annabelle was on edge. Her nervous breaths made the smothering sensation worse. Lan tried to feel for magic that she could use. It flickered, but her attempts were like moving through mud. What was wrong with this forest? She kept her focus on Marlow in front, scared to look at what might jump out from behind the nearest tree.

Just when Lan thought she might burst from stress and exhaustion—*drop*! She gasped and stared at the sky. Through the trees, she saw the sun had sunk behind a cloud. For the first time since she'd arrived, it began to rain!

The summer sprinkle cut through the tense air. Lan's shoulders sagged in relief. Marlow crowed, his mouth turned to the sky. Annabelle laughed and spun like a dancer in the rainfall. Lan couldn't get enough. It felt wonderfully refreshing on her face. She hadn't realized how hot her skin had gotten under the sun and protested when Annabelle urged them to keep going.

"Why can't we stop here tonight?" said Lan. "There's always tomorrow to walk."

"We do have corn," said Annabelle reluctantly. "Let's find a spot with shelter."

Lan silently thanked whatever Silvan gods existed for cutting them a break at last. She threw in a shout-out to her own ancestors as well, just in case they had an eye on her. But after an hour huddled in a grove of twisted silver-bark trees, Lan no longer welcomed the sputtering rain. It had made everything damp. She longed for a fire. Annabelle wrapped herself in her dark blue cloak, the smell of fish on it pungent. Marlow handed Lan his plain black one.

"I'm not cold," he insisted.

Lan took it gratefully and tucked her head in the hood. The desert's dry smell still clung to it, laced with the lingering scent of dandelions that had followed Marlow since the western valley. She stopped shivering, but the green corn did little to fill her belly. Lan longed for a bowl of instant phở. In Toronto, she would've complained about how the seasoning failed to rival her mother's homemade broth, but there was a time and place for the packaged kind. Her dad had really perfected them.

"Rice noodles," Lan tried to explain to the other two, "but there's all sorts of secret spices in it—and it's hot. Perfect for a night like this."

"No chance you can conjure us a bowl about now?"

"Marlow, I'm so tired I can barely make a potato grow."

"Maybe when we get to Asta. I gotta broaden my menu beyond plain porridges."

"Can we stop talking about food? It's making me hungry . . ."

"You're always hungry, Belle."

The sky darkened. Lan's eyes adjusted with it. The quarter moon shone brightly, but it was impossible to see far. The clouds were thick. Only a sliver of light streamed through the foliage. Lan leaned against a trunk. She could tell from the other two's deep breathing that they were drifting off. She squeezed her eyes, willing rest to come. A deep sense of unease still nagged her, driven away briefly by the rain but present once more. She reached for her spear, reassured by its weight in her hand. Though he'd passed out, Marlow's fingers were wrapped around his bow.

Lan's gaze drifted to Annabelle. Her face was scrunched up, restless, as if fighting in her sleep. The sooner they got out of here, the better, Lan thought. The weariness in her muscles caught up to her, and her eyes grew heavy.

She almost didn't hear the first creak.

THE CREATURE IN THE NIGHT

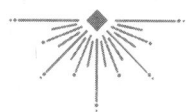

Lan's head snapped to the direction of the noise. Fear gripped her so tightly that she could scarcely breathe. She tried to tell herself it was likely innocent—a deer or rabbit out for a nighttime wander—yet, they hadn't seen any animals in these woods. The realization troubled her. She listened for the sound again. Maybe she had dreamt it.

Crack! A branch snapped. The leaves rustled. Annabelle stirred.

"What's going on?" she murmured, lifting her head.

"I thought I heard something," Lan whispered.

"What?"

"Listen."

But there was only silence. After a minute, Annabelle's head drooped back onto her hands, her breathing steady. Lan frowned, torn between wanting to wake her and letting her catch her much-needed rest. Whatever had moved sounded larger than a deer. Even in the stillness, Lan couldn't shake the terror rising in her with every second. Something was wrong. She felt it now in her gut and in the nasty ooze of magical residue all around. Slowly, she got to her feet, her back pressed against the tree bark. She squinted at the darkness—and saw it.

A large creature moved into the grove. Twice Marlow's height, it towered, the moonlight glinting on its short silver fur. It stood on two legs and began to move slowly but deliberately toward them, a few dozen feet away. Lan gasped. This was no moonlit stroll. She heard a low growl and bit back a curse. Panicking, she knelt by Marlow, who was closer, and shook him. Annabelle opened her eyes again, confused and alarmed.

"What is happening?" she whispered, her back to the approaching beast.

"Something's coming at us! Marlow," Lan whispered urgently, "wake up."

He was awake at once and sat up.

"You all right?" he said. He reached for her.

Before she could answer, the beast let out a bellowing roar that shook the trees around them. A shower of leaves and a branch dropped from overhead. Marlow and Annabelle dived out of the way. Lan stumbled trying to rise, hands over her head.

"Get up," said Marlow, pulling her up as he spoke. Another roar shook the grove. Annabelle gasped at the threatening shadow.

"Is there any chance this thing hasn't seen us?" she said in a panicked whisper. "Maybe it's friendly!"

"I seriously doubt that, Annabelle," hissed Lan. "It's making a beeline!"

They backed against the large trees behind them. Lan felt the same powerful magic that she'd sensed in the Cognitor's clearing—the thick blanket that had blocked her spells, but this one had no golden hue. Throwing caution aside, she scrambled to direct magic through her spear. Nothing happened. She might as well have been back to day one on the riverbank, fumbling through the residue. Chills crept down her spine. They were definitely not about to be offered tea.

"The trees," Annabelle said. She sounded more scared than Lan had ever heard. "They moved! They're blocking us."

Marlow and Lan stared. Annabelle was right. A tremor ran through the ground. The silver-bark trees tightened around them to create a wall of trunks, sealing off every gap they might've squeezed through. *This creature was controlling the forest!* Lan had never seen magic so strong. They were trapped. Just when she thought she'd pass out from fear, things grew worse.

The creature spoke.

"Your escape plans won't work."

Its growling voice filled the grove. Beside her, Marlow swore. Lan felt his hand grasp hers and squeeze. She was breathing hard and could not move. She couldn't even feel hot or cold or wet—only terror. From the corner of her eye, she saw Annabelle grip her dagger so tightly her knuckles shone white in the moonlight.

"What do you want?" Annabelle shouted. The breathless note of fear in her voice made Lan more scared than she had ever felt in her life.

"Straight to the point," it said. "I like you."

"We're just passing through!"

"And this isn't personal. We all must eat to live, wouldn't you say?"

"Are you saying you want to eat us?" said Marlow, his voice hoarse.

"It is rare that I find a feast in my grove."

"But we're just kids!" said Lan.

The creature stopped in its approach and laughed. "Precisely! Children have the most heart, and that is what I feed on. You three have some of the heartiest hearts I have ever encountered!"

Annabelle's mouth dropped. Lan's stomach plummeted. She could see no way out. The heart-eater resumed its steady path in their direction. Steps away, it loomed as tall as the trees, and Lan could see the outline of a snout and gleaming black eyes. The word *werewolf* came to her mind.

"I don't want to be dinner!" Lan squeaked. "I didn't join this quest to be dinner!"

"You won't be," said Marlow firmly.

"Then how are we gonna beat this thing?"

Without warning, Marlow dropped her hand. He drew and fired. The creature ducked, then charged with shocking speed. Lan screamed and dived aside. When she lifted her head, Marlow had fired again. His arrows missed. It moved in, focused on Annabelle, who stood nearest. Lan tried to direct her magic but yelled in frustration. Nothing worked! Instead she threw the spear. The beast dodged. Annabelle took the chance to roll away.

Marlow's third arrow hit the creature in the shoulder. It staggered, snarling, but did not stop coming. Lan grabbed a rock and turned to throw it. Annabelle was back on her feet, blade in hand. She grabbed the spear off the ground and spun back to back with Marlow—and for a second, Lan could only stare. Sharp jabs, quick parries, feet light and fluid, they fought together like instinct. Annabelle's blows perfectly matched Marlow's shots. The beast began to retreat, grunting. Their hits were landing! Could they have a chance after all?

As suddenly as hope had flooded her, it vanished. Lan cried out as her body jerked backwards. Ropes had slithered out from somewhere behind her and wrapped themselves around her waist and both wrists, holding her so tightly it was hard to breathe. A second later, she realized with dread that they were not ropes: the trees were alive. A sinister feeling pulsed through the air, so cold that it seeped through Lan like melting ice.

Her vision blurred with angry tears. This could not be how she went out! Hazily, Lan saw branches and vines whip at Marlow and Annabelle in fierce attacks. She heard Marlow shout her name. The heart-eater, she realized with dread, had abandoned the other two to the trees. It came to her, limping but determined. Lan lurched forward, straining to break free. She kicked at the ground. The roots were unmoved by her efforts. The rock dropped from her hand, and she collapsed on her knees on the damp earth, dizzy and gasping to regain her breath. How to fight back? Her fury slipped away, and fear clouded her mind. Without her magic, she had nothing. This was why Annabelle resisted witchcraft, Lan realized. It was impossible to rely on. Useless when she needed it most!

Was this the end for her? Maybe she wasn't meant to take part in this story at all. Lan closed her eyes. Disappointment overwhelmed her. What a failure she was! She stifled a sob thinking of her warm bed in Toronto and her father's face. What had possessed her to barge in and come so far for—what exactly? An adventure? To prove she was more than the sad sack she'd been all year? She was no hero.

"Lan!"

Her eyes flew open, and her heart clenched. Behind the approaching heart-eater, the trees fought on of their own accord. A thick branch swung for Marlow's head. Annabelle rushed to block it, and the force of the impact split the spear clean in half.

Lan felt the crack reverberate through her body, as if all the residue trapped in the stick had suddenly been released at its breaking. Fear from seeing the other two in danger willed her to focus. She had to help!

Sudden energy rushed to Lan's hands.

Her magic hadn't left her! She wasn't helpless! And they would *not* go out as some creature's midnight snack. Lan stopped struggling and reached out her palms. She felt no colourful bubbles, but something like sludge seeped between her fingers.

Come on, trees. Come on, wind.

She was too late. Lan gasped. The heart-eater lunged at her face and grabbed her from the waist, raising her a foot off the ground. With a growl, it lifted her chin with a long claw. Her energy evaporated.

"A witch," it said with mild interest. "A poor one."

Lan smelled a sickening sweetness on its breath. The claw pierced her chin, drawing blood. She bit back a sob at the sting. *Think!* What could she use?

"My trees won't respond to a weakling like you," the heart-eater continued. "They know to obey my power and mine alone."

Lan strained to see past the heart-eater just as vines shot for Annabelle's ankle and wound up her leg. She dropped to the ground with a cry. Lan's brain sped through a million wild possibilities in a second as she watched . . . and her eyes landed on the leather bag, tossed open at Annabelle's feet. Her snowflake pyjamas spilled over the forest floor.

In an instant, Lan's head cleared with blinding determination. If the forces in the grove wouldn't listen to her spells, then Lan would make her own.

LET IT SNOW

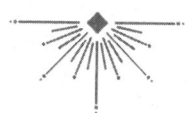

Reaching beneath the heart-eater's crushing grip on her side, Lan thrust out her right hand and forced her mind to zoom in on her no-longer-white pyjamas. She was too far to see individual snowflakes, but she knew that outfit inside out. She'd worn it since they'd landed in Canada. At the same time, she pictured the rush of Toronto snow, coming down hard and fast in early January. It was her least favourite time of year, and she tried to channel the distaste into her spell, promising to the universe, *If this works, I'll never complain about winter again.*

A whooshing sound rose, filling the grove. Before the heart-eater could turn, a giant snowball sped through the air and hit it squarely on the back of the head, knocking it to the ground. Lan dropped from its grasp and scrambled out of reach. She stared.

Like in a holiday postcard picture, snow was coming down all around, heavier by the second. It fell not as fluffy white flakes, but rather as the muddy pebbled-filled slush that coated Toronto streets for four months in winter. Already, Lan was soaked and streaked with grime, struggling to make sense of the chaos she had unleashed. Marlow and Annabelle seemed bewildered, their eyes wide with fear at the strange storm. They had cut themselves free with Annabelle's blade. The silver-bark trees had paused without the heart-eater's magic guiding them, but the creature was getting to its feet.

Instinctively, Lan spun both arms and sent a wave of slush barrelling toward it. She focused her energy on where the heart-eater was lurching against the onslaught. The storm responded, but it tugged against her grip like a wild animal breaking free.

All around, the grove bowed in defeat. The heart-eater stumbled. Hunched over, it turned from Lan, slipping in the mud and wind to get away. Her muscles strained. The snowfall slowed—then abruptly, it died. Lan was shaking. She did not even feel the cold. The creature got to its feet and bounded toward where the trees were opening to create an escape path, as if in surrender. She dropped her guard a moment too soon—

The tendrils around Marlow's and Annabelle's feet lashed out lightning-fast like a life-and-death game of jump rope. The roots swept them off balance, and they tumbled. With a crack, the side of Annabelle's head hit a dead branch so hard that Lan was sick. Marlow had tucked his head in his arms, rolling safely, but he came up too late. The heart-eater swerved and made a swipe for Annabelle, lying still. Marlow scrambled for her fallen blade and launched himself in front of her.

Lan hardly heard the panicked cries coming from her own mouth. She sent flurries flying into the heart-eater's face, but it moved with razor-sharp efficiency: claws cut through Marlow's side, and he collapsed on his knees. Red blossomed on his white shirt. The creature swept him up in a flash and ran. The trees parted.

Abandoning all magic, Lan raced after them, willing her legs to speed up, but she was losing ground. She might've been a skilled sprinter at home, but there was no way her short limbs could catch those loping strides. At best, Annabelle was passed out, and in seconds, Marlow would be gone—

Suddenly an arrow whistled past, narrowly missing her head. Lan gasped and stared as it hit the beast right between the shoulder blades. It howled and dropped Marlow, disappearing empty-handed into the woods at last. Had Annabelle gotten up somehow? Lan's body felt like pudding. She staggered to Marlow, fell beside him, but she had no idea how to stop so much blood at once.

Crackling footsteps made Lan start. What more could happen now?

"You're safe, little witch," said a voice so close to her that Lan fell over in shock.

As if from nowhere, a woman with a round face knelt by Lan's side. She wore a short-sleeved leather top, tight pants, and a forest-green cloak. Her skin was dark brown and rough like tree bark. Her eyes, gentle and black, twinkled in the strands of starlight. Braided vines bearing small red flowers sprouted from her head, straight from her scalp, as though she'd emerged from the foliage itself. An *elf*, thought Lan, except her ears were not pointed. Magic hummed around her body. She had a crossbow in hand, which she set on the ground, nudging Lan aside and moving closer to Marlow. Lan realized she must have fired the shot that saved him.

Smoothly, the woman cut through Marlow's shirt with a knife pulled from her boot and bound the fabric tightly around his side. She unfastened her cloak and wrapped it around him. Then, she stood. Though not much taller than Lan's mother, the lady steadily lifted Marlow in both arms, as if he were a toddler rather than a tall fourteen-year-old boy. Lan watched with her mouth open.

"Annabelle . . ." Lan managed to say. She looked at the grove, obscured by trees.

"I'm Phoenix," said the lady. "My brothers are with your friend. Can you walk?"

Lan nodded and got to her feet. Phoenix gestured to follow. Her head spinning, Lan trailed after her to the clearing and drew a sharp breath at the scene that awaited her.

THE RIDERS

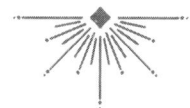

For a moment, Lan was convinced she was dreaming. Were Phoenix's brothers horses? Riders? *Centaurs?* Even after the magic she had witnessed in Silva, the sight of them stunned her. With racehorse bodies and human heads and torsos, two centaurs bent over Annabelle. They looked up at Lan and the woman, Phoenix, who was carrying Marlow. The smaller centaur spoke in a strange language. Phoenix picked up her pace, set Marlow gently on the earth, and examined Annabelle. The second centaur, older and broader than his companion, walked toward Lan. She froze.

A few feet away, he stood and stared at her for several seconds in silence. A palm-sized star-shaped scar marked the centre of his chest. Lan focused her gaze on his dirt-streaked face, his matted brown shoulder-length hair pulled back, and his dark eyes. They made her feel self-conscious, like he was waiting for her to make the first move. What did one even say to a centaur? Lan gulped and took a step forward to show she was not afraid but tripped over a root. The centaur caught her with his right hand, supporting her frail body.

"Steady," he said. She was surprised by how smooth his voice was and staggered to get her footing. "You'll want to get on."

He straightened, taller than she'd realized, and turned so that she faced his side. He held out a hand.

"Who are you?" said Lan.

"You may call me Ruse."

"I've never—" Lan began, but stopped. Her voice, broken from crying herself hoarse for the past hour, sounded foreign. She'd wanted to say that she'd never ridden a horse but thought it might sound impolite. She cleared her throat.

The centaur seemed to understand. He beckoned his companion over.

"This is Zephyr," said Ruse. "He'll help you up. You're safe now."

Tentatively, Lan nodded and took Zephyr's hand. He lifted her. Lan swung her leg over Ruse's back, landing clumsily with a grunt. She could barely stay upright.

"Hold on," said Ruse. He turned and walked to Phoenix, kneeling on the ground.

Her expression was guarded. When Ruse stopped beside her, she lifted Annabelle, bundled in her blue cloak, and positioned her in front of Lan on the centaur's back.

"Will they make it?" said Lan, fearing the response.

"They're alive," Phoenix answered but said no more. She waited until Annabelle was safe in Lan's arms before letting go. "You'll have to hold her carefully. My sister, Kestrel, will be able to help back in our camp."

Lan nodded. She cradled Annabelle's head against her shoulder, making sure she was stable. She felt so small, her eyes closed and her face scratched. Both of her wrists showed red welts from where the branches had grabbed at her. Her shirt was torn at the hem, a long scrape visible underneath. It was hard to picture her in action now, with her brown eyes flashing and strength clear from a distance. A sizable bruise had risen on the right side of her head. Lan pressed her cheek against it, trembling, her tears wet on both their faces.

Phoenix leapt easily onto Zephyr's back. She supported Marlow, slumped in front of her. Lan noticed that the trees had receded, no longer pressed together to form a wall. The magic that controlled them had disappeared with the beast. The path that she, Marlow, and Annabelle had come through earlier the previous day—what now seemed like ages ago—lay visible once more.

They moved, Zephyr with Phoenix and Marlow in front, and Ruse steps behind. Zephyr sped to a gallop, rounded a bend, and disappeared from view, but Ruse did not pick up his pace. Lan did not look back at the grove.

She was still wrapped in Marlow's black cloak, the smell of dandelions steadying, but Lan could not stop shivering. Her senses were coming back to her, and the first thing she felt was *pain*. Her arms screamed with the strain of holding Annabelle, but she did not let them falter. She felt her wrists, her ankles, and her waist throb where the trees had held her. Her side was definitely bruised. She was damp all over.

It was pitch black in the forest. Lan stopped trying to make out her surroundings. Everything around her felt blurred, including time itself. She could not even say how long they rode for. There were stretches when it felt as if she had been on Ruse's back for days being lulled to sleep, and moments when she jerked awake, the panic rising in her chest and the need to get to Marlow overwhelming. His face had looked so pale, wrapped in Phoenix's dark green hood. When she couldn't bear it any longer, Lan leaned forward to ask if they could speed up. Then she saw the flickering orange of a fire on a slope ahead. In the same moment, she suddenly noticed that the air around her grew heavy, not unlike Hà

Nội's spring heat. That was odd, Lan thought. Sweat beaded on her forehead.

"Where are we going?" said Lan. "Is Marlow there?"

"Your friend is looked after as we speak," said Ruse. He trotted up the slope, and Lan leaned forward, clutching Annabelle and struggling to keep her balance.

They crested the hill and came upon a circular campsite. Lan gasped, uncertain if she was indeed still in Silva. It was like nothing she'd imagined. Two trees bowed with red flowers dominated the far side of the sandy clearing, much larger than the saplings around them. They looked like the trees that lined Hoàn Kiếm Lake in her hometown every spring. Lan wanted to rush over and look more closely, but she couldn't move from Ruse's back, her arms still wrapped around Annabelle.

In the centre, a low fire blazed, the flames just tall enough to provide light. The scene reminded Lan of Sol's earthy pods, as she had seen in the Cognitor's vision. Yet certain parts about the clearing felt familiar, reminiscent of her home in Việt Nam for reasons she could not understand.

A large bamboo-like structure with a slanted top stood at the far end. It had no walls, no floor, only a post in each of the four corners. Vines draped over the roof sealed the cracks in the rounded planks, creating a dry semi-curtained refuge, lined with furs along the soft ground. Zephyr and Phoenix stood, visible through the foliage, beside a second lady in a dress. Lan guessed the woman was Kestrel, Phoenix's sister. She was big with strong arms, similar in height, with the same delicate red flowers for hair. The two women knelt on either side of Marlow, whispering. His eyes were closed and his body eerily still. His blond hair flickered in the firelight, the only sign of movement.

Ruse and Lan drew nearer. The figures rose. Ruse asked a question in the tongue Lan didn't recognize and got an answer in the same language. The young centaur, Zephyr, approached and tilted his head in greeting. He waited. Unsure of what he was expecting, Lan did the same.

"May I?" he said to Lan. He held his arms toward Annabelle.

She nodded and gave a tiny sigh of relief as the weight lifted. Zephyr trotted to where the women sat with Marlow. He lay Annabelle down beside them.

"Can you dismount on your own?" Ruse asked Lan.

"Yes," she said automatically, then paused and looked at the ground beneath her. It took a couple tries to slip ungracefully down and face her rescuer.

"Thanks for—saving us."

The words felt inadequate. If the riders hadn't appeared, all three of them would've been food.

"What do they call you?" said Ruse.

"Lan. My friends are Marlow and Annabelle."

"This is my home," said Ruse. He opened his arms. "Zephyr and Phoenix, you've met. Kestrel is our healer."

"Are Marlow and Annabelle gonna be okay?"

"Go on and see."

Lan bit her lip. Her hesitation surprised her. They were just across the clearing, but she suddenly felt scared to step closer.

"You fear what you will find," said Ruse, watching. "A warrior does not shy away from the truth."

"But I'm not a warrior," said Lan. "They might be, but I'm definitely not."

"And what makes you so sure of that?"

"I can't do what they can," said Lan. She met Ruse's steady eyes. "I can't fight. The one thing I managed with my magic, I couldn't even control properly. It's not fair I'm the one who made it out unhurt."

"I'm not convinced you did, Lan. Look at yourself."

Lan looked down at her hands and clothes. Red welts lined her wrists, so deep that the scrapes had drawn blood. The ring around her waist where the largest branch had held her felt chafed, her shirt crumpled and torn at the side. For some reason, her sandaled feet were covered in bruises and scratches. Her head throbbed looking at them.

"It doesn't serve to ascribe blame after a fight," said Ruse. He gestured toward the others. "You, too, need to rest."

They approached together. Marlow and Annabelle lay on mats of furs and thin woven sheets. Annabelle could've been sleeping, her face wiped clean of dirt and blood. Marlow was not so peaceful. He was sweating, his hairline wet. His face was white. Bandages wrapped tightly around his midriff.

Zephyr, Phoenix, and Kestrel stood up to face Ruse and Lan. They nodded again, and Lan copied them. She couldn't voice her questions out loud, but they understood.

"The girl will be fine," said Kestrel. "She'll make a full recovery with rest."

"And . . . him?"

"We have reason to hope. He's a strong boy."

"Thank you," said Lan. She felt relieved, but her fears were far from gone. She could not take her eyes off them. Her body was stiff, unable to move closer.

"Takes a strong witch to hold her own in that grove," said Phoenix kindly. "You're not the first to cross the heart-eater's path. Luckily, we heard you on our ride."

"Are you elves?" Lan asked her.

Phoenix laughed, but her sister looked annoyed. Kestrel ignored Lan's question, gesturing instead at a coconut shell full of steaming pearl liquid by Annabelle's head.

"Drink," she commanded. "It will help."

"How?" said Lan, but she took the bowl anyway.

"Sleep," she said, "the best medicine."

Lan took a sip. The warm liquid tasted like diluted honey. It filled her with calm. She drank deeply and felt her body grow heavy. Kestrel waited until she'd drained the bowl, then nodded at an empty spot on the bamboo bed. Lan sunk in and let the furs envelop her. The last thing she saw was Annabelle's face, her tangled waves of brown hair framing her drawn cheeks, just inches away.

RUSE'S HOLLOW

Lan opened her eyes and lay still for several minutes, blinking at the sunlight streaming through the bamboo slats of the roof above her. Something was thumping rhythmically close by. She tried to rise, propping herself up on an elbow, but the simple movement made a wave of dizziness flare up.

"You're in no state to get up," said a sharp voice.

Lan started and immediately collapsed again. When she opened her eyes slowly and turned toward the source of the sound, she saw one of the flowery women from the previous night sitting on a large log crushing something with a stone mortar and pestle like Lan's mother used to do for fancy meals before Tết. The thought made her hungry for the extravagant meals they cooked for Lunar New Year: crispy nem, xôi gấc—red sticky rice—and of course bánh chưng and bánh giầy, the legendary savoury cakes that symbolized the earth and sky.

The lady was dressed in plain brown, her plant-like hair twisted into a giant bun that would've impressed Annabelle. Lan pushed herself up to a sitting position, noticing then that she was covered in furs. She shrugged them off.

"You're Kestrel, right?" said Lan, struggling to remember.

"Yes. You called me an elf."

"Oh—um, right, sorry about that."

Lan glanced around, and her eyes fell on the figures of her friends beside her. Annabelle looked so worn and still in her sleep. It made Lan uncomfortable. The white bandages wrapped around Marlow's side ruined any illusion of peace. She reached out and touched them. Both were freezing, despite the humid heat in the clearing.

"They look awful."

"They'll live," said Kestrel. "Her fever just broke. She should wake soon."

"How long have I been out?"

"Long enough. I'll whip up another batch of that sleeping potion today."

"What are you making now?"

"Something for the girl's head."

"I can help if you show me."

Kestrel laughed in answer. Her voice had a strange accent to it, different from Marlow or Annabelle's. The words wove together like a lullaby.

"I mean it," said Lan, feeling slightly put off.

"I believe you, but it's taken us centuries to master these remedies."

"If you're not an elf, then what are you?"

"Aren't elves those little helper critters in woodworking shops?" said Kestrel with a sniff. "Or does it mean something different wherever you're from?"

"Well, I guess there are different kinds," admitted Lan. "Some of them can be quite tall . . . I wouldn't say I'm an elf expert."

"We are tree nymphs, silly. There is a nymph for every tree, every stream. Ruse has lived in this Hollow for ages, and Phoenix and I have shared it with him. It has been our home since he protected us as saplings fifty years back."

She pointed to the border of the clearing, where the two towering red-flowered trees grew, bent in a close embrace.

"That's you?" said Lan in awe. "You remind me of the trees by the lake in the city where I grew up, but they're a long way from here."

"A long way, you say? This forest is one of the oldest ones to thrive in any world. Perhaps we started off as distant cousins years ago, us and your trees. Seeds have drifted through portals as long as they've existed."

"How did you know I come from another world?"

"It's my job to read bodies, and yours bears the marks of a crossing not long ago."

"What mark is that?" asked Lan, looking down at herself as if expecting to find a stamp of some sort.

"Not one visible to your eye," said Kestrel. "At least not yet. It appears somewhat like—oh, I don't know—baby skin?"

"*Baby skin?*"

"Like a snake."

"You're saying I look like a snake to you?"

"Of course not. You look like you've just shed a layer. You're all raw and shiny."

"Is that a bad thing?"

"No, it's natural to leave a bit of your old self behind when you make a big trip. Makes room for new things to stick. We all do it—people, snakes, trees—some in more visible ways than others."

"Sorry if this is rude," said Lan, "but are you the same thing as a tree guardian? You're a whole lot nicer than the ones we've met."

"No, nymphs are spirits, much like human souls, with the ability to move between physical forms. We have the power to *create* tree guardians from our bark."

"But *you* don't?"

"I don't need to, beyond the odd one to run an errand here or there—or to prank Zephyr. He's easily skittish, but keep that between us."

Lan smiled. She took the potion Kestrel offered her and sipped obediently, but she couldn't stay silent for long. The very air teemed with questions, bursting with so many smells that Lan could not keep up. Though it was early morning, and the fire was dead, the clearing danced with shadows flitting in and out of focus.

"Why haven't we met more of you?" said Lan. "Nymphs, I mean, if there's one for every tree and river?"

"How many strangers stop you on the street to say hi?" said Kestrel. "We aren't on display for your amusement. We show ourselves when we want, take any living form as long as we stay a day's walk from our roots. Many nymphs never leave their homes. They're happy in the shape they were planted. You've probably run into plenty without knowing. Phoenix and I like our human bodies, but many don't. Ruse once claimed he saw a nymph in dragon shape. Can you imagine? That would be a hard form to hold."

"Does it hurt you to not be in your tree?"

"It can get draining if I don't return often. It is my life force after all."

"So what happened when Ruse saved you? Was Zephyr there too?"

"Zephyr is younger than that. Tell me, do you know why outsiders call this place the Weathering Woods?"

"No, I asked, but Marlow couldn't say."

"This forest has stood far longer than Asta's orchard," said Kestrel. She emptied the contents of her mortar into a separate bowl, added a new batch of ingredients, and continued crushing. "But everything changed when those seeds were brought to Silva."

"Who brought them?"

"They were ordered by the Silvan ruler as an amplifier for the kingdom's magic. Likely brought to the capital by merchants or traders. Along the way, they had a bad run-in with a witch or two. A fight broke out on the eastern road. The whole forest changed. Have you noticed how the air and trees feel different in this Hollow?"

"Yes," said Lan. Her hair was getting frizzy, and her shirt was sticky with sweat. "It feels warm, almost like my home."

"That's because the rest of Silva's weather is controlled by the meteorologists up in their towers in Asta. It's always sunny, neither too hot nor too cold, with just enough rain to keep everything growing. These woods are the exception."

"Who controls the weather here?" asked Lan.

"We do."

"You mean, the nymphs?"

"I mean, everyone. Whatever residue that spell left in the woods centuries ago made the forest particularly sensitive to changes in weather, as caused by the whims of all beings who call this place home. It's allowed for pockets of different plants to flourish, much like the orchard in Asta."

"So this clearing we're in—"

"Ruse's Hollow is the product of many homes blended together: that of the centaurs and of the nymphs that live nearby, including Phoenix and I. If you stay longer, you'll start to leave your own mark too."

"What's the rest of the forest look like? It was so dark last night, I barely saw."

"It greatly depends. I've heard the north is foggy, cold, and wet from the mists rolling in from the cliffs. Other parts are too dry for me to venture, and rumours are the southern coast is perpetually caught in storms. To each their own, I suppose."

"That creature we ran into, the heart-eater—"

"He is well practised in exerting influence over his grove. It takes ages to master that much control. Even I could not."

"But if *anyone* can change the weather in the forest, what if I want it to rain and someone else wants sun in the same place?"

"You'll find you're more in agreement when your needs are aligned and entwined with the natural world. Nevertheless, you're right. Some parts of the woods are always in chaos over who gets to grow where. You asked for mine and Phoenix's story. Ruse saved us when a nasty bunch of stone pines were ready to rip us from the ground. His scar is from that fight."

"He fought off their tree guardians, like we did?"

"With the older nymphs who have passed on. Phoenix and I decided that we wanted to learn how to help, so we wouldn't be helpless if anyone was in danger again."

Lan opened her mouth to ask more, but then Ruse himself appeared at the far end of the clearing, where the terrain dropped off into the sloped ravine. Phoenix and Zephyr followed, draped with ropes. Kestrel stood, and Lan saw relief on her face.

"The sun is well up," she said.

The centaurs spared Lan only a glance before they settled by the empty firepit. Kestrel called out a few words to her sister, and Phoenix approached.

"Lan, is it?" said Phoenix. She planted her spear, ropes slung around it, in the dirt and looked Lan up and down. "What are three kids doing crossing these woods alone?"

"It's a bit of a long story."

"Let me guess—orphans headed to the capital?"

Lan stared. She didn't bother to mention that she was neither an orphan nor going to Asta. At least, she didn't plan on going.

"Do you meet a lot of orphans headed to the capital?" asked Lan.

"Anyone who's after anything goes to Asta."

"What did the others want?"

"Second chances?" Phoenix said, shrugging. "The forest isn't kind to strangers, but I hear it's rough out west. No one ever heads to the valley anymore, not in years."

"Did you rescue others too?"

"Zephyr and Ruse guided two on their way," she said. "They didn't stay long."

"We have to get going too, as soon as my friends are better."

"You might have some time to wait."

Lan made a face. She had to believe they'd all be back on their feet in a few days, even if the odds weren't great. Her stomach turned uneasily. Waiting was the worst.

"Get yourself food," Kestrel instructed, pointing to a cauldron beside the fire with her pestle. Something soupy smelled good. Lan gladly obeyed, getting up cautiously. It took her two tries to steady herself.

The creamy broth was nothing like the clear soups Lan was used to eating with her family. It had too many beans for her taste and some strange grain, but she couldn't be bothered to care. The honey cakes that followed were delicious.

The sun rose high over treetops laden with spring flowers. Kestrel ordered Lan down to the stream to wash. She stumbled across the dirt paths, tripping on roots amid the giggles of tree nymphs, and found the creek in minutes. Lan sunk into the cool water. In the shallow riverbed, sunlight flitted across her face. A rush of feelings came over her—exhaustion that lingered in her bones, a loss of what to do while she waited for Marlow and Annabelle to recover, and the strange mix of comfort and hesitation at being in this unfamiliar Hollow. Her toes squelched in the mud. Small fish nipped at her ankles.

Lan lost track of how long she sat in silence, submerged to her eyes like a frog. Her fingers grew pruny. She tried to ignore the thought of hidden tree nymphs watching and judging her gross clothes and icky hair. Carefully, she rinsed away the layers of grime and gods knew what else coated her body. As the gunk floated downstream, Lan could almost feel the current carry the events of that horrible night along with it.

When Lan got back to the Hollow, the camp appeared empty except for Zephyr, who stood alone by Marlow and Annabelle as if keeping watch. Wet clothes and furs hung to dry on a line strung between two saplings, just like the clothesline Lan's mother had rigged herself on their old balcony. The young centaur glanced up as Lan returned, his arms crossed and his face impatient.

"*Finally*," he said. "I was tasked with looking out for you."

"I was *right* down the hill," said Lan grumpily. "My walk to school is longer, and I'm *not* helpless."

"That's what I told them. Kestrel wouldn't listen. She says you're very fragile in your condition—don't get mad at me! I'm just repeating."

His front hoof pawed the ground in a fidgety manner. In the light, Zephyr looked infinitely younger than Ruse, like a teenager, whatever that meant in centaur years. His hair was black and neatly braided, his eyes bright. They examined her with curiosity.

"Kestrel says you're not from here, not like the other two," he said.

"I—um, I guess not really," said Lan awkwardly. "I just wanted to help."

"Good thing for them that you did."

"But I should be getting back before long."

"Back to where?"

"Toronto, I suppose."

"Is that your home?"

"Well, it's where I'm supposed to be. I don't know . . . It's hard to explain."

Lan stood dripping from the river water, wondering how she could excuse herself politely but was spared the need to escape when Zephyr abruptly changed the subject.

"Wanna go for a ride?"

"Oh, um, yes, I do. Will Marlow and Annabelle be okay alone?"

"Every nymph in this clearing's got eyes on them. Well, maybe not *every* one. The peach blossoms are throwing quite the party downstream. But the rest aren't far."

"Can we go see?"

"See a nymph party? Ruse would have my head if I brought you there. No, we're going for a nice gentle stroll somewhere I can justify when we inevitably get yelled at."

"Is Kestrel going to be mad we left?"

"Absolutely, but you'd rather sit here and do nothing?"

"No."

"Then hop on."

Lan grabbed hold of Zephyr's hand and clambered awkwardly onto his back. She tried not to sway as he began to move.

"You don't have to squeeze your legs so hard," grumbled Zephyr. "My shins are bruised from you kicking around trying to get up. A truly ungraceful display."

"Sorry. I've always wanted to ride, but I never got to learn."

"No centaurs willing to give lessons?"

"Um—I guess you could say that," said Lan. She did not have the heart to tell Zephyr that she came from a world so empty of magic it didn't even have creatures who looked like him.

"The trick is sitting upright," said Zephyr. "Keep your back straight and try not to move around so much. A strong centre means you'll stay balanced through all the bumps and turns. You won't get far by clutching on tighter."

Lan tried to relax and keep her balance. Zephyr moved slowly. He pointed out the names of nearby tree nymphs they encountered, at least the ones in human form that Lan could see. Some waved and peered at her curiously behind winding trunks or perched atop branches. Others flitted shyly between the foliage. Now that she listened, an undercurrent of laughter and whispers followed their walk. She realized that she had never spent so much time outside the city, never recognized the pull of bustle and silence that sat in the outdoors. It wasn't scary or wild at all but bursting with life. That mixed feeling of solitude and company reminded her of being in a library.

"Everyone's so friendly," said Lan. "The pines we met in the western valley didn't give us this kind of welcome. They sent a whole tree-guardian army after us."

"Tree guardians are only called on under threat," said Zephyr. "No offence, but you're hardly a threat here."

"We didn't do anything there either. Marlow might've taken some firewood and sap for his arrows early on, but then we just wanted to pass."

"Pines are famously cranky, especially when it comes to strangers barging in. They don't play nice with just anyone. Either way, you have to know who you're dealing with, and take only what you need. That looks different among foreign trees."

"It all sounds so complicated. How are we supposed to know what's okay if every place is different?"

"You take the time to learn."

"What about you? Have you ever left this forest?"

"What for?"

"Don't you get curious about what else is out there? I always did."

Zephyr shrugged and simply said, "This is home."

Lan looked around. Rays of sunlight danced on speckled leaves. Colourful mushrooms poked out of the damp dirt, and dewdrops sat suspended in spiderwebs. The air smelled so clean. Amid it all, she could almost understand what Zephyr meant.

They returned to camp to an upset Kestrel who did not accept Zephyr's answer of "fresh air" as an excuse for disappearing. ("We live in a forest!") Lan was sent straight to bed with another sip of potion to help her rest. When she woke the following morning, Annabelle was stirring. Lan resisted the urge to prod her. She did not have to wait long. A few minutes later, Annabelle's brown eyes blinked open. She pushed herself upright, bewildered, and took in the towering trees, quiet clearing, and Kestrel bent over something by the fire.

"How are you feeling?" said Lan at once.

"What happened? Where are we?"

"It's okay. We're safe," said Lan. "You've been out for a couple days, but—well, it's a long story—centaurs and nymphs and woods that change weather. They're friendly. That's Kestrel. She's the reason you're alive. I can fill you in later. Are you okay?"

Annabelle's bottom lip quivered. Then she buried her face in her hands and burst into tears. "This is my fault!" she sobbed.

"How do you figure that?" said Lan, taken aback. She tried awkwardly to pat her head.

"I was stupid enough to think we could make it!"

"Well, you were right, weren't you?"

Annabelle sniffled and stared down at Marlow beside her. Her eyes widened, and her fingers brushed the hair from his forehead.

"Kestrel is a healer," Lan said quickly. "She said he'll be fine soon enough."

"I was wrong," whispered Annabelle. "This was a horrible idea. I didn't know what I was doing. My grandmother warned me."

"Well, you can't give up now!" said Lan. "We're halfway there. He'll wake up, and you'll get to Asta to do what you were meant to. I've got the poppies in my pocket! Proof of a heart!"

"Your book never said anything about a happy ending."

"Well, it probably would've if I'd read that far. These types of books all have happy endings. I've read enough of them to know."

"I can't put Marlow in more danger. And you have to get back to your family. I've kept you both long enough."

"I'm choosing to be here," said Lan, stunned by Annabelle's dejection. She would've given anything to see the resolute glint return to her eyes.

"Well, it's over. You don't have to anymore."

"So what?" said Lan. Frustration rose. How could Annabelle take them this far only to quit? "You're returning to the Academy? It's just as dangerous to go back."

"At least I'd know the way," said Annabelle with a half-hearted shrug. "I'm so tired I can barely move now. Everything hurts. I should've stayed put, like I was told."

She blew her nose on her sleeve and began to cry so hard her whole body shook. Lan was at a complete loss. Her anger slipped away as quickly as it'd arrived. What would Marlow think when he woke? What could any of them do now?

"For the record, I'm glad you didn't stay in that awful place," said Lan quietly. "I came through the portal because someone needed me. That's what the Cognitor told us. If you didn't decide to go, we would've never met."

"Does that really matter so much to you?"

"Of course it does! Don't you see how much I've learned since I got here? I never thought I could fight a beast! Heart-eater or not, I wouldn't trade this week for anything."

"That's nice of you to say, but you're still planning on leaving, aren't you?" said Annabelle. Her shoulders were stiff, and her eyes as hard as the morning they'd met on the riverbank. It made Lan want to shrink. "How can you tell me to keep going, that it'll be all good and worth it in the end, if you're not even willing to stick around and see?"

"You never seemed to care much about me staying either way . . ."

"Because I thought I could do it on my own! Well, I can't."

"What are you saying?"

"Isn't it obvious? Marlow was right. You're the witch we need to complete our journey to Asta. Without you, there's no chance. They're *your* poppies, not mine—proof of *your* heart. I'm not going to force you, of course—do whatever you want—but I'm done. My quest is finished."

FATE IN HER OWN HANDS

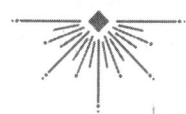

Lan sat at the river's edge, dangling her feet in the murky water. The stream was just down the hill from the northern crest of Ruse's Hollow, and Kestrel had granted permission for Lan to go on her own. Around her, wild berries burst from bushes, and tall flowers sprouted in pockets around groves. The air was heavy with the approaching weight of a large storm. Lan wondered whether it might whisk her back to Toronto. After all, the Cognitor had said she would find her way home the moment she decided her time in Silva was up. This had to be it. Lan couldn't go all the way to the capital like Annabelle had asked. In all likelihood, Annabelle had been exhausted and not known what she was saying. She'd come to her senses when she recovered.

From her pockets, Lan pulled the crumpled poppies that she'd gathered at the valley's edge and smoothed out the petals. They had not wilted or been torn. The bright flowers were as crimson as the ones on Phoenix's and Kestrel's trees. Hoa phượng, Lan remembered, that was what they were called in Vietnamese. Even if she gave these to Annabelle and Marlow to carry, would they stay in perfect condition on the road to Asta? Lan wiped away a stray tear that had fallen without her noticing.

"Why are you crying?"

Startled, Lan jumped up and slipped on the wet rocks of the riverbed. Ruse caught her before she tumbled in, clucking disapprovingly.

"A warrior should learn to have better balance," he said, righting her. "And pay attention to your surroundings."

"I told you I wasn't a warrior," said Lan. "In fact, I was thinking of running away when you snuck up on me like that."

"I wasn't sneaking. I was simply walking. Warriors don't sneak."

"What is it with you and warriors anyway? Some of us aren't! Kestrel isn't."

"Of course she is. You think cheating death isn't worthy of the title?"

Lan paused, her head tilted as she considered Ruse's words. He looked amused.

"I thought it meant you had to be good at fighting and shooting things."

"You're mistaken. It can mean much more. That's why I'm telling you."

"You don't have to stand here and talk to me," said Lan. "I'm sure you have lots of centaur-y things to do."

"Old habits," said Ruse. "I taught folks of all sorts when I was younger. Centaurs have a long history of training heroes. Haven't you heard? It's impossible to resist."

"I have heard actually," said Lan. Tales of old wise centaur teachers had been scattered across stories she'd read all her life. "Why did you stop teaching?"

"I trained Zephyr when he joined us, but I'm getting old and feeling the weight of these woods. Most of my kind have moved farther west. They don't like rain."

Ruse cast an eye at the darkened sky peeking through the treetops.

"I guess we should go back before it starts pouring," said Lan, squeezing out her wet trousers.

"Not before you tell me what you're running away from."

"Oh, well, it does seem a little harsh when you put it *that* way."

"I am simply repeating your words."

"It's not that big a deal," said Lan.

She started to climb up the slope to their camp but paused mid-path and went on. "My parents would probably say I'm being dramatic, but things have been confusing since they decided to move . . ."

"Tell me."

Lan hesitated only a second, and then everything tumbled out. All at once, she was recounting to Ruse each detail, from the moment she'd found out about her family's plans to the defeated look in Annabelle's eyes that very morning.

"So you see," she finished, minutes later, out of breath, "it feels like I'm being pulled in all these different directions, but somehow, I still don't belong anywhere! Zephyr asked me yesterday about my home, but I don't even know what *home* means. It's just these little pieces, and Annabelle wants me to go with them to Asta, but I can't lead anyone! I can't even tell you where I'm meant to be."

Ruse listened patiently, and at her feet, Lan vaguely noticed tiny dandelions blooming, aging, and wilting in fast-forward motion. They mirrored her quickened breath. Blades of grass grew all around, thick and coarse rather than the slender kind in Canada.

"Annabelle is not asking you to lead," said Ruse when she stopped talking. "She is lost and seeking comfort from a friend. You can provide that, can't you?"

"Of course, but—"

"In helping her, you may come to know more about this *home* you long for, if it is indeed one place. I see nothing wrong with the pieces you described."

"It doesn't make sense. Home shouldn't be pieces. It should be a big solid thing! For me, it's all scattered."

"Even scattered pieces can make a whole. Look down." Ruse gestured at the weeds growing underfoot. The forest was always bursting with strange plants. Lan found it hard to distinguish which ones were her doing.

"The Weathering Woods responds to the energy of every living being in order to define the environment. You have been here only a few days, and yet you are already creating changes much like Kestrel's and Phoenix's trees, growing in a grove that had never before seen their kind. I have seen homes grow and take form over and over again."

"I don't live in the Weathering Woods," said Lan. "I wouldn't be able to change anything at home. My world isn't magical."

"I wouldn't know about that, but you can always try and see what you grow. It isn't easy, but those without the luxury of one place to call home must make do."

"It's unfair that I have to try so hard to make a place truly mine."

"Perhaps, but isn't that what Annabelle is doing by fighting for her coast?"

"I guess so," said Lan, "and I want to be where I'm needed most now. But I really do want to try out for the track team too, like I promised my friend, Manav. It started off as a bargain so he'd get me this book, but I think I actually want to do it now."

"Can you not help Annabelle and return in time to keep your initial promise?"

"I probably could. Time doesn't seem to be moving there. My parents are safe."

"And you think your way isn't clear?"

"Well, I'm still a half-baked witch who can't control my powers or fight."

"I'm afraid the forest is short on trained witches who can teach you magic, at least in a way that would serve you. We have our own way of weaving spells that relies less on outside residue and more on our own strength. But the second part . . . I do know someone that would be eager to show you a few tricks."

Lan looked up, hardly daring to believe she'd understood his meaning correctly. "Would you teach me to fight like a real hero?"

"I'm retired, Lan," said Ruse, "but I'm sure Phoenix would love to oblige. I can ask for you. She's more than capable, and her style will suit you more, given your—shall we say, limited limb situation."

"I'd like that very much," said Lan, "but I'm not sure I'll be able to learn much if I'm still worried about my friends."

The thought of Marlow still unconscious turned her insides cold again.

"Consider it," said Ruse. "Take your time. You need only ask when you're ready. Now we should return before Kestrel starts to fret."

Lan nodded and followed. Then, with a loud crack of thunder, the grey clouds brewing above them erupted. Lan gasped at the sudden cold. The ground turned to mud. In seconds, she and Ruse were drenched in the monsoon-like rain. Though Lan could barely see, she grabbed on to Ruse's hand. They ran uphill, and a weight seemed to lift from Lan's chest with every step. By the time they reached the Hollow, she was smiling.

Kestrel, ever protective over her patients, was peeved to find Annabelle so distraught when she woke. Lan was ushered away to let her rest. They only saw each other briefly the next day, but it was long enough for Lan to realize that Annabelle was not going to change her mind.

"In case you haven't noticed, Marlow still hasn't woken up," hissed Annabelle. They were sitting side by side on the bamboo cot, whispering at nightfall. The nymphs had returned to their trees, and the centaurs were dozing on the other side of the Hollow.

"Of course I've noticed!" said Lan, stung. "Kestrel told me today he was better."

She had seen it too. Marlow's breathing came easier. His heartbeat was steadier, and his forehead cool and dry.

"He looks awful," said Annabelle. The corner of her mouth lifted in a wry smile. "That's a first."

"He'll be up soon," said Lan. She had to believe it. "He'd tell you to keep going. What will you do if you don't go on?"

"I hear the woods are a good place to start over," said Annabelle drily. "I could take up the healer's life like Kestrel, save stupid kids who stumble across my path. Maybe by then, someone else will have saved Sol."

"You don't really believe that, do you? I mean, it's your quest."

"The only one who really believed that was Marlow, and he nearly died for it."

Lan stayed silent. Annabelle's beaten voice broke her. There was nothing else she could say, except that—but saying it would make it very real. If Lan promised she would go to Asta, there'd be no turning back.

"He always used to sneak me apples when I was ill," said Annabelle out of nowhere. She began to cry again. "He never got sick. Never got a scratch on him. I was in the infirmary every week."

"Were you?" said Lan, surprised.

"Oh, not for any training thing," Annabelle said. She managed a small smile. "Those kids couldn't touch me, but the air—I felt in my whole body I wasn't built for it. I came down with stuff all the time."

"That's how I feel about Toronto winters," said Lan. "I'd joke that I wasn't born for it. The snow saved us in that grove though—ish. So I can't complain now."

"Complain all you want. Marlow definitely listened to his fair share of my gripes. I don't know how he never told me to shut up."

She paused, and then continued in the silence that Lan left.

"First time I met him, I was throwing a tantrum in the middle of the training field. This incompetent joke of a teacher made me sit out for terrorizing the other seven-year-olds—their fault for putting a blade in my hand. All I did was dance like my grandmother taught me. Didn't think I could be punished for being good at it. Anyway, I look across the field to where the older boys are sparring, and he's staring at me. Challenged me to a round later that day. I lost." Annabelle shrugged and smiled sadly. "But I think we're about even now."

"You know he'll be okay, right?" said Lan. She reached a hand out. Annabelle returned her squeeze, but she did not seemed reassured.

"It's still my fault. You don't know how horrible it is seeing him like this. Whatever he thought of the Academy, he loved being on the field, moving. Somehow, he was always good at it . . . But don't tell him I said that."

Suddenly, Marlow's eyes fluttered as if he'd been listening all along. He stirred. Lan's heart skipped a beat, and Annabelle's breath caught.

"Annabelle?" he murmured.

"Right here," said Annabelle instantly, bending over him.

"Were you talking about me?"

Annabelle began to laugh. She leaned in and hugged him. His arm squeezed tightly around her waist. Lan felt her face wet with tears. Marlow reached with his other hand and found hers.

"You're okay," he said. "What happened?"

His eyes squeezed shut again, and he fell back.

"Tell you everything when you're better."

"I am better."

But a minute later, Marlow sank back on the furs and lay fast asleep.

"You told her *what*?"

Lan woke to the sound of Marlow's voice. He was sitting upright, staring at Annabelle in disbelief. The colour had returned to his face.

"You can't be serious," he said.

"I'm not putting you in danger again," said Annabelle stubbornly. "My grandma was right. I should just stay put, be patient, and let the big people deal with it."

"You're gonna hang out in the Weathering Woods until someone else saves Sol?"

"Why not? It's comfy."

"Because, Annabelle, Sol is your home! This isn't you."

"Well, I almost died being me, and so did you! Stop arguing with me. You're making my head hurt again."

Her voice was hard and resolute, but Lan saw tears stream down her cheeks.

"Annabelle, you can't quit—"

"I'll go," said Lan.

Her voice was so quiet she wasn't sure they heard, but Marlow stopped talking.

"What did you say?"

"I'll go," she repeated.

Lan sat up. Her hair was matted, damp from the humidity, and her eyes full of gunk and half-laden with sleep. Her body hurt from lying on the bamboo, and the rainfall had made every part of her grimy and coated in mud. Her mother would have cried aloud to see her this way.

"What are you saying?" Annabelle whispered. "What about your family?"

"Rồi sẽ qua nhanh," said Lan. "That's what they kept telling me when we were apart: time will pass quickly. I'll see them again, but I can't let you give up halfway, so we're going together if that's what it takes."

"If you mean it, then I—I'll think about it," said Annabelle. She wrapped her arms around her knees, looking small. "It helps, a lot. I didn't expect you'd say yes."

"*I* knew you'd come to your senses in the end," said Marlow, smiling. "You didn't have it in you to resist."

"Resist having my heart eaten by a terrifying monster? Or did you mean the endless walking?" said Lan.

"Not helping . . ." mumbled Annabelle, glaring at them.

"Resist being with us, of course, just like the Cognitor told us!" said Marlow. "And using your powers like that awesome snowstorm!"

"I've still got a lot to learn," said Lan. "That reminds me. I have to talk to Ruse."

"The centaur?" said Annabelle, looking up. "About what?"

"Lessons. If I'm going to stay, then I'd better get practising."

ENERGY CREATES ENERGY

Phoenix greeted Lan that afternoon with a newly whittled stick in her hands. Lan had forgotten how good it felt to really move again. The nymph's style was close to Annabelle's fluid dance, and she quickly got lost in the practice. Phoenix was a patient teacher and waited for Lan to adjust to the forest's strange magical residue.

Her powers felt different than in the valley but more stable than before. Magic moved through her like a breeze, not as colourful but noticeable at every turn. Her spells intermingled with the current of energy throughout the rest of the woods. Phoenix taught her to notice the air and ground, to ask for their help rather than fighting against them when working a spell. They moved around the clearing to not bother the nymphs in one place for too long. Lan didn't pause until Zephyr came and whisked her off for a break.

Within days, Lan's riding improved so much they were moving fast, and she no longer stumbled pulling herself up on Zephyr's back. Her newfound energy surprised her, and the Hollow held no shortages of distractions, from picking up phrases in Centaurian and Nymph to Kestrel's subtle magic. Marlow and Annabelle were still confined to bed, faced with a slower recovery under Kestrel's watchful eye. Lan walked alone around the surrounding woods—the sweet mango blossoms, cranky old guava fruit, and ever-flirty peach trees with velvety pink sprigs in their short curls. Even the ancient pomegranate shrubs that few dared to bother began to recognize Lan and whisper to her by name. It was a shame so many delicious fruits were not in season.

As Marlow grew steadier on his feet, Lan saw with some annoyance that the young nymphs were taking notice. Even with their muddy feet and rougher skin, they made for a beautiful picture. Lan still wore Annabelle's Academy clothes. Rough with wear, they weren't so flattering. The outfit was cozy, but Lan would've welcomed a nicer option. It puzzled her. The lack of fancy clothes hadn't bothered her in Toronto. Then again, none of the kids at her school made her feel all sunny and warm like Marlow could. She practically glowed each time he looked at her. It was downright annoying.

"You get used to it," Annabelle said, watching Lan glare at the nymphs one day.

"I don't know what you're talking about," Lan said guiltily, turning away.

"Oh please, I've been his best friend for five years. I know that look," said Annabelle, rolling her eyes.

"I don't know what that means!"

"It means you're like every other girl making moon eyes at a handsome guy. I'll admit it. That swoopy hair goes a long way. It's totally normal."

"But not for you?"

Annabelle sniffed. "He's not my type."

Lan raised an eyebrow. "Pretty sure he's every single nymph's type."

"Well, not mine. To be honest, guys have never much held my interest. But in any case, you don't have to worry about the nymphs."

"Because we'll be off soon, right?"

"Marlow has to get better first."

Annabelle had not regained her old drive, but flashes of her strength returned. It made Lan hopeful to see her moving again, training on her own, and exchanging stories with Ruse about their different traditions from the coast to the forest. Lan grew surer each day that their time in the Hollow was drawing to a close. The thought both saddened and relieved her. So much of the woods remained unexplored, and Lan's chest ached to think of her new friendships cut short. The impossibility of any future together weighed heavily.

"Why so glum?" Zephyr asked as they rode out of the clearing in late afternoon. The air was muggy. Lan's shirt stuck to her uncomfortably. "You know the nymphs never mean anything by it. They flirt with everyone."

"What? No, why does everyone think—that's not it," grumbled Lan. After the talk with Annabelle, Lan had decided to firmly ignore the inconvenient effect Marlow had on her, in the hopes that it'd disappear.

"The ground's perfect for a gallop, and you haven't even asked me to go faster."

"Okay, can you go faster, please?"

Zephyr muttered something under his breath but picked up to a lope. They cantered in silence. The breeze calmed her. As they moved, Lan practised grabbing hold of the residue trailing through her fingertips like spun silk. Flowers sprouted wherever she willed them to: dandelions, roses, and giant sunflowers, her mother's favourite.

"You've grown," Zephyr noted, slowing to a walk.

"You think so?"

"In many ways. It'll be interesting to see how the stars cross in your life."

"The Cognitor in the fields said they couldn't see my future," said Lan. "Can you? Centaurs are supposed to be good at that sky stuff."

"More as a faith we follow than a mystery we try to solve," said Zephyr. "Besides, as Ruse would say, the future is your doing, not the sky's."

They both looked up through the trees, where the sun had taken on the dim orange glow of sunset, with traces of the rainbow clinging to the edges of the clouds. Kestrel would want them back soon.

"I'll be sad to leave," said Lan quietly.

"I know. As will I."

"I finally feel calm, like it's enough just to be here, you know? I can't remember the last time I felt that way. Definitely not in Toronto. Not unless I was reading and imagining I was someplace else."

"The forest can have that effect on people."

"You don't happen to know a way I can come back, do you?"

Lan hardly dared to voice the question. She wanted to go to Asta for Annabelle, but the thought of never returning to the Weathering Woods felt too permanent to accept.

"I'm no witch," said Zephyr, "but I've heard the orchard in Asta can do just about anything you ask."

"Even let me go back and forth between worlds?"

"Even that."

"Tell me how," said Lan, leaning so far forward in her eagerness that Zephyr had to steady her.

"The trees in that orchard are the original source of Silva's residue, the power of kings. Many species exist for all sorts of spells, but when it comes to crossing realms, the pomegranate's what you'd want."

"Pomegranates?"

Lan's mind flashed to scrambling up trees in her grandparents' garden and looking down onto laden shrubs bearing the grenade-like fruit that her mother cracked open, spilling shining seeds like jewels.

"How do you know this?" she asked Zephyr. "And what's so special about them?"

"Nymphs like to talk. I like to listen. I've heard just one seed would do the trick, but it depends on the person and the fruit. Magic like that gets very dangerous, but if a spell is cast right, even the gods aren't immune."

Lan considered his words. She had to admit that kind of power was tempting. If she could go back and forth between her world and Silva, she'd never feel alone or bored again! She wouldn't have to say goodbye to her magic.

"Don't forget," said Zephyr lightly, "Asta's orchard is forbidden to people for good reason. Its residue may reach across the land, but working with a seed itself—a spell like that doesn't always do what you want it to. Best to leave it to the witches who know what they're doing."

"It feels silly to be learning all this magic just to leave it behind when I go."

"You can't continue wherever you're headed?"

"Not in my world. There's not an ounce of magic to work with."

"But energy creates energy, remember?"

Lan was silent. After a while, they turned and rode back to the Hollow. Dusk set upon the forest. A warm glow of firelight appeared ahead. They mounted the hill at a gallop and entered camp, where Marlow was hanging wet clothes on the line and chatting to two redheaded apricot nymphs. The others were erecting a slender wooden structure around the fire, strung with flowers and herbs.

"Full moon tomorrow," Zephyr said. Lan slipped smoothly off his back. "I almost forgot. Ruse always does something special."

"Like a ceremony?"

"A simple one, for gratitude or reflection and the like."

"I do that, too, at home," said Lan. "We set out water and fruit for our ancestors. We send it to them with incense, these smoky nice-smelling stems."

"Ruse prefers bonfires, but same idea."

"Wait a second," said Lan, suddenly remembering the circled day on the calendar on her bedroom wall in Toronto. "If it's the full moon in May tomorrow, it must be the seventeenth. I know because it's my birthday."

THE FULL MOON

"It's not a big deal," said Lan to Kestrel, who was making bite-sized honey cakes with Marlow.

For a nymph who rarely ate human food, she was an excellent chef. Annabelle had left to get firewood with Ruse, thrilled to finally regain her independence.

"Twelve is a big birthday," Kestrel was saying. "A magical number, a complete rotation in our calendar—apparently yours too. A step into adulthood, many would say."

Lan made a face.

"She's right," said Marlow, who was sprinkling lavender on top of the honey glaze. "Back at the Academy, it was a graduation. They make you do a full set of exams to celebrate. Annabelle had hers last year. She hated every minute."

"Back in Toronto, I'll probably have instant Jell-O," said Lan. They stared at her. "It's like this powder that turns into sweet gloop . . . Not as bad as it sounds. My dad bought it a lot for me when we first moved."

Kestrel fished the last cake from the fire and swept the lot away on a wooden tray. Marlow looked at Lan and tipped his head toward

Kestrel's vacated spot on the log beside him. He was still peaky, his jawline pronounced, his light hair messy and pushed to the side. Lan knew he was too weak to even string his bow, but he had not lost his poise. If an army of elves (the scary kind) suddenly marched into camp, he'd be ready to meet them.

Lan picked up a couple of knives from the firepit alongside a handful of smooth stones cast aside and passed a pair to Marlow. She sat beside him. They began to whittle in a comfortable quiet, Marlow making arrowheads and Lan trying to not cut her hand open like Phoenix had showed her. Marlow was wrapped in the dark green fabric of a borrowed cloak. The potion stains on the hem marked it as Kestrel's. His clean shirt was thin enough to see the bandages underneath.

"Do you want your cloak back?" Lan asked.

"Keep it. It suits you, matches your hair."

With Kestrel out of sight, Marlow reached into his pocket and pulled out a mini honey cake that he handed to Lan.

"For you," he said, looking proud of himself. "Happy birthday."

Lan looked at it and tried not to laugh. "Aren't they all supposed to be for me?"

"Slow down, birthday girl. They're to share. Besides, I made this one specially. Not that there's anything different about it, but it's from me, personally."

Lan took the cake and bit in. Honey from the centre oozed out and filled her mouth with sweetness.

"Not bad for a first attempt at baking," she said. "I'd say you might actually like being Kestrel's assistant."

"She's incredible. Almost a shame we have to leave. I mean, obviously I'm happy we're going." He glanced quickly in the direction Annabelle had left, as though making sure she hadn't somehow heard. Lan followed his gaze.

"If you like it here, you can always come back," she said.

Marlow stopped whittling and looked at her, his eyes their usual bright green in the daylight. His forehead was creased. She waited for him to say something, but then someone coughed loudly behind them. They started.

"Sorry to intrude." Kestrel had returned, a bowl in her hands.

"You're not intruding," said Lan.

"Clearly." Kestrel held up the potion. "Marlow, your medicine."

"Thanks, Kestrel, I can apply it myself."

"Right away." She turned and left to join Zephyr by the cauldrons.

"I know you hate watching," said Marlow, shrugging the cloak off his shoulders.

"Not looking," said Lan. She focused intently on her misshapen rock carving and swung around when he said, "Finished."

"Now I know I'm not cut out to be a healer."

"Not at this rate," said Marlow. He nodded at the stone beginning to take a blade-like shape in her hands. "You've gotten so much better. I saw your practice last night. You looked great."

"I thought you were sleeping."

They were interrupted again before Marlow could answer. A laugh cut in from the edge of the clearing. Annabelle and Ruse had returned, firewood in hand, deep in conversation. Her face was scrunched up but in a good way.

"Last call to get yourself cleaned up, because I am starving!" Zephyr shouted.

"I'm gonna to pop down to the stream and wash before we eat," said Lan, rising. "Zephyr knocked me into a mud puddle earlier."

"Want me to come with you?" said Marlow.

"You shouldn't be moving too much," said Lan, echoing Kestrel's caution. She laughed at Marlow's unimpressed grimace. "Don't eat without me!"

It might have been her imagination, but he looked sad to see her go. Lan left the clearing, taking in the smell of the woods that she had grown to love. A few apricot nymphs darted around the bushes and smiled as she passed. She reached the stream and dipped her bare feet in. The water brushed her ankles. She filled the pouch tied to her hip and scrubbed her face, hands, and nails of dirt. A delicious smell was already wafting from camp. Lan hurried back to find a feast spread over the logs.

"Finally! You're back!"

Annabelle pulled Lan over to rows of roast corn on the cob, a steaming cauldron of Lan's favourite tomato and fish soup, jugs of berry juice, a pyramid of lavender-topped cakes dripping honey, bowls of wild fruit, and stubby miniature baguettes just like the ones from the streets of Hà Nội.

"Do you do this every month?" said Lan in amazement.

"Your birthday called for adding something extra," said Ruse.

The seven of them gathered around the logs and sat, food balanced on woven-leaf plates like the banana-leaf wraps from Lan's childhood.

"To a giving and forgiving month ahead," said Ruse before they ate. "To Lan."

Marlow, sitting across in the circle from Lan, winked at her as he took a drink. The fire suddenly felt warm on her skin. Beside her, Annabelle leaned in for a hug.

"Happy birthday," she whispered. Lan's heart swelled to see her smiling again.

"Zephyr told me he and Ruse can take us out of the forest," said Lan. "After that, we're practically in Asta! I know you're still healing, but we'll be ready to leave anytime you want. You'll be home in Sol soon."

"Wow," said Annabelle softly. "Without you—well, we really needed you. I did. Now it's as much your quest as mine."

She leaned over and laid her head on Lan's shoulder. Her eyes closed. Opposite the circle, Marlow and Zephyr were laughing at something Ruse had said. Lan's stomach settled in a comfortable fullness. Phoenix and Kestrel began to sing in their own tongue. A few nymphs whistled from the nearby trees. It reminded Lan of the raucous karaoke nights her parents had hosted with old friends many years back. New Year's Eve always got loud with eighties hits, and her mother's voice could've rivalled a nymph's.

When Lan glanced up again, Marlow was looking at her across the fire. He rolled his eyes at something Zephyr whispered in his ear and brushed him off. Then he stood and walked over to sit at Lan's other side.

"How's it going, birthday girl?"

"You need a haircut," she answered.

"Do I?" he said, running his hand through his hair. "I rather like how it's grown."

"If you like the lost-in-the-woods look."

"I'd say I'm pulling it off," he said. "More fun than being the golden boy."

"The scars add to the look," Lan said without thinking. Her eyes moved down to his side, where his bandages were still visible under his shirt.

"Kestrel says I'll be good as new soon. Then we're off, right?"

Lan caught his hesitation but said nothing. They sat side by side, the full moon so bright above them that it barely seemed like night. The others had gotten up to dance. Lan was surprised by their grace but remembered how fluid a good fight felt. The moves were two sides of the same coin. She leaned on Marlow's shoulder, Annabelle's head still perched on hers. The fire crackled pleasantly.

"I have something for you," said Marlow, his eyes still on the dancers.

"You already gave me a honey cake."

"This is for real."

Lan sat up. On her right, Annabelle stirred and sat up too.

"I don't need anything. Tonight was more than I would've gotten in Toronto."

"Well, you're getting it anyway," said Marlow. He reached into the pouch at his waist and drew out a necklace of braided cord with an arrowhead pendant.

"It's from all of us, actually," he said, nodding at Annabelle, who was watching. "My idea, though, for the record. May I?"

Lan nodded, unable to say anything back. He leaned in and looped the necklace around her neck. His cold hands brushed her skin. Goosebumps rose along her arms.

"The arrowhead is mine. It's actually from the fight in the heart-eater's grove. Phoenix picked up some of the strays. Annabelle braided it."

"The vines are from Phoenix's and Kestrel's trees," Annabelle chimed in, "woven with centaur hairs."

"I don't know what to say," said Lan, her voice tight. The pendant sat perfectly between her collarbones, and a shiver went up her spine as it rested on her skin. It was made of black stone, like Annabelle's dagger. She fingered the sharp edge, dulled for her to wear safely. Tears pricked at her eyes.

"*Thank you* is the typical response," said Marlow, "and you're welcome."

"But do you know what this could mean?" said Lan slowly. She pulled the red poppies from her pocket and held them out. "I think we have two of the items we need."

"Courage in large supply?" said Annabelle. "Yes, the arrowhead from overcoming the heart-eater, and the people who came to help . . . That does make sense!"

"You're right," said Marlow. "It took all of us to make it out of there that night."

"And a good story is the easiest item!" said Annabelle, "We practically have one already! I'm starting to believe we might actually have a shot."

A BURST OF YELLOW

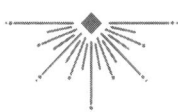

Within the week, Marlow recovered in leaping strides. He and Annabelle joined Lan every day in the woods. They were sent to fetch traps and water with Zephyr or herbs with Kestrel while Phoenix and Ruse tracked larger prey farther out. Kestrel showed them exactly how to pluck the parts they needed so the plants would grow back quickly.

"Doing anything worthwhile takes care," she lectured, emphasizing her words by bopping them all on the head with a handful of mint.

Annabelle was talking more about Sol with each passing day, lingering on the sunny weather and her sister, Daisy. Lan could tell the forest didn't agree with her much. Even Lan missed seeing more of the sky.

"We should leave on the half moon," said Ruse one evening. "It's a lucky day for long journeys. If we go at dawn and move fast, we'll hit the main roads by midnight. Zephyr and I will keep you safe until you reach the open fields. The heart-eater isn't the only danger in these woods."

They looked to Annabelle, who slowly nodded. "Thank you," she said.

"That's in two days," said Ruse. "Mind you start getting ready."

Marlow's expression was calm and unreadable. They dispersed before dinner, and Lan saw him disappear behind Phoenix's and Kestrel's trees out of the clearing. She hesitated for a second, then followed. It had rained the previous day. The shaded ground was still damp and the tracks of Marlow's boots imprinted in the mud. Lan had been down this way only once. It was a small trail Marlow and Kestrel often came through to gather plants for his medicine. The weeds were dense, and Lan was grateful for his footprints to make sure she was going the right way.

The prints ended where the path cut off behind a wild berry bush. Lan pushed the brambles aside and fell into a clearing. Her mouth dropped. The field was dotted in yellow flowers, golden like the hills by the riverbank in the western valley. Marlow sat with his back to Lan. His face was turned to the sky.

"I never knew this place was here," Lan said. She stopped beside him. A freshly made flower crown of marigolds and dandelions sat in his lap.

"Kestrel only showed me last week," said Marlow. He held out the flowers. "Made this for you."

"Did you expect me to come after you?"

"I hoped you would."

Lan sat and took the crown. It was larger than the ones by the river. He had gotten better at making them. She smiled.

"You know what's weird?" she said. "I thought I knew this forest so well, or at least the area around our Hollow. Turns out I've never seen this clearing, and it's closer to us than the stream."

"I wish I had longer to explore. I'm just getting to know my way. It's strange."

"What is?"

"Not wanting to leave."

"Why's that strange?"

"It is for me," said Marlow. He ran a hand through his hair, pausing as if trying to find the right words. "Can I tell you something?"

"Of course."

"It's like—I've never said this out loud. Annabelle's always had Sol, even if it's only a memory now. It gives her this big solid thing to push off from."

"I know exactly what you mean."

"You know what my big solid thing was?" said Marlow. He glanced at Lan. "Annabelle. The moment I met her, everything made sense. My fixation on training, being admired, and rising in the ranks—she changed it all for me in a heartbeat. The day we met by the river, you asked me why I followed her and left everything behind. I never wanted to admit it, but she's the only thing that ever mattered. Maybe it's pathetic, but going with her was the easiest choice."

"It's not pathetic," said Lan. "It's like riding, what Zephyr told me when I was starting out. If your centre is strong, you'll keep your balance through whatever comes. Maybe Annabelle was your centre."

"I suppose that makes sense. There's so much I want to do here, but I feel like I'm betraying Annabelle. I mean, you had to be the one to convince her to keep going. That should've been me. If you hadn't stepped in, I don't know if I'd have been strong enough to."

"I don't think of it that way, and Annabelle doesn't either. I know it."

"Deep down, I know it too. I'm just so used to following her, I'm not sure what to do with myself now that I want . . . different things."

Marlow's cool demeanour slipped. His voice cracked. Lan took his hand.

"You know, I used to get so nervous whenever people got close," he whispered. "So many tried. They wanted to, and I was scared each time that they'd ask one question too many and figure out that the only worthwhile part of me beneath the flashy surface was Annabelle."

Tears fell fast down his face. He wiped them away. Lan briefly registered how odd it was that she did not want to get up and run. If it had been anyone in her world, she would've squirmed right out of there. Instead, she waited until Marlow stopped crying, and said, "Maybe this is a good thing."

"How do you figure that?"

"Well, we're making sure Annabelle gets to Sol, right? After that, it's up to you, isn't it? I'm sure you could follow her there if you wanted, or stay in the capital. Or you could come back to the woods. You don't have to make up your mind now, but isn't it kind of exciting to have something new entirely for yourself?"

Marlow smiled, his face still wet.

"That actually really helps," he said. "Does having a birthday automatically make you smarter?"

"Always have been, you're just starting to notice."

"Hey, I've always noticed you. Speaking of which, people are gonna start to wonder where we've gone."

"Right," said Lan. Marlow rose and offered her a hand. She took it, suddenly aware of how dark it had gotten.

"Thanks for coming after me," he said, pulling her up. The flower crown hung lopsided over her head. For a moment, it seemed like Marlow wanted to say more, but he cleared his throat and dropped her hand.

"Anytime."

They pushed through the berry bush, and the clearing vanished from view. Lan ruffled the stray weeds off her cloak. Her steps dragged back to camp.

"We were starting to get worried," said Ruse when they trekked into the Hollow.

"I told you they'd be fine, Ruse—give them some space," said Zephyr.

"Just needed a walk," said Marlow. Annabelle stared curiously.

"Make sure you eat well tonight," said Ruse, nodding at the roast on the fire. He sounded like Lan's mother. "You have a busy day ahead."

That night, for the first time since coming to the Hollow, Lan was unable to sleep. She lay listening as Zephyr and Ruse rode out late for an evening run. Kestrel sat until the fire died out and disappeared to rest in her tree. After the centaurs returned, she heard them talking in low voices before quieting down to sleep. The camp was still. At dawn, Lan got up, sniffling in the chilly morning air.

Their final day was upon them. Lan knew she had to be brave for Annabelle, but she couldn't stop the tears when they came. It reminded her too much of the morning in Nội Bài International Airport when her whole family had come to bid Lan and her father goodbye. Vivid as ever, the memory pierced her, sharp as glass. For something to do, she grabbed the pieces of flint by the fire and struck them fiercely over and over, sending up sparks that would not light. She was shaking. Footsteps approached behind her.

"Can I help?" Marlow took her hands and eased the flint away. He struck it once steadily, and the flame caught.

"Annabelle's counting on us. I know what you're gonna say," she said.

"I had my cry yesterday. Feel free to take yours," he answered. He put his arm around her. They stood by the flames as Lan sobbed, trying to not wake the whole camp.

"You know, it's not a bad thing if you want to cry," said a soft voice. "Don't hold back for my sake."

Lan had not heard her coming, but then Annabelle was on her other side, her arm looped through Lan's.

"I'm sad to leave too," she said.

THE RIDE OUT

It was their last evening in Ruse's Hollow. Even after she had eaten her fill of dinner, Lan did not want to get up. She sat alone, fiddling with her arrowhead necklace. Annabelle was talking animatedly with Ruse. Marlow was nowhere in sight, and the thought made Lan frown. A whole party of nymphs in human form had joined them for the evening, filling the clearing with loud jokes in their language and laughter. Zephyr was chatting in their midst. Lan knew Kestrel would order them away soon to ensure everyone had a good sleep before dawn.

There was nothing more to be done. Their pouches were full, their bags loaded with loaves of fresh bread, honey cakes, dried meat, and berries. Their clothes had been scrubbed clean earlier that day in the stream, rubbed with lemon, the tears mended using a rose thorn and loose thread. Lan had pricked her fingers a dozen times in the effort, wishing she had listened more carefully when her mom had tried to teach her to sew.

Marlow's voice startled Lan out of her thoughts. He had reappeared suddenly, his hair messy and expression unreadable, a steaming cup in his hands.

"Tea?" he said. "Figured you could use help getting to sleep tonight."

"Oh, thanks," said Lan. She refrained from asking where he'd been. He looked lost in thought but gave her a reassuring hug. Across the fire, Annabelle stretched and headed toward bed.

"You coming to sleep?" said Marlow.

"In a minute."

Phoenix emerged and sat in his spot beside Lan. Her long red hair was loose. She held a half-empty drink.

"How are you finding the farewell festivities?"

"Is this a usual nymph party?" said Lan. "Honestly, I'm not sure it's my scene."

"Gods, no," Phoenix laughed. "Our parties are something else. Kestrel's keeping a firm hand on this one, for your sake. If you come our way again in a few years, I'll show you what I mean."

Lan smiled. She drank the rest of her tea in two gulps, linden flowers still sweet at the bottom of her cup.

"Whatever path you walk on, Lan," said Phoenix gently, "I hope you can always see yourself the way I saw you on the night we met."

"Crying and running out of breath after a werewolf monster?"

"A warrior. It'll be thanks to your heart if the quest succeeds." Phoenix stood, her hand resting a moment on Lan's shoulder. "I'll see you at daybreak once more."

Kestrel was raising her voice above the din, ordering nymphs back to their trees. Lan smiled and headed to sleep. She curled up beside Annabelle, staring at the shadows on the bamboo roof twisting in firelight. She could hear the occasional murmur of lighthearted voices, a twinkling laugh, over the crackle of the dying flames.

Lan looked behind her when she got up shortly before sunrise, the half moon still hanging in the barely grey sky. She stared at the indent her body had made in the blankets over the past weeks. It took a moment to tear herself away.

Marlow had joined Annabelle by the fire, eating a bean bun and sausages. Lan saw him say something to Annabelle. She shook her head.

They had carefully packed, but Lan kept glancing around the Hollow, unable to shake the feeling that she was forgetting something important. At Kestrel's insistence, she ate her breakfast and washed it down with tea, tasting nothing. She tried to seal every detail of the clearing in her mind, from her scattered pile of practice swords in one corner to the nosy nymphs poking around Kestrel's newest potion. Phoenix's and Kestrel's trees stood as tall and elegant as ever, but the rest of the clearing was changed. Instead of the soft dirt ground that had covered the Hollow the night they'd arrived, a ragged layer of grass dotted with dandelions carpeted it. Even Lan could tell the magic was her doing.

Phoenix approached her as the sky began to lighten in earnest. "You should get moving."

They nodded and stood. Phoenix pulled Lan in for a goodbye.

"Take care of that heart of yours," she said. Lan couldn't quite manage to smile.

Marlow and Kestrel were hugging. He was saying something in her ear, and her response made him laugh. Kestrel drew back and unfastened her own cloak, which he had frequently borrowed. She shook it out and wrapped it around him. Then, with a squeeze of his hand, she turned to Lan and embraced her.

"Remember us kindly wherever you go," she said.

"How could I not?"

Lan led the way to the edge of camp. The centaurs waited by the main path where they had arrived the first night. Marlow mounted smoothly onto Ruse's back, their belongings secured behind him. Annabelle vaulted on Zephyr with the same ease and reached out to help Lan up in front of her.

"Stay alert," Zephyr said over his shoulder. "This won't be a leisurely stroll."

"We'll meet again in good time," said Phoenix. Kestrel reached up and clasped their hands once more. "It's not farewell."

They turned away from the nymphs and the Hollow. Only when descending the slope did Lan realize Phoenix spoke in her own lullaby-like tongue. Lan had understood nonetheless.

As they raced down the hill, Ruse picked up his pace and began a gallop. Zephyr followed, faster than they had ever ridden before. Lan did not recognize their route. The trees rushed by in fuzzy shades of brown and green, strange and twisted, though it was hard to see clearly. The speed knocked the wind from her lungs. It took everything to stay on. Annabelle reached for her hand, her touch warm.

They stopped to eat, then rode again until sunset turned the sky pink, snacking along the way and noting unusual tracks to avoid. Time passed in a blur. When the sky darkened, Ruse halted at a spot downstream of the river they had been following.

"Stopping so early?" said Zephyr. "It's not dark yet."

"Better to rest and get a fire going. Been a long enough day. We'll stay the night, start fresh tomorrow."

The three dismounted and unloaded their bags. Lan could barely move from the sores on her thighs and bottom. Her body was stiff. She refrained from complaining given how far the centaurs had travelled to bring them to the road. They hobbled down to the river to wash, then set off to find kindling. Ruse and Zephyr rested in the water, talking.

"Watch out, bear tracks," said Marlow, steering Lan aside as she headed deeper into the bushes. He pointed to the ground, where a giant print lay. "That's the largest I've ever seen."

"More this way too," said Annabelle. "Let's get a fire going quick."

They hurried in building one. When the centaurs returned from the river, small flames were growing. It was colder than it had been back in the Hollow. Lan recognized distinctive maple leaves and oak trees that lined Toronto streets in this part of the Weathering Woods. They towered above her, and no nymphs came out to greet them. She shivered and wrapped Marlow's cloak more tightly around her, nibbling on fried dough. As hungry as she was, the packed food didn't taste quite the same so far from the Hollow.

"Should we be worried about the bears?" Annabelle asked the centaurs.

"Or whatever else is out here?" added Marlow. "I didn't recognize the tracks around where we stopped for lunch."

"Bears won't attack a large group without reason, and we certainly will not be giving them one," said Ruse. "Forest-dwellers are nothing to fear when you're with us. Better them than what's on the other side of the stream."

"What's over there?" said Lan.

"Witches," said Ruse, "unlike any you'll meet in Asta. Pirates and thieves with powers as old as Silva itself. They say the seeds of the royal orchard came from that land up north. It is called Maare. Independent but connected, like Sol on the western coast. Rumours have it that the children up there grow wings in their youth and fly."

"Is that true?" said Lan.

"Who knows? We only know enough to stay clear of their land. Maare is largely beaches and cliffs, but people do breach the northwest ranges of the forest from time to time."

"You've never seen them?"

"I've seen enough to heed caution and know my place."

Lan wrapped her arms around her knees and tried to not listen to the strange sounds of the woods. They were so different from the noises around Ruse's Hollow, though she couldn't place exactly why. Now that she thought about it, she hadn't seen any nymphs since they stopped at noon. Their absence was jarring. Every few minutes, Lan turned, looking into the darkness, unable to tell whether the low growls she heard were real or imagined. Phoenix's and Kestrel's absence felt achingly pronounced.

"Can you hear the noises or is that just me?" Lan whispered to Zephyr beside her.

"Different nymphs, animals, even running water," he said. "It sounds foreign because you're used to the Hollow."

"I miss them. It was so easy to be there," said Lan. "Almost like home."

It was the first time she had voiced the words aloud.

"Only because you embraced it as such," Zephyr said. "Now you know it's a feeling you can make."

"Like it's that easy," Lan said. "I wish you wouldn't sound so mystical sometimes. You're only—what, forty years old? My parents are more ancient!"

"You'll miss me soon."

Lan's heart twisted knowing he was right. When she turned to tell him so, Zephyr was already asleep, head drooping with a light snore. Lan tucked her hands under her head beside Marlow and

Annabelle on the ground of fallen leaves. Ruse stood alert on guard. Her eyes fell shut before she knew it.

They reached the edge of the forest by mid-morning the next day. As they broke through the treeline, Lan stared at the field in front of them, disoriented. They had been deep in the woods for so long, the open space looked foreign. The sun was too bright without the cover of the trees. She felt naked without their protection.

"This is where we part," said Ruse.

No one moved. They stood, looking out where miles of grass greeted them.

"You are safe out of the woods," Ruse continued. "We are just north of the Paver's Road. Use the sun to find your way."

Marlow was first to dismount. His face was a mask of calm. Without a word, he reached for the bags. Annabelle slid down to join him, and Lan followed, her movements rigid. They shouldered their belongings, the weight of the food heavy. The centaurs faced them and bowed deeply. Marlow, Annabelle, and Lan bent their heads in return.

"Thank you," said Annabelle. Her voice was quiet but clear. "If you ever feel like a vacation to Sol . . ."

"We'll know who to ask for," said Ruse, smiling.

Lan was too sad to say a word. She reached out to hug them one more time.

"Take care, little warrior," said Ruse.

"And take heart," said Zephyr, ruffling her hair.

With a final nod, the centaurs disappeared into the woods. The trees closed in on them. Annabelle stared for a long moment, frozen. She drew a shaky breath.

"Come on," said Marlow. He gently turned her around to face the field.

"Ready to confront a king?" said Lan with all the confidence she could muster. A spark of magic crackled at her fingertips, eager to answer her call.

"Yes," said Annabelle.

"Good. It's time to get you home."

THE BRICKSIDE INN

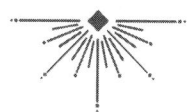

"Keep a hold of your magic, would you?" said Annabelle, jumping back as a sudden burst of pollen flew from Lan's hands into her face. She coughed.

"Sorry," said Lan hastily, wiping her palms. "The residue is so different here than in the forest! It's like those bubbles in the valley again. I'm not used to them anymore! How do witches learn magic when it keeps changing everywhere you go? You're right, Annabelle, it's so hard to count on."

"Well, I didn't mean you had to stop altogether. Keep practising if it helps you. Who knows what we'll run into next? We might need help again."

"That's a change of attitude."

"Honestly, ever since I found out Daisy was practising, after what the Cognitor said in the fields, I've been remembering . . ." said Annabelle. "The times I saw my grandmother do magic, I didn't even realize that's what it was—a spell to fix a leaky rafter, bring a boat to shore on a windless day, make a fish grow in the pot. She still did so much by hand. Maybe I was wrong to blame the craft instead of the witch."

Her words meant more than Lan let on. Maybe she had it in her to learn properly and be a good witch. Lan stretched her palms out and felt an immediate rush of magic respond. The surge made her head light. Close to Asta, the air was heavy with residue.

They walked for a while in silence, glancing often at the sun to check they were on the right path. Annabelle led the way. Lan tried to not look behind her at the receding treeline and caught Marlow staring back at the forest more than once. She distracted herself by trying to double her water supply. It was the hottest day yet, a dry heat that felt unbearable beyond the shelter of the woods. All three were sweating through their clothes, hair sticking to their foreheads.

They hit the road by mid-afternoon, dark purple bricks baking in the heat. Without a sliver of shade to stay cool, they continued walking and tore through their supply of fruit. After so long, the hardness of paved ground almost hurt Lan's feet. Though their pace quickened—the path sloped gently downhill—the heat did not let up.

Only when sunset bathed the fields in a pink glow did they stop. A stone building had come into view. It stood by the side of the path, several others visible beyond it in the distance. They squinted at the houses in the fading light. The rolling hills obscured a farther view, but Lan guessed that Asta's walls would soon appear on the horizon.

"We're getting close to the city," said Marlow, taking a long drink. "It'll be weird seeing humans again."

Ruse had once mentioned how Silva's population largely resided within the capital or on nearby farms. Few had cause to approach the woods since the desert spell. Life in Asta was plentiful, a trade hub with fulsome apprenticeships around every corner. Lan's stomach somersaulted in excitement to see it at last. It was worth staying in Silva to see the town. The forest nymphs might never have visited the capital, but they liked to wander and talk. She'd heard much about the colourful shops and cobblestoned streets—and most of all, how currents of magic powered the city like electricity.

"I heard no one lifts a finger without using magic in Asta," said Annabelle, peering in the direction the brick road led. "Witches back in Sol used to scoff at the class offerings, two-for-one quick spells to master over a weekend and the like. Sold like cheap trinkets with no respect for the craft."

"Maybe they have a different way of doing things," said Lan. A two-day magic lesson sounded pretty useful to her right now. Might she have time to sign up?

"We should find a place to stay the night," Marlow said, bringing them back to the sweltering heat and hazy road. He nodded at the nearest building. "Let's try there."

They drew closer, close enough for Lan to see a stone well around the back and a wooden sign swinging in front with letters reading The Brickside Inn.

"Convenient," she said, waving at it. "An inn. How are we supposed to pay?"

"Offer help? Stories? Leftover honey cakes? Plenty of options," said Annabelle. "Do you see anyone?"

"The windows are open," said Marlow. "No innkeeper leaves windows wide open if they're not home."

He stepped forward and rapped on the door. A moment later, it swung open.

A large woman stared at them from the door frame, her curly black hair taking up so much space that it blocked out everything behind her. She was dressed in a simple but stylish burgundy gown. Her dark eyes widened as she took them in.

"Hello," said Marlow, managing a dashing smile despite the heat. "We're looking for water and shelter, one night only. We've got food to share, stories too. Happy to clean up after ourselves."

The woman blinked once, then said, "Your stories, I'd like to hear. You've got yourselves a deal."

She stepped aside and welcomed them into a dining room with round tables and a stone floor. A faded doormat read Welcome to Rosa's in fancy script.

"Are you Rosa?" asked Lan.

"Proud owner of the Brickside, only bit of civilized life this far out of Asta."

Lan frowned. She glanced up and saw a carved sign above the mantelpiece reading The Last Homely House to the West. She stopped herself from scoffing.

"Excuse my welcome," said Rosa, clearing plates and cutlery as she swept around the room. "Few commoners use this road. My guests are mostly loggers or king's watch. You don't look like either."

"I'm sure we look pretty ragged," said Annabelle at the same time Marlow murmured, "I could pull off both."

"Not to mention, we're in the middle of a heat wave and all. No fools out if they can help it. Don't know what those meteorologists in the castle are thinking. They do mess up a few times a year, especially when it comes to tempering that hot sun. Take a seat. I'll get you some drinks. Then we'll talk."

They ditched their bags and sat at the nearest table, set with a vase of blue flowers in the centre. Wide windows lit the room. This place was the closest Silva had come to her own world so far, Lan thought, but it was weirdly where she felt least at ease. She did not like the innkeeper's haughty tone. Nonetheless, when Rosa waltzed in with three tall glasses, Lan could have cried to see fat ice cubes floating in her drink. The lemonade-like liquid revived her like a potion. Rosa returned with a pitcher and fresh fruit, then spun a chair around to face them.

"What brings you stragglers eastward down this road?"

Lan and Annabelle let Marlow talk though mouthfuls of grapefruit, recounting their midnight departure from the Border Academy across the enchanted desert. He omitted their reason for leaving and pretended Lan had been with them all along.

"It's so bad out west you're coming this far to start a new life?" said Rosa.

"Who wouldn't want to live in Asta?" Marlow said smoothly before Annabelle could make a retort.

"You're saying you made it through the Weathering Woods without getting eaten by lions and tigers and who knows what else is in there?" said Rosa, her eyebrows raised. "I've met king's watch soldiers who cower at the prospect of venturing anywhere near."

"As they should," said Marlow. "We got lucky."

Rosa leaned back in her chair and stared at them with a mix of suspicion and reluctant respect. "Are they true?" she said. "All the stories they tell about the woods to scare kids?"

"We never saw any lions or tigers," said Marlow. "Maybe they were hiding."

"What about the centaurs? Heard they can be dangerous. Patrol once had a bad run-in. The gatherers don't like the nymphs much either. They're so picky about their pretty flowers, can't even spare a few branches."

Lan couldn't stop her angry huff. She felt a sudden longing for Ruse's Hollow and an eagerness to leave the conversation behind.

"Rosa, if you'd be so kind as to excuse us," said Marlow. He leaned forward and flashed a smile that made Lan's heart skip a beat.

"I know I'm dying for a proper shower after all the trudging around in this heat."

"Oh, of course." Rosa stood at once and gestured to the wooden stairwell, her prying eyes instantly replaced with hostess professionalism. "Take any room you like. Doors are labelled, keys in the locks."

Lan eagerly pushed her chair back and gave Marlow a grateful smile. He returned it with a wink.

"How do you do that?" she whispered as they headed upstairs. "I thought we'd be stuck listening to how she's the last welcoming harbour before the terrifying wilderness."

"It's a special skill of his," said Annabelle in grudging admiration.

"I just asked nicely," said Marlow, pushing open the first door on the landing. "We all wanted out."

"I think we've got our story down though," said Lan. "The way you told that . . ."

"She was captivated," said Annabelle. "Can't wait for you to finally tell the king."

"He'll be so moved by our long journey, he'll have to help you," said Marlow.

Lan flashed Annabelle a hopeful smile and received a tentative one in return. They stepped into the room. Two double beds with ugly quilted sheets took up most of the space. A small nightstand and wardrobe were cramped in the corner. Moth-eaten curtains fluttered half-heartedly before the drafty window. A lantern sat on the sill but instead of a light bulb or candle inside, a golden pulse emitted a warm glow. Lan poked it. It bounced lazily at her touch like a cat being disturbed from a nap.

"I want to leave early," said Lan, looking back at the others the moment the door closed. "We're so near the end, and I don't like that woman. I can't stand to hear her talk a second longer about the forest, as if she knows anything about it."

"You're right," said Annabelle. "Let's go before she's up."

"First stand-up shower in months though," said Marlow, peering into the bathroom. "Look, Annabelle, it actually works unlike that rusty old Academy faucet."

"Good, you could use a shower."

"How rude . . ."

He came out ten minutes later, shrugging on a shirt. The long scars on his side were apparent but well healed.

"Water doesn't even run dry once your time slot is up," he said as Annabelle stood to take her turn.

"How far do you think we are from Asta?" Lan asked.

"At least a few days in this heat," he answered, sitting on the bed opposite her. "We can stop at inns along the way."

"You think the other innkeepers will be like Rosa?"

"People of Asta really pride themselves on their city," said Marlow. He paused. "That's kind of why we're here in the first place, isn't it? Protect the capital at the cost of the rest. Nebulo's gonna be tough to get to."

"How are we going to make him listen, if he doesn't want to help?" asked Lan.

"He has to!" said Annabelle, poking her head back into the room. "My people are dying, and it's his fault. We've got the items we need to see him! That's the deal. Everyone knows it."

Lan didn't understand much about politics, but the closer they drew to the castle, the harder it became to believe that they could simply march in and demand the attention of a king, even *with* his price of admission.

When Annabelle emerged from the shower, her hair twisted in a stringy towel, Lan got up to wash and heard the other two continuing their conversation in low voices. The cold water soon drowned them out. Even though they had been walking all day, Lan's limbs didn't ache nearly as much as they had climbing out of the valley. Unfortunately, that meant it was harder to sleep. The unfamiliar mattress was too soft, the quilt scratchy on her skin. By the time she drifted off, Annabelle sprawled beside her, the first birds were already awake.

ASTA

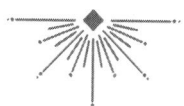

Over the following days, houses and inns grew more frequent along the widening brick road. At one stop, Annabelle fixed the well out back in exchange for a night's rest. At another, Marlow milked the neighbour's pink cow, and they got a bottle of strawberry milk and water in return.

Each morning, Lan felt the pulses of magical residue around her more strongly. The colours in the air were brighter than they had been before. She began to test out new spells, refilling their water, freezing it into ice, or doubling their fruit. Glimpses of magic became more obvious with every stop. They no longer saw just enchanted lanterns but also self-sweeping brooms, jars of rejuvenation potion that made Lan all jumpy, and even a floating menu that sent their orders straight to the kitchen. People called out comments like "Remember to get another dose of that cleaning potion the next time you're in Asta!" and strange pets ran underfoot with fluffy tails in vibrant hues.

Soon, the imposing walls of Asta rose before them. Cut from large slabs of stone, they towered impressively even as the wrought-gold gates were flung wide open and unguarded. King's watch soldiers meandered down the road in shiny uniforms, laughing and drinking at inns as though on holiday. They were clearly not anticipating any security risks.

Marlow, Lan, and Annabelle stopped for their last night at a quieter lodging a short distance off the main road and did their best to freshen up for a presentable entrance. Marlow even managed to talk the innkeepers into lending them new clothes, with an honest promise to return them clean and pressed in a week's time. Donning the deep red vest over her white top made Lan smile at her reflection in the mirror.

"Nice to see my daughter's old outfits getting some use," the man remarked as they came down the stairs. He ruffled his newspaper and leaned back in his seat. "You lot look fine enough for a royal visit."

"As a matter of fact, would you know the quickest way up to the castle?" asked Lan, tucking loose hairs into her attempt at a braid. "We'd like a closer look."

"You've clearly never been round these parts," he said with a laugh. "Getting to the castle's about the easiest thing you can do. Paver's Road runs right through Asta, takes you straight to the steps of King Nebulo's home. Can't miss it."

"If he's that easy to find, why are all his guards hanging out here?" said Marlow.

"King's watch? Those fancy folks aren't for him. You think a powerful wizard like that needs his own guards?"

"We've seen the soldiers everywhere along the main road. Gates are wide open. What else are they here for?"

"Oh, don't you worry about that. They've got other things they're guarding."

Lan felt a pulse in the air at his words, as though the magical residue around them understood his meaning and responded. Specks of violet flickered in her peripheral vision.

"We'd best be off," said Marlow.

Lan's heart pounded the closer they drew to the walls. They followed the same purple-bricked Paver's Road right to the main gate. Lan saw bicycles, horse-drawn carts, wagons, and harried cabbage merchants bustling casually down the lane. Annabelle's face was drawn and nervous beside her, chewing on her bottom lip. No one spared them a second glance as they passed under the shadowed arches and entered Asta. Lan clutched her arrowhead pendant in one hand and the poppies in the other.

"Can you believe it?" Annabelle breathed. "We're here."

Pulses of magic thrummed through Lan like music in the gym at a dance party. She walked, eyes wide with wonder. Vivid colours swirled in the sky, matching the rainbow-painted buildings with flowers blooming from balcony sills. Tall lanterns glowed purple every few paces. People teleported up and down the winding cobbled streets left and right, appearing and disappearing from random corners in broad daylight. Annabelle was right. Signs advertised discounted magic lessons, sold in packages for household needs (basic tidying spells with a cleaning potion starter included) or transportation 101 for short-distance teleporting over two days' time. Seeing the colourful displays sent a pang of longing through Lan.

"Anyone can learn here," said Lan, staring at a group of beginners practising the step and pivot of a waterfall spell in the square. Barrels of water sloshed over the stones. An instructor in light blue robes was calling out directions. "Everyone's a witch."

"Knowing a couple of go-to basics doesn't make you a witch," said Annabelle. "I told you from the start, didn't I? In Sol, you're not considered a full witch until you invent a new spell. It's not enough to copy. You have to create too."

"These sure do come in handy though," said Marlow.

"And it'd really help to have a proper teacher," said Lan sadly.

"You know, if you want to come back to Silva sometime," said Annabelle, "visit me in Sol. I'll get you a real teacher, no problem. At this rate, my grandma will probably do it. You'd like her. She's intense, but in a good way like you."

It was the first time Annabelle had spoken about what might happen at the end of their quest. For weeks, Lan had focused on getting them to Nebulo. Now she allowed herself a second to imagine . . . How long might she be able to stay in Silva afterward? Perhaps she'd go back to the Weathering Woods with Marlow, and then see the western coast for herself, hopefully in all its non-deserty glory? The idea tempted Lan more than she wanted to admit. She could easily get used to this world. The local fashion certainly beat her own world's sale-rack clothing, and her newly acquired bartering skills would've impressed a Vietnamese grandmother. The lack of rice noodles wasn't ideal, but she could work on getting that spell right.

"Watch where you're going," said Marlow, pulling on her arm. Lan stopped as a wagon rumbled past, loaded with vegetables and potion crates. When the bulky cart cleared, Lan looked up and gasped.

The castle loomed before them, a hundred paces straight ahead. The white stone ramparts shone amid the multicoloured houses of the city. It was smaller than Lan had imagined but still large enough to dwarf her school back in Toronto. A wide balcony ran along the second floor, the railing polished gold. The magical energy around the place was a thick, dark purple. Stained clouds above the turrets floated by in the same hue as the ones in the valley on the day Lan had arrived in Silva.

They were nearing the end.

They sped up without a word. Lan reached for Annabelle's hand and gave her a reassuring squeeze. Annabelle felt clammy, but she had never looked more composed. The borrowed ribbons in her braid matched her blue top; her knife was on her hip, her chin held high.

She gave Lan a nervous smile. Lan tried to return it without thinking of the task still to come. Seeking an audience and convincing a king was no small thing. Her stomach fluttered with every step uphill.

"Relax," Marlow whispered beside her. "You look like you're about to face a death sentence."

"We can't all be you."

At the base of the castle stairwell, a king's watch guard appeared as they approached, her helmet in one hand, brown hair spilling over her shoulder pads. She looked hot and impatient, as though she'd been demoted to the noon shift when the sun was at its peak.

"Can I help you?" she said, cutting off their path.

Lan swallowed, but before she could speak, Annabelle stepped up. "I come from Sol, and we're here to see the king," she announced.

A beat of silence met her words. Lan held her breath, waiting for the derisive laughter that would certainly follow—but it didn't.

"Sure, I can get you on that list," said the guard easily. She turned and beckoned behind her. Another young guard appeared with a clipboard in hand.

"Captain?" he said.

"Get these kids on the waiting list to meet King Nebulo."

"Right away. Your names, please?"

Lan tried to hide her shock. Would this be easier than she'd thought? The young guard took down their names with an elegant fountain pen. The pages on his clipboard flipped through lightning-fast as if they knew precisely where to file their info. Lan peered over the top of the document and saw a few lines of writing that read:

Annabelle of Sol, Marlow of Mireille, Lan of ? on business of restoring coastland and saving home.

"I assume you possess the required items to gain entry?" said the male guard. He held out a hand.

"Yes, of course," said Lan. She handed over the poppies and removed her arrowhead necklace. "That's our proof of a heart and courage in large supply. Um—do you want the story now?"

"Absolutely not. King Nebulo will assess the story upon entry. For now, we will evaluate your items and keep them if they qualify."

The captain held out a clear palm-sized tube with a gold bottom, like one that might be found in a lab. She crushed the poppies and jammed them inside. The tube began to emit a vivid pink glow. Lan, Annabelle, and Marlow stepped back.

"Hmm, impressive," said the captain. She shook the tube, and it emptied. "This will do. We'll hang on to it. Next?"

The guard handed her Lan's necklace.

"Oh, please don't dissolve that!" said Lan. "It's a gift. Can't you check it without evaporating it? I thought we just had to present them. I—I'd like it back if possible."

The captain frowned and exchanged an annoyed look with her companion. Nonetheless, she put the tube back in her pocket, rummaged around, and pulled out a collapsible golden scale instead, the kind they used to weigh meat or fresh noodles at the street market. In her hands, it grew to a suitable size for the pendant.

"I'll use the rare-items scale, though this object hardly warrants it," she grumbled. "You can ask for it back when you meet the king, if he decides to fulfill your request."

A tiny bell-like sound came from the scale when it was finished weighing. Lan had no idea what the meter read, but the guards seemed satisfied. They nodded and pocketed the pendant.

"Sign here," said the one with the clipboard.

Annabelle took the quill and made a loopy signature in the box. The words began to disappear, sinking right into the page.

"That's all I'll be needing for now," he said, taking it back. "Give me a minute to check on your wait time. Then you can be off."

"I wouldn't mind exploring the city for a few days," murmured Lan.

"Well, you're looking at fourteen months now, so that'll give you plenty of time."

"*What?*" said Annabelle and Lan in unison.

"Would you like a sightseeing map to help with your stay?"

"Sorry, did you not hear anything I said?" said Annabelle, her voice growing louder with every word. "This is an emergency! My people are dying!"

"What are the other requests for?" said Marlow.

"Spell distribution, infrastructure expansions, adoring compliments, all sorts," said the guard. "Everyone's got something to say. We all have to wait our turn."

"And they all carry the price of admission?"

"To varying degrees. Our system has been in place for a long time."

"Shouldn't some things be prioritized? Like starvation, for example?" said Annabelle. Marlow put a hand on her shoulder.

"Please," he said to the guards. "We've travelled a long way, across the enchanted desert and Weathering Woods to get here. We just want a few minutes of audience."

"It's the least your king can do," Annabelle muttered audibly.

"It wouldn't be fair," said the captain, taking over for the younger guard with the clipboard. She put her helmet on. "Why should you get to skip over people who have been patiently waiting? Who's to say your issue is more important?"

"Maybe the hundreds of people slowly dying on the southwest side of Silva?"

"King Nebulo is dealing with urgent matters as they come up.

I assure you he has more reliable informants than kids walking through the front door of the castle."

"Is there any other process available?" Marlow said quickly as Annabelle puffed up angrily, ready to start yelling again. He stepped forward. "Somewhere else we can put down our names? I'm happy to explain further if you've got the time."

"Sorry, kids. Have yourselves a grand time in the greatest city you'll ever see and come back in fourteen months."

Annabelle was shouting again. The guards promptly tipped their visors and disappeared into thin air. Lan blinked, stunned. She tried to take the first step up the castle stairs, but an invisible barrier shoved her. She fell backwards onto Marlow, who caught her with one arm while using the other to restrain Annabelle from running straight into the blocking spell, shouting at the top of her lungs. People were starting to stare.

"Belle, please stop kicking me—we're gonna find another way," he was saying.

"We're here *because* of him in the first place! It took us so much to get here, and all we get is a pat on the head from some guy with a clipboard? Let go of me, Marlow! You should've just let me yell at them!"

"Come on, Annabelle, what would that have done?" said Marlow. He cautiously let go of her wrist. "Let's not burn bridges before we come up with another plan."

"I don't want to plan! Right now, I want to give them a piece of my mind, and I'd feel a whole lot better if I had!"

"I was trying to save our chances. People usually prefer guests who *don't* yell at them."

"Well, your pretty manners didn't work, did they?" she cried, rounding on him. "It's easy for you to be cool when it's *my* home we're talking about! I *should* be upset! And they should have to hear it!"

Marlow looked for a second like he wanted to argue, but Annabelle stopped struggling then and crumpled in on herself, sobbing. She trembled like a wilted flower. Marlow sighed and pulled her into a hug. She wept miserably, clutching his shoulder.

"Okay, I'm sorry," he said. "I shouldn't have cut you off."

"It's not fair . . ."

"I know."

They moved to a nook to the side of the castle to avoid curious pedestrians. Annabelle cried until Marlow's shirt was wet. Lan tried and failed to conjure up tissues, her hands shaking. The gears in her head were racing as she fumbled to understand. This couldn't be the end. They had to make Nebulo listen. But how?

Lan wasn't one to cause a scene, at least never in public. Hiding was easier, but that was not an option. They had to do something, and it had to be big. By the time Annabelle sniffed and looked up, an outrageously genius plan had begun to form.

"I might have something," said Lan quietly.

"What now?" said Annabelle, wiping her face with her sleeve.

"I'm not sure Nebulo would've paid attention even if we did get to see him. Not if he's expecting adoring compliments from his visitors like that guard told us."

"Don't Astans care about anything but themselves?"

"Maybe some do, but people act this way in my world too. Since moving—well, let's just say some of the questions I've gotten about Việt Nam prove that loads of people don't know a thing beyond their neighbourhood! They can be so rude without even realizing."

"So what are you saying?" said Annabelle warily. "*You* told me keep going. You got us here! This can't be it."

"It's not," said Lan. Her ears were ringing, but her head felt clear with purpose, just as it'd been in the grove right before she brought down the snowstorm. "I'm saying if he's not ready to listen to you, we're going to have to make him pay attention."

"Do you have an argument that'll convince him to hear us out?" said Marlow.

"No offence, Marlow, but as Annabelle said, asking nicely didn't work," said Lan. "Tried your plan. We're doing it my way now."

"Your way?" said Marlow and Annabelle at once.

"Make a grand entrance they can't ignore."

They stared at her blankly.

"Think about it," she said. "Nebulo's power is concentrated at the castle. He's got king's watch to keep things running, but the rest of them? Our last innkeeper said they were busy guarding *other things*."

"So?" said Annabelle. "We don't want other things."

"No," said Marlow, catching on. "But an attempt to steal something valuable might capture their notice enough for us to demand an audience. A proper one."

"I bet if we go after what they're guarding, they'll march us right into the throne room before Nebulo himself," said Lan.

"How do you know we won't end up before some justice of the peace or clerk?"

"Because it'll be big. We're not stealing flowers from the farmers' market here."

"What exactly are we after then?" said Annabelle. "What is this *something big* supposed to be?"

"The only thing in Silva more valuable than the king," said Marlow, realization dawning. He looked at Lan in awe, eyes bright with excitement. "You're incredible."

"I sure am," said Lan. She couldn't resist throwing her hands in the air for effect. "They're guarding the source of all spells. We're going into Asta's royal orchard."

OPERATION ORCHARD

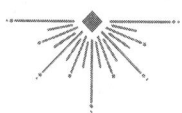

As the afternoon wore on, Lan, Marlow, and Annabelle picked their way through the crowded city, seeking a spot away from prying eyes. This did not prove to be an easy task. It was a beautiful day, and people happily milled about eating savoury rolls off food carts, wicker baskets in hand. Every few minutes, a colourful plume of residue shot into the sky like a firecracker, a sign of someone practising magic nearby.

At last, they stopped at a small fountain far from the castle grounds to regroup, sandwiches in hand. A goat bleated, tied to a lonely sapling. Lan wondered if that nymph minded being used as a post. No one else approached.

"We should do this as soon as we can," said Lan. "What's the plan?"

"Midnight makes sense," said Marlow. "Cover of darkness will help. We can go early, scope out the guard situation. Do you remember which side of the city it's supposed to be on, Annabelle?"

"Somewhere east. The orchard's famous, even in Sol. We can walk along the eastern wall and keep an eye out. Gotta be hard to miss."

Yet when sundown appeared on the horizon, they still had not found an opening. The eastern end of the city was emptier and darker. Purple street lamps pulsed once every couple blocks. The streets were slippery with smooth stone and tilted downhill. They stopped, changed out of their nice clothes to avoid tearing them in a fall, and hid them in a crack between giant slabs of rock.

"This is ridiculous," said Annabelle, shaking out her Academy clothing. "Those main gates cannot be the only way in or out of the city."

"We've walked the length of this wall," said Marlow, frowning. "And I'm not about to do it again."

"Sol is built in open air," Annabelle said. "As it should be. None of this border nonsense. Asta is a fire hazard."

Something in her words jogged a line in Lan's brain: *No one lifts a finger without using magic in Asta.* What would a witch do?

"The passage could be hidden," she said. "Annabelle, didn't you say something about waterways or air tunnels in Sol?"

"Sure, back when magic used to run on the coast, we had all these canals intersecting the city that people would hop on or send things through. What's that got to do with the orchard?"

"Maybe they've got something similar here."

"Across a ginormous stone wall?"

"The passages could be hidden by magic. What better way to protect an orchard?"

"Can you feel anything?" said Marlow. "The spells can't be too obscure. All the guards have to get through daily, and most of them aren't skilled witches."

Lan closed her eyes and reached out along the smooth stones of the eastern wall, trying to feel where spots of residue were strongest. With the amount of energy in Asta, it was impossible for her to decipher individual traces.

"There's magic everywhere," she said. "I can't tell what's what."

"The guards would know," said Annabelle. "We can go back toward the castle. The next shift will be coming from there, and we can follow."

It was their best bet. They retraced their steps to the main road and did not have to wait long before a dozen guards strolled toward them in uniform, chatting nonchalantly. Annabelle pulled Lan quickly behind a tree. They tiptoed after the troop, keeping their distance until the guards stopped. Lan peered around the tall oak that the three of them hid behind.

The king's watch stopped around a lamppost, its purple glow flickering in the evening air. One of the guards with a red plume on her helmet placed a hand on the metal pole. Lan squinted, trying to see what the guard was doing. Before she could make out anything else, the group joined hands in one swift motion and vanished.

Lan, Marlow, and Annabelle stared, stunned. Slowly, they made their way toward the spot. No trace of the guards remained. It appeared perfectly ordinary.

"Did you see what they did?" Marlow asked Lan.

"All I saw was one of them touching the lamp," Lan said. Lightly, she ran her fingers over the cold metal. A shiver rushed down her spine, the presence of magic overwhelming. "Then it's like they evaporated."

"You might as well try," said Marlow.

"Better hold on to me in case."

Annabelle and Marlow each placed a hand on her shoulder. Lan drew a deep breath and laid her palm flat on the lamppost . . .

A surge of energy knocked her back a step. She kept her balance, but her jaw dropped. Her surroundings had disappeared.

Lan was no longer looking at the cobblestone street with its dark houses and tilted sidewalks. Instead, a glistening web of silver strands amid a purple background surrounded her. It was like she had entered a different dimension. Bulbous dots connected across her vision. She tried to touch one of them, where the thin lines intersected, and saw a blurry view of a fountain they had passed several streets away. The spot pulsed for a second when touched, a rippled reflection, then faded back into the nebulous violet setting.

"It's a map," Lan breathed.

At once, understanding hit her. She touched another silver point farther away and saw a corner of the castle. Another showed the square where witches in training had spilled barrels of water earlier in the day.

"Uh . . . nothing is happening for us," said Annabelle. Lan could hear her voice but not see them with her hand still on the post. "What's going on?"

"I think this is their bus route," said Lan.

"What's a bus?"

"Never mind, I mean this must be the main transportation system. I can select a place, and I think the poles take us around, like teleportation stops."

"I'm guessing they don't have a stop in the middle of the orchard?" said Marlow.

"Somehow I doubt it, but I'll check."

Lan pressed her finger on the stops eastward of where they stood. The first one showed a spot outside the walls—she could see the farmlands stretching far—but no orchard in sight. She tried again and realized immediately that this second destination was where the guards must end up. They were standing in front of wooden gates, though certainly not the main entrance of Asta. These doors were modest and firmly shut. A few more glances around the map confirmed for Lan where they stood.

"There's no transport stop inside the orchard, but it shares a wall with Asta," said Lan. She removed her hand, and Marlow and

Annabelle came back into view. "The soldiers are guarding a section that sticks out. Trees must be right on the other side of these stones. They don't look hard to climb, but someone's bound to see us in the city. We can use the lamppost to get outside by the farms with no one around. We'll climb in from there."

Annabelle bit her lip nervously, her eyes moving up the length of the wall.

"Any chance you can magic us some safety gear?" she said. "Maybe a nice net?"

"Um, I'll look into that in a minute," said Lan, grimacing. "First, we have to get out of here before someone wonders what we're up to. Grab on."

Marlow and Annabelle held her arms tightly. Lan plunged her hand through the haze of magic again and pressed it against the pole. Glimmering threads reappeared in the purple fog. They enveloped her senses. She sought the right stop, then pushed firmly on the knot of silver. This had better work, she thought. Willing the residue to carry them through, Lan leaned in—and fell.

Her stomach dropped. She was suddenly weightless, the sound of whooshing in her ears, just like when she'd come to Silva in the storm. It was deeply unpleasant. Lan somersaulted through the mist and landed ungracefully on her back with a grunt of pain on the hard impact.

"Ow," Marlow was mumbling. He pushed himself off the ground and reached over to help her up. "Are you okay?"

"Fine," said Lan, stumbling to her feet. "Annabelle?"

"Looks like you were right," said Annabelle. She was already standing, gazing at the empty fields bathed in starlight. Lan followed her gaze to the sky and saw the tangle of constellations not unlike the web of silver that had carried them to this spot. A single lamppost, glowing a dim violet, stood behind them on the outer perimeter of the castle wall. Lan touched the post with her finger and jerked back quickly. It was burning hot.

"The system's connected by lampposts," she said. "They mark every stop."

"We used the symbol of a seabird in Sol," said Annabelle. "Stone carvings or reliefs etched on fountains, the sides of buildings. They're anchors to establish the pathways. Usually, our transit is supervised. I'll admit this is a clever design."

"And clever of you to figure it out," said Marlow to Lan.

"I'm used to transit maps. You should see Hà Nội."

"Add that to the list," said Annabelle. "But we have to move now. Guards are gonna appear any second patrolling the grounds."

"Grass is tall enough to hide us if we lie on our stomachs," said Marlow, already leading the way into the fields.

They settled uncomfortably on the ground, which sloped slightly uphill. Sharp weeds poked through their clothes. When she glanced back, Lan saw the double wall encircling Asta, the orchard nested between its two layers. Cast in shadow, individual trees were hard to make out, but large coniferous tops loomed in the centre. She figured with all the time spent by Kestrel's side, Marlow could probably name the exact species.

"An orchard that size's gotta have real powerful nymphs," he said in a low voice.

"Maybe they'll be friendly?" said Annabelle.

Marlow made a dubious face. Lan couldn't help but share his pessimism. Phoenix and Kestrel had been loyal to Ruse's Hollow, and by extension, their guests. However, Lan had met enough of the other nymphs to know most were happy frolicking in their grove, content to leave creatures to their business as long as their own roots were secure. They were not so nice when threatened by strangers.

"I'd rather face guards than angry trees," said Lan. "We'll need to cause a ruckus big enough to get their attention and see the king—but not to get speared on the spot."

Lying low in the grass a few dozen feet away, Lan, Marlow, and Annabelle watched a pair of guards march past. The king's watch soldiers did not bother to stop and examine the recently used lamppost in the corner. Their armour glinted in the moonlight. They were talking, but not loud enough for Lan to decipher the words. One glanced up the walls before moving on.

"They're awfully poor guards," said Marlow. Lan felt him fidgeting beside her, fingers on his arrow fletchings. His restlessness was kicking in. "The captain at the Border Academy would've pummelled me for being that careless. I could fire from here and take them out in ten seconds."

"We're not taking anyone out until we get in that orchard," snapped Annabelle. "If we get caught too quickly, they'll take us for orphans causing mischief and throw us in a dump on some random street. We need to be intentional enough to scare them."

"We need to climb," said Lan.

"And we'll need to make it to the top between patrols," said Annabelle. "Let's wait a couple more rounds to get a good sense of their schedule. Do we have *any* gear?"

Marlow rolled onto his back and rummaged through his belongings. He pulled out a small coil of rope vine, tucked away from the forest. "It's on the short end, but does this help?"

Lan took the coil and examined the weaving. It was one of Phoenix's own braided vines for hunting. The material was strong. She pulled it gently from one end. It grew. Longer and longer, she drew the rope out until it had multiplied to the significant length of the wall. At least, she thought it was the same. It was hard to judge.

"Who's the better climber?" said Lan, holding the rope out.

There was a moment of silence. Annabelle looked disgruntled.

"Uh—probably me," said Marlow. He took the rope. "I'll make the climb and pull you both up. Take turns and wait between patrols."

"You sure you can make that climb freehand?" said Lan. It was so tall that it hurt her neck to stare at the top.

"Child's play."

"Let's not get cocky," muttered Annabelle. "Remember the lake trip?"

"Did you have to bring that up?"

The next round of guards came into view about fifteen minutes later. Lan's body was starting to go numb from lying still on the ground, kept awake by pure adrenalin. She could tell Marlow was itching to move, but Annabelle insisted they wait for one more patrol to pass.

"To make sure!" she hissed. "What if that time gap was shorter than usual?"

But the following guards came through another fifteen minutes later as expected. Marlow slung the rope around his body, his bow and quiver in place. He shifted into a lunge, eyes focused on the figures retreating from view. Before Lan could even think to whisper *be careful*, he was sprinting. An arrow in his hand before he reached the wall, he leapt easily onto the stones and began to scale, using the arrow tip to help with his holds.

"You don't have to look so impressed. We did drills like this at the Academy all the time. He grew up with it," said Annabelle under her breath. Lan quickly shut her mouth. "I could beat him on the water any day, but this—we never had anything like this where I'm from. Sol's a beach."

"You don't have to feel bad, Annabelle. You're great at a million other things."

"When I want to be," said Annabelle softly, shrugging. "I

remember complaining non-stop when I arrived at the Academy. I thought the training was rigged against me—all these desert and mountain exercises, so little of the sea. I resisted learning them at all. Turns out it wasn't personal, just how things worked. Marlow's from Mireille, deep in the mountains. It's like he was born for this."

"He hasn't been there since he was a baby," whispered Lan. "You think he remembers?"

"I think our bodies do. What you said before about not being built for the winter cold—maybe our bodies know home."

Then what if home changes?

Lan didn't voice her thought out loud. She knew Marlow disliked naming Mireille his homeland. She'd seen his face whenever it came up. Annabelle hadn't considered that with her attachment to Sol. Still, as Lan watched Marlow reach the top of the orchard wall, she could almost believe something in his skill was instinctive. No one was simply that good. With a one-handed grip, he stowed the arrow back in his quiver and pulled himself over the edge, disappearing from view just in time.

The next pair of guards that passed included the one with a red plume on her helmet who had initially taken the rest of the group through the lamppost portal. Unlike the other patrols, these soldiers carefully felt the post and checked around the area. Lan held her breath as one of them pointed at the ground. She prayed their footprints weren't visible. Knowing he was there, she could also see Marlow's flattened form at the top of the wall, but the king's watch didn't seem to notice from their spot. They scanned the rocks above them and then kept walking, apparently satisfied.

"Get ready," Annabelle whispered. "You're up next."

Lan was on her feet and running before her brain even clued in. Without a backwards glance, she reached the wall and saw the thin braided vine slithering down toward her. *Gods almighty*, she realized with sinking dread, *I've made the rope too short*. It dangled ten feet above her, swinging tauntingly. Lan gulped and began to climb. In an instant, her instincts from her tree-climbing days in her grandparents' yard in Việt Nam kicked in. She saw nothing but the next foothold. Her chipped nails were soon caked with dirt from gripping the cracks in the stones. Then her hands grasped the rope, hanging on for dear life. Ten minutes later, Marlow was pulling her up the edge of the wall. It was wide enough to lie on with her ankles peeking out the other side. Lan collapsed on it, panting hard.

"Guards will be by any minute," said Marlow, drawing her closer into the shadow. "Watch your breathing."

"Sorry."

"It was a good climb."

"Give me the rope." Lan took the loose end and tried to extend the length farther for Annabelle. Exhausted and arms aching, she only managed a few extra feet before the next patrol passed and Annabelle was racing toward them, her dark braid and clothing blending in with the night. She hesitated a second at the base before climbing. When she reached the rope, she took a minute to tie a makeshift harness knot around her waist.

"That would've been smart," Lan murmured beside Marlow.

"It's really hard to do that mid-climb," he said. "I never learned properly, but Annabelle made sure to. She's not a fan of heights."

"And what are you scared of?" Lan said automatically.

"Ask me later."

Annabelle's hands were shaking when she reached the top.

"The next quest we pick, I want it to be by the ocean," she breathed, rolling onto the ledge, "where I can swim and dive and sail instead of all this trekking around."

"You picked this one," Marlow pointed out, earning him a glare.

The three of them lay huddled, their stomachs flat against the stones. Marlow hastily hoisted the vine up as the next shift passed underneath. The guards looked up at the last flash of movement, the rope's tail whipping over the ramparts. Lan held her breath, realizing then that the sky was starting to lighten. After a careful check of their surroundings, the guards stopped whispering and moved on.

"Honestly, I need to have a talk with this Nebulo guy about the quality of his king's watch," said Marlow. "They're dismal."

"Get in line," said Annabelle.

"You have to admit," said Marlow, "Operation Orchard is bang on schedule."

"You couldn't think of a more creative name?"

"Hey, it was your quest first. You think of one."

"Operation No-More-Desert/Gonna-Get-Sol-Back?"

"Very catchy. Easy to remember. It's perfect."

They laughed, but Lan couldn't bring herself to join in. Marlow's confidence, however welcome, felt too optimistic. The residue around the orchard was dark and ancient. It made goosebumps rise along her skin.

"Something tells me we haven't seen the worst of this place yet," she murmured. "Especially if the guards are so unbothered."

"Maybe it's because they don't expect anyone would dare break in," said Marlow.

"Maybe . . ." said Lan, but she wasn't so sure. "Isn't that their job though?"

"You'd be surprised how bad people can be at their jobs. Anyway, we still have to get down first," said Annabelle, looking with distaste over the other side.

Lan shifted and peered into the shadows of the orchard. Trees were planted in neat rows a hundred strong. The largest stood in the middle. Shrubs and herbs lined the border. In the distance, rosy light spread like watercolour over the grey sky.

Beside her, Marlow smiled, a hand shading his eyes against the light. He carefully pulled himself to his knees and said, "What a perfect day for mischief."

THE POMEGRANATE

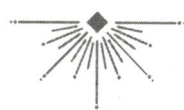

Lan's feet hit the soil with a thud. She'd had to push off to avoid landing on the blueberry bramble at the base of the wall and now narrowly caught her balance. She untied the rope around her waist and waited for Annabelle to be lowered down.

The thrum of magic was so strong that Lan could barely hear herself think. She was amazed they'd made it this far. As she recovered her breath, she caught hints of whispers through the air. Nymphs? She didn't see any nearby. A glance back showed Annabelle halfway down the wall. Lan took a few steps into the nearest trees. Their leaves reached out as if curious to greet her. Traces of residue ran through her skin at their touch, but she had no idea what to do with them.

"Tell me how to use this magic," she whispered to the orchard at large, Longing lacing through her whole being. The longer she stood under the branches, the more her hands burst with greater power than she had ever held. It terrified and thrilled her at once. Her body felt awake and rejuvenated. Right here was the heart of Silva's strength, the game-changing source of all spells and residue that had coursed through the land for centuries. A deep Longing to understand the forces overwhelmed her. There was so much of magic left to know.

"Please be careful," said Annabelle. Lan spun around.

Annabelle approached cautiously a few feet away, her knees scuffed, a hand on her knife hilt. Lan had not heard that wary note in her voice since their first day on the riverbank—at least not directed at Lan. Her eyes were creased in concern, and her body, tense. Dimly, Lan registered Marlow free-climbing down the rocks far behind.

"I'm not doing anything," she said. "This energy—it's flowing to me on its own."

"You don't know how to hold it."

"You're the one who told me to practise."

"Small steps, like what you've been doing with our supplies. The magic in this orchard is something else entirely."

"Maybe I can learn."

"Not here. Lan, you promised—"

But Lan froze. Roaring filled her ears. A scream died in her throat. Over Annabelle's shoulder, she watched in terror as Marlow's right foot missed a step and slipped off the rocks, taking the other foot with it. Annabelle turned to follow her gaze and gasped.

Even at the last second, Lan did not believe he would fall. For a moment, Marlow held on, his arms straining, dangling a hundred feet in the air. As if in slow motion, they watched his left hand give way—he plummeted faster than Lan could've imagined. Annabelle shrieked and ran toward him.

"Save him!" she cried.

"I'm trying!"

Lan's gust of wind caught Marlow twenty feet off the ground but slammed him into the wall. She flinched, praying he'd managed to shield his head in time. He fluttered limply on the fading breeze and landed on the blueberry bush. Annabelle was already pulling him out when Lan reached them. Marlow groaned, clutching his side. His hair was damp with sweat. Lan was so relieved to see him conscious that she threw her arms around him.

"Are you okay?" she panted.

"I think my ribs are bruised," he said weakly. "Missed my head when I crashed though, luckily. That could've been it."

"Sorry, but in my defence, you were doing fine dying on your own already."

"I've never fallen . . ."

"We need to move into the trees," said Annabelle, helping him up. "Do you hear that? The guards definitely know we're here."

Loud voices and clanging armour punctuated the enchanted orchard's stillness. Someone was blowing on a shrill whistle. Lan half expected to hear the creak of front doors opening. They hurried under the cover of the branches.

"This orchard is magic all right," said Marlow, looking up as they moved.

"You can feel the residue too?" said Lan. "It's so strong. That blast was the most powerful thing I've done!"

"Uh no, actually, I meant these trees don't grow in the same climate, so it must be enchanted soil."

"You're a nerd."

"Plants are cool! You didn't complain when I made you all those flower crowns."

Lan smiled and snuck a glance at him. He was paler than usual, but his expression was unwavering. His green eyes shone. Relief flooded her at the thought of their close call. If she hadn't summoned that gale in time . . . but the magic had responded so easily! Asta was teeming with residue, far easier to work with than the forest's. Lan could almost believe it was possible to control. What she might give for a bit of time to test it out.

They wove their way through the rows of trees but were forced to slow down as Marlow's steps began to falter. Annabelle waved off his apology. They stopped in the shade of shrubby trees bearing fruit.

"Do we just let them find us now?" Marlow said, slumping to the ground.

"We should put up a fight when they do," said Annabelle. "Make it convincing."

Lan wondered whether Annabelle simply wanted an excuse to beat up Astan soldiers. It wasn't a terrible idea. Part of her longed to see how she'd fare in a real fight with everything she'd learned from Phoenix. That razor-sharp focus was something she'd never felt anywhere else. She was pondering which weapon she'd choose, given a range, when she saw it: a red grenade-like fruit lay innocently on the bed of fallen leaves and dirt several feet away.

Cold descended on Lan as if she'd been plunged into an ice bath. Her body grew still. Marlow and Annabelle were busy talking. They had not noticed that the one thing that could change the course of her life forever was suddenly well within grasp. She reached for it, Zephyr's words echoing in her head.

When it comes to crossing realms, the pomegranate's what you'd want . . . just one seed would do the trick.

Temptation rose in Lan. It was such a simple solution to all of her worries. She could grab a handful, go back and forth between Silva and her world anytime she wished. Her heart swelled at the thought of taking lessons in Asta's square and seeing Annabelle home to Sol. She could even stay with Marlow and grow older beside him. Of course, Zephyr had cautioned against its power, but he was no witch. He had never felt the magic of this orchard. Lan had only had one taste of what she was capable of in the midst of this much residue, and it'd been enough to stop death itself.

Lan turned the fruit over in her hands. The thin, smooth skin felt too easy to puncture. Hundreds of seeds were tucked inside. Each contained the power that she had spent so long dreaming of, even from her days in Toronto longing to escape! She'd never be bored again. Lan could almost taste the sweetness already, the smell reminiscent of her days in Hà Nội and the trees in her grandparents' yard. She ignored the others rising, calling her name. Her head felt fuzzy, her senses clouded.

Without another thought, Lan broke the pomegranate.

TREE GUARDIANS (AGAIN)

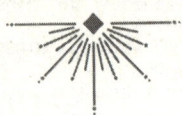

An ear-splitting crack shook the ground. Marlow and Annabelle dropped to their knees. The fruit, split in two, lay a foot away from Lan, its seeds glistening like rubies. She reached to grab it, but another ginormous rumble sent them sprawling. Somewhere close by, something very big roared.

"What do you think you're doing?" Annabelle was shouting. She'd drawn her blade. "You promised me you'd be careful! Are you trying to get us killed on the spot?"

Lan got to her feet, confused, failing to fumble a response. Her head was still hazy, but her senses were suddenly acute. Everything sounded loud. Before she could manage a word, Marlow leapt to his feet. He grabbed his bow and pulled Lan behind him. She looked up. At once, she understood the source of the roar.

"What—?" said Annabelle, staring up at the shadow rising to block the sky.

"Tree guardian," breathed Marlow. "That is a redwood."

"What have you done?"

The wooden giant lumbered in their direction, as tall as the orchard walls themselves. Unlike the stone pines, the redwood guardian was humanoid and deliberate. Its bark was soft, deep red. Slowly, as though time were no issue, it reached them in three steps and peered down, expressionless, with knotty holes for eyes.

Lan's courage curdled like sour cream. Magic flickered faintly at her fingertips, but the guilt washing over her took centre stage. What *had* she been thinking to risk their lives? She had helped them get this far only to screw it up at the last minute! Annabelle was trembling— in anger, fear, or perhaps both. Only Marlow held still, his bow drawn and steady. He waited for the giant to bend low before firing.

The shot landed squarely in its left eye. It reared. Lan took advantage of its moment of imbalance. She threw her arms wide and sent a barrage of fallen fruit rushing at its chest, exploding in a multi-coloured mess. When the giant stumbled, its footprints left gaping indents in the dirt.

The three of them scattered. Lan ducked behind a tree. The frantic sound of guards clamouring drew closer. As she regained her breath, preparing for another blow, Annabelle yelled. "Catch and run straight!"

Lan turned just in time to grab one end of the braided vine falling toward her. She ran. Out of the corner of her eye, she saw Annabelle take off. Her slim form ran fast as a deer toward the giant and wove around its feet, the rope tangling through the trees behind her. Lan snuck a glimpse at the redwood guardian's head as an arrow flew from somewhere to her left. It landed next to the other eye. She gripped the rope tightly and did not stop moving. Faintly, she heard Annabelle shout from far across the trees.

"Get ready! Don't let go!"

The rope strained so tightly that Lan gasped, pulled several feet along the ground. Her hands burned. It was an impossible game of tug-of-war. Sweat trickled from her forehead and into her eyes.

With a crash as loud as the one that marked his appearance, the tree guardian tilted forward and fell to its knees, trampling a dozen smaller saplings. Lan winced. She tied the rope to the nearest tree and bolted toward the creature.

"Annabelle?" she shouted. "Marlow?"

Trees sped past her. Lan could almost hear their voices, annoyed and accusing. Shadows flitted among the branches, sending chills. The nymphs that had lost their lives today were on her. No wonder they didn't like to associate with strangers. Lan kept running even as guilt stabbed her. No one was in sight. Her heart pounded loudly in her ears. Cramps rippled through her stomach, but she barely noticed. Lan whispered their names again. No answer.

"Darn it," she muttered. She slowed and moved closer to where the giant was groaning. It seemed to be rising, shaking the branches close by. Shadows of nymphs darted wildly. Several rows of trees away, Lan caught the unmistakable shining armour of the king's watch through the trunks. Her panicked cry came out raspy.

Ignoring the pulsing of the orchard's magic or her own head—she was no longer sure which—Lan inched forward until she was close enough to see the scene. The redwood giant knelt in a web of rope, looking dazed but unharmed. Its arms had been bound, but the vines were starting to snap. Lan hastily sent a spell to rebind and strengthen the restraints. In the commotion, no one seemed to notice.

Directly in front of the giant, Marlow and Annabelle stood back to back, weapons drawn. Metal flashed from the swords of a dozen guards surrounding them, yelling and drawing closer. Annabelle's braid had come out. Matted waves of hair framed her face as she twirled. Lan stared. She looked like a picture-perfect giant-slayer. On the other side of the redwood guardian's body, the soldier with the red plume on her helmet faced Lan, red hair visible underneath, waving her guards forward. She was frowning, one hand on her hip. Her expression was half shock, half-grim determination. Lan turned and saw the soldier closest to her kneel to load his crossbow.

With the trees as cover, Lan crouched and crept up behind the guard. She rammed into his side. His bow dropped. The bolt flew wide. He dropped with a yell. Lan elbowed his helmet hard enough to bruise her arm. Before his fellow guards could reach her, Lan drew the fallen guard's sword from the sheath on his side. He swiped at her legs from the ground. She jumped and spun in time to parry the first thrust from the guard rushing at her. *Just like practice*, she told herself, ducking the next blow.

An arrow landed in the shoulder of another guard. Someone was yelling, but Lan could not tell whom. She pushed through the startled king's watch, straining to reach the others in the centre. Movements came without thought. Then Annabelle was by her side. The guard between them fell with a kick to his chest. Lan had a moment to stare at the half-injured soldiers closing in before a sharp whistle cut through the chaos.

The woman with the red plume had raised her arms. This close, Lan could see her young face, freckles dotting her nose. Sudden heaviness settled around them like the air before a storm. Wind ruffled Lan's hair. Even the redwood giant stilled. Marlow had drawn his last arrow, poised in wait. Lan felt residue pool at her fingertips but held back.

"You call it, Belle," she heard Marlow say.

But it was too late. Before she could say a word, a whirlwind of leaves overtook them. The guards dropped first. Lan caught sight of red flower petals, just like her poppies', whistling toward her face before the world went black.

NEBULO

"At least we're in the same cell," said Marlow, rubbing his wrists. The bruises around them showed signs they'd been cuffed on the way down, not that they'd been conscious. Lan had only come to minutes prior, and she was relieved the other two were not yelling at her for her moment of stupidity that had nearly taken their lives.

Their weapons were gone. Lan knew it was costing Annabelle to not comment on the loss of her knife. They sat in the stone cell behind metal bars. No sunlight reached it, which suggested they were far underground. Straining for a bright side, Lan wondered glumly: How many people could say they'd been locked in a dungeon? Certainly none of her classmates back home. Her stomach was grumbling, hunger making her knees weak. Annabelle was crying softly in the corner. Lan scooted over and held her in silence, thankful when she did not move away.

A loud clanging made them jump, disoriented. The redheaded guard with the plume was opening the cell door. Marlow was on his feet, ready to meet her.

"Good, you're awake," the guard said, beckoning. "Come."

She did not bother to wait or cuff them but left the door wide open and walked down the hallway without a backward glance. Her black boots clacked against the flagstones. Exchanging a quick look, Marlow, Lan, and Annabelle hurried after her, jogging to keep up.

"Who are you?" asked Lan. "What's happening?"

"I'm the king's general. What's happening are the consequences of your actions."

"Where are you taking us?" said Annabelle. The guard took her time responding. They passed several flights of stairs in the torch-lit corridors.

"The throne room," she said at last.

Lan inhaled sharply. She forced her face to remain impassive, but her insides were shouting in triumph. They'd done it! Marlow caught her eye, his lips turned up at the corner. Beside her, Annabelle sniffed and looked up, holding her breath. Lan's stomach was doing flips again, terrified that one wrong move would break the spell and send them straight back to the cell.

The guard made a sharp turn, then stopped so brusquely in front of a wooden door that they almost ran into her. She spun to face them and glared, her eyebrows creased and her freckles inches away. Her red curls spilled out of her helmet, which she wore with the visor up.

"We're about to exit the dungeons. Stay close to me. Think of running or fighting, and these are going back on." She rattled the handcuffs attached to her belt. Then, she hoisted up the heavy metal bolt holding the door closed. It let out a groan as though it was being woken up too early. She shoved her full body into the door, which creaked open. When all of them had squeezed through, she rammed it back and latched the bolt.

Through the halls of the castle, they followed the guard, their shoes echoing on the marble in the wide passages. It was an ornate building, and Lan caught glimpses of Annabelle looking up at the tall pillars. Large windows flanked their walkway. Dark curtains, pulled aside by golden rope, revealed a clear blue sky over the green shrubbery of the royal gardens. She guessed it was the afternoon.

They reached the end of a hall, passing two servants in red outfits rushing past, and came to the doors of the largest elevator Lan had ever seen in her life. The guard waved her hand, and the golden doors slid open noiselessly. She ushered them in, stepping briskly. The doors closed at her nod. Instead of walls, the inside held mirrors, polished clean. For the first time since she had arrived in Silva, Lan saw herself fully, untouched by water's ripple or grime from some dusty inn glass.

Her hair had grown longer and wilder than ever, falling loose of the rough braid from the night before. Her heavily tanned face was grimy and scratched, though she could not tell what from exactly. Annabelle's red Academy shirt was torn and stained with orchard dirt. Yet Lan was taller, her shoulders broader. Her reflection shocked her. Beside the others, she did not look entirely out of place.

Lan did not realize she was staring until the elevator bell dinged to signal their landing. She saw Marlow smile reassuringly at her in the mirror. The golden doors slid open. They crossed another hallway to the entrance of the throne room.

The first thing Lan felt was magic. It hummed as strongly as it had in the orchard, but this residue was restricted, like in the Cognitor's cornfields or heart-eater's grove. Lan could not use any of it herself. She flexed her fingers. Dark purple residue seeped in.

They stepped inside. The throne room was not large, but high ceilings created a spacious impression. Stained glass windows depicted scenes of knights with unicorns, fire-breathing dragons, centaurs, and nymphs. Marlow's eyes seemed to linger on a dancing nymph in a white gown. The art cast coloured shadows on the marble floor. Flanking the centre aisle that led to the throne were two rows of guards in gleaming armour, their visors down so that no faces were visible. The throne itself was as lavish as the rest of the castle, raised on a platform and lined with gold leaf. Lan had never treaded anywhere that rivalled this place in grandeur, not even the Hà Nội Opera House.

But more remarkable still was Nebulo himself: a cloaked figure lounging casually on the throne before them. The man was bald, his skin unnaturally tanned and shimmery as though he were part illusion. A circlet of entwined golden vines rested on his head, his body draped in a midnight robe. His startling violet eyes held a certain warmth in them, which reminded Lan of the Cognitor's. A smile crossed his dark, full lips as he stared at them approaching.

They followed closely in their guard escort's footsteps—the only sound that reverberated around the chamber. When they reached the dais, the king stood and extended his arms wide. He opened his mouth to speak. Lan looked to Marlow, expecting him to tell their story, but Annabelle got there first. She stepped forward. Her hands were planted on her hips, her chin jutting out.

"We came a long way for me to say what I got to say, so you're going to listen."

Nebulo's mouth fell open in surprise. There was a sharp collective intake of breath. A loaded silence hung in the room. Lan caught Marlow's eye and bit back the urge to smile. The corner of his lip was turned up, amused.

Then the man on the throne laughed. Tension eased, but no one spoke or moved. When he finally stopped and drew a breath, he waved a hand and said something that Lan didn't quite catch, but all the guards nodded, turned, and left. The redheaded guard stayed by the king's side.

"I daresay you've earned my time," said Nebulo. He took the dais steps slowly toward them, looking neither angry nor concerned. "I hear you gave my guards some trouble at the orchard this morning. Seems they're out of practice."

The redheaded guard cleared her throat loudly.

"Ah, Mira," he said, smiling at her. "You must admit I'm right. Look at them. They're children."

"It's a mistake to underestimate children, sir."

"Of course. Six guards and a redwood giant down, though?"

"No serious injuries," said Mira, looking miffed. "It was a young cohort."

"Don't fret, it's no critique of your command. Simply, I'm . . . rather impressed."

Mira sniffed.

"We were turned away at the gates, even though we came so far to seek an audience with you and brought the items you asked for," said Annabelle. She glanced at Lan quickly before continuing. "For the trees lost in the fight, I'm sorry. We couldn't wait, so we sought to see you another way."

"I see," said Nebulo. His smile faded. Standing mere feet away, Lan realized how inhumanly tall he was. "I had the noon shift rescan your *heart* and *courage*. If your story is as impressive as the first two items you brought, you must have quite the tale."

"A sad one, thanks to you," said Annabelle. She looked to Marlow, hesitant, as if unsure whether she wanted him to speak instead. He nodded at her encouragingly, and Annabelle continued. "I come on behalf of Sol."

"Sol?" Nebulo murmured. "The independent people of Sol have never come as far east as Asta before, let alone sought audience with the Silvan king. I'm honoured."

"Honoured when it's your fault? We didn't have any need to until your desert destroyed everything! When I was little, the coast held all the fish we could eat for centuries to come, and the sky turned the brightest blend of colours with every spell . . ."

Her voice cracked as she kept talking—of the splash of whale pods breezing by on a clear day, children coasting on air channels with makeshift boards, and music-filled ceremonies in the central arena, where bonfire sparks reached as high as the stars. Lan could not see her face, but she could hear tears tightening her throat. She glanced at Marlow. He stared at Annabelle with glowing pride.

"Everyone at the Border Academy knows we only get Asta's scraps. No one in the capital cares about the kids on the wrong side of the desert, so the grown-ups in charge don't care either. They think we'll never amount to more than lowly patrols on the farthest corners of this land. I'd rather search forever for an end to this curse than go back to that awful place!"

Annabelle finally stopped, dissolving into sobs at the end of her tale. Nebulo had let her speak without interruption, his face impassive. Now in the silence, a single tear trickled down his cheek. His form appeared to solidify, free of the mirage-like effect that Lan had noticed when they first walked in.

"I have not heard this story yet, Annabelle of Sol, but I can tell you speak truly," he said solemnly. "Why has no one sent word to plead your case sooner?"

"All our communication channels were blocked when the spell hit. Our witches said something about the residue being a mess."

"I suppose a strong blocking spell would have that effect," said Nebulo. He seemed to be considering a curious math problem. "Quality of magic often depends on the residue available, positive or otherwise. I did not anticipate it . . . but what of the ice giants to the northern range? I understood them to be a threat to Sol as well."

"They only became a problem when your people crossed the mountains. My grandmother, Marya, fought them in her time. We've always held them off in our own way. Our borders have never been breached."

Nebulo gazed down at his clasped hands and did not speak for a long time. Marlow approached Annabelle and put his arm around her. Lan went to take her hand. The king's eyes met General Mira's when he finally looked up. She had been standing at her post by his throne, unmoved. Something passed between them. She gave the slightest shake of her head. Nebulo sighed.

"I'm afraid I cannot help you," he said.

"What?" Annabelle gasped. Her cry plunged through Lan like a blade.

"What do you mean you *can't*?" cried Lan. "You have the orchard's power at your command! You can do anything! Everyone we met said so."

"You must understand that the desert spell has brought much prosperity to the eastern range of Silva. Without cause to cross the forest, Asta and the surrounding farms have thrived from growth right at home. My people would never—"

"*Your* people! At our cost!" yelled Annabelle. She pushed Marlow and Lan off and lunged forward, but Nebulo raised a hand. She stilled, frozen in place. Mira was swiftly at his side. He dropped the spell, and Annabelle fell to her knees, winded. Nebulo's form began to shimmer again, and his skin deepened into a sickly orange tan.

"Wait, you wouldn't even have to tell them!" Marlow blurted out. He rushed to Annabelle's side and knelt to help her up. He struggled to compose himself before speaking, and his next words were careful and firm. "If no one goes west now anyway, they'd never know if Sol was restored. You'd be popular across the land, not just in the capital!"

Marlow's voice bounced off the throne room's walls. Nebulo paused and considered his words. Lan held her breath. She saw Mira shift. For a long moment, Annabelle's sobs were the only sound present.

"You make a fair point, but I couldn't if I wanted to," said Nebulo finally. "Magic like that is beyond my power to work a second time, even to reverse. The original spell took the amplification of half the trees in the orchard, some of which will take ages to bear fruit again. It weakened my power for years afterward. No one would sacrifice that for *your* country. An ordinary witch risks losing their power altogether. I cannot ask it."

"If we can get a message to the witches in Sol, they would come," said Annabelle. "It would take a long time, but—"

"There's another way," said Lan quietly. "A quicker one. You have me."

STRAY WITCH IN SILVA

All eyes turned to Lan. She stepped forward, wishing she'd had a moment to freshen up and look more heroic. Instead, her hair was scraggly as ever and her clothes reduced to rags. She did not have a weapon in her hand. Nebulo examined her curiously, and Lan felt a flowing sensation come over her like she was being scanned.

"A witch," Nebulo said, surprised. "Untrained but strong. You see the magic she carries within her, Mira?"

"Her signature's the one we found on the ropes binding the redwood," said Mira.

"Fascinating," murmured Nebulo. "If I'm not mistaken, you are not born to Silva. It is written across your body, though difficult to immediately tell. This was not a recent crossing. You've even learned some of Silva's languages, instead of relying on the universal translator."

"The what?"

"One of my ancestors, an ancient king of Silva, built a membrane in the fabric across worlds that allows us to understand each other in the language of our choosing, with some exceptions. What you may perceive as your tongue might not be the one we're speaking, expressions and all. The opposite also holds true. Now tell me, how did a stray witch come to accompany two Border Academy runaways?"

"I was lonely. I asked a portal to open, and it brought me here," said Lan. Her chest tightened. Nerves seized her. "Honestly, I'm not sure how. Back where I'm from, there's no residue anywhere. I didn't know I was a witch. I just found a weird book at the library fair, and next thing I knew, a magic storm dropped me in the western valley."

"A book brought you here?" said Nebulo.

"Brought me to them. Annabelle and Marlow . . . it was their story."

"Any indicators on this novel of yours? Any peculiarities that you noticed?"

"No author. A gold dandelion on the cover, I think. And a chocolate stain."

Nebulo looked at Mira, and they nodded as if the detail explained everything.

"Witches leave signatures on every spell they cast," said Nebulo. "A mark, a colour, often only a smell or trace of distinct feeling in the residue. A trained witch can pick out patterns, identify the wielder. Of course, signatures may change, but certain threads remain constant."

"Your signature smells a great deal like chocolate, new books, and a keen sense of Longing," said Mira.

"Um, is that a compliment . . . ?"

"It makes it clear that the book was summoned by you," said Nebulo, "or more like created. The spell could've taken any form, though books are a popular choice of portal in many worlds."

"How did I manage that unintentionally, without any residue?"

"All worlds have residue, some more than others—but that is not what makes a strong spell. The heart of magic always rests with the witch herself. You have a lot of power in you—I can see it—enough to tear a hole in the world."

"Does that mean other people from my universe can cross into Silva too?"

"Of course. Not just Silva, but as many worlds as stars in the galaxy, though few can bring themselves all the way through without help. You must've truly wanted it."

"You're saying there are other portals around us then?"

"Infinite. Crossing worlds is not so radical if you know what you're doing. Witches travel often between realms, especially in Silva, ever since the orchard was planted. In fact, many who settle in Asta are not originally from this world at all."

"When I came, I wondered if I was meant to be here for a *big reason*," said Lan. "I wanted proof that it was supposed to be *me*, but anyone can come and go?"

"Coming and going was never the hard part. People browse other worlds for fun every day, but you chose to stay and help someone who needed you, even at great cost."

"I want to make sure Annabelle gets home before I go back to my world," said Lan. "That's our quest. We have to finish what we started. You said you need the help of a witch to reverse the desert spell, one who won't mind draining their own powers to make sure it works. I will help. Use me."

"Do you understand you might lose your magic, perhaps forever?"

"I do," said Lan boldly, but she couldn't stop her voice from wavering. "I went all my life without it. Marlow and Annabelle have, too, but Sol deserves to be restored."

Nebulo and Mira exchanged another long look.

"Come with me," he said finally.

Nebulo swept his robes up and led the way. They followed him out of the throne room. Mira brought up the rear. Annabelle looked at Lan as they walked, uncertainty on her face.

"Do you mean it?" she whispered. "I know how much your magic means to you."

"Not as much as home means to you," said Lan. "I will, if I can."

Down the hall on the left, Nebulo stopped and waved a hand in front of a black obsidian door. It opened soundlessly. Lan peered around him into the room. At first glance, it looked like an old office. Wooden shelves lined the round chamber, filled with books, jars, and dried plants. Papers and quills were scattered on floating desks.

"Come along," said Nebulo. "For your own safety, don't touch."

A hush descended over the space as if it were sacred. An enormous topographical map took up the centre of the room. Lan recognized it at once as Silva. The river running through the western valley ended in a waterfall she had not seen in her time there. The forest dominated a large portion of the landscape, tapering out in cliffs over the northern coast. Lan remembered the area was called Maare. A golden patch depicted the Cognitor's cornfields. The map breathed. Miniature trees swayed, water flowed, and fat clouds floated low above the scenery.

Mira stayed by the door, but the rest dispersed throughout the room. Annabelle headed immediately to the southwestern coast, which was clouded in an unnatural mist, obscuring the land itself. Marlow stopped at the forest, leaning in close as if trying to pick out individual trees that he recognized. Lan followed Nebulo to Asta and the orchard on the eastern front.

"This is my workspace. These trees were planted centuries ago by my ancestors," said Nebulo. He pointed to the castle's orchard, which showed a plot of trampled trees. The map had updated live from their morning fight. "We have not made contact with the people of Sol for centuries. I assumed they wanted to be left alone and cast their own protection spell to avoid the prying eyes of outsiders."

"No one even knew *you* had the power to see into Sol," said Annabelle tersely. "I'll suggest that, though, after we're through. I'm sure they'll be happy to keep the borders drawn. What do you need to start?"

"It's complicated. We will need to lift the blocking curse first to see into Sol, clear out all that foggy residue. I can do that myself. As for the desert... That spell took a large amount of baobab root, which has not grown enough since, not to mention several other plants. The original amplifiers are required to reverse the spell. It's possible that with another witch's power, we may not need the same proportions."

Lan's thoughts darted to Kestrel in the forest and how careful she had been to never take more than each plant was willing to give. She'd always given them a chance to grow back healthier. Nebulo's magic was undoubtedly strong, but he had pushed the limits of his own power beyond nature. She thought of his hazy form, waves of magic flickering as though they were clinging to his body. But Annabelle needed this.

"So you'll try it at least?" said Lan. "No matter what it means for Asta?"

"I'll keep the desert around the northern range, but with your help, we can attempt to lift the spell over Sol. The question is if you are truly willing to make this sacrifice."

"I'll give up my magic if I need to," repeated Lan. "It's worth it, for Sol. Otherwise, why am I on this quest?"

"That's exactly it. You might be paying a higher price than your power alone. Tell me, do you want to stay in Silva, Lan?"

Lan's mouth fell open, taken aback by the abrupt question. "Why?" she asked. "What's that got to do with Sol?"

"The tree guardians in the orchard act when their magic is threatened. Any root, leaf, or fruit threatened triggers the strongest to respond. I couldn't help but notice that a pomegranate breaking open incited the disturbance this morning. Care to explain?"

Lan forced herself to meet Annabelle's brown eyes. They were gentle, almost pitying, and held no blame. It made Lan's stomach twist with guilt.

"I got a bit carried away," said Lan. "I thought it might help me cross between worlds at will. I didn't want to leave forever and never see anyone from Silva again."

"I thought it'd be something like that," said Nebulo. "Fooling around with magic that strong would have only resulted in a curse. You are lucky you did not get a chance. Of course, you are welcome to carry on in Silva if you wish, but I must warn you that undertaking this spell will likely send you back to your world."

"What do you mean? You won't let me stay in Silva if I help Annabelle?"

"Please, I'm not the villain you might think," said Nebulo, waving a dismissive hand. Lan caught a bitter glance flash between Annabelle and Marlow, leaving a heavy feeling in her gut.

"Your time in our world is tenuous and dependent on fervent Longing to maintain your consistent presence. That is the case for all witches who cross worlds. From what you have told me, that deep desire to stay in Silva might drop without Annabelle's quest to spur you. Not all your Longing will dissipate, perhaps only a smidge, but even that is enough to send you packing."

Lan froze. Marlow looked horrified. Annabelle seemed simply lost.

"But I summoned the portal once," she said. "Could I do it again? Or find another in my world?"

"Certainly, but that will be up to you. No one can help. No guarantees. So I imagine you'll want some time to think it over."

"What happens if I delay?"

"Then you could stick around a while longer, enjoy all the wonders of Asta, which are endless. I'm sure your friend can wait a little longer or find another way."

Lan looked at Annabelle, desperate for direction. But Annabelle shook her head. She smiled wistfully.

"You were right from the start," she said. She crossed around the map and clasped Lan's hands. A single tear fell down her face, but her eyes were bright. "It is our quest, and I won't ask this of you. It's your choice."

"I can't do that to you," said Lan. She knew the moment she voiced the words that they were true. She'd never been able to deny Annabelle a thing. "You've been away from home long enough. I don't want to say goodbye, but if I could stay, I'm scared I'll never leave. I can't do that, so I should probably get home."

"Lan," said Marlow. He appeared by her other side. "Silva is as much your home as it is mine. You know that, right?"

"I suppose it can be many places at once." Lan tried to brave a smile but could not quite manage it. "Don't people say that we can always find a way home?"

"I wouldn't be surprised if Silva sees more of you down the line," said Nebulo. "Is this your decision?"

"It is," said Lan firmly. Nebulo nodded.

"Get them dressed and fed," Nebulo said to Mira. "Fetch Asriel and Marisa to the orchards. Use my notes from the last spell in the syllabus to gather what we need. The best time for this spell is dusk, when the borders between realms are thin. We'll reach Sol more easily."

"Understood," Mira said.

They followed her out. Lan looked back at Nebulo, bent over his enchanted map like a general preparing for war.

A SPELL FOR SOL

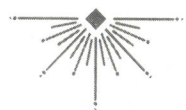

F ood will appear as you wish," said Mira, showing them into a queen-sized bedchamber. "The menu will send your orders straight down. You only have a few hours before dusk. Get some rest."

Weariness seeped through Lan's bones. Nearly a day without food was making her faint. Marlow and Annabelle were staring at her as if she might spontaneously combust. It made her uncomfortable.

"You think I'd be able to get bún riêu here?" said Lan, trying to distract herself. "Not on the menu, but we are in a magic castle . . ."

"No harm in asking," said Marlow. Lan shrugged and did her best to explain to the hovering menu what she wanted. It snorted, disgruntled, but sent her order anyway.

"Lan—" Annabelle said gently. Lan cut her off.

"It's the only way, Annabelle. I just hope it works."

"If it doesn't, we'll find another way. I believe that now, and I wanted to say thank you."

"Hey." Lan smiled. "What kind of hero would I be if I kept sabotaging the quest to stay longer? You'd hate me."

"I wouldn't hate you. In Sol, everyone makes their own decisions, even kids. We aren't put in classrooms to learn the same things for years, like you described in your world. We learn from our land and people, following whatever we're interested in or curious about. My grandmother always said the worst blow to a warrior is taking away their choice, like Nebulo did to us. So I'd get it, whatever you choose."

Lan sank on the bed at her words and began to cry. They gathered around her and wrapped her in an embrace. She could not remember the last time she had been held in this way. Not since before her family had moved. The thought made her sob harder. How could it be that Silva had come to feel more real than her own life?

"You saved me several times over," said Marlow quietly. "Every minute you practised, every chance you took... We never would've made it without you."

"Kind of seems like you saved me too. And I'm sorry I touched the stupid fruit. It felt like a shortcut..."

"I get it," said Annabelle. "If I thought it could give me what I wanted, I might've done the same."

"You've always taken the slow and steady way, Annabelle," said Marlow gently. "You're good at that."

"Maybe that's the secret," Lan murmured, "taking care."

She drew a shaky breath, then started as a bell tinkled by the table. Marlow stood to investigate. A steaming bowl of crab noodle broth materialized before them.

"No way!" Lan exclaimed. She picked up the soup spoon and took a sip. It had a distinct taste she could not place, but the right flavours were there. "This is amazing."

Marlow and Annabelle ordered their own bowls, and Lan taught them to handle the chopsticks. They were made of slippery stone, not like the wooden ones she knew.

Lan did not think that she could fall asleep, but the moment she sat on the plush bed again, her eyes fell shut. They blinked open hours later to a darkened room. Marlow and Annabelle were awake. They were whispering, their backs turned to her, but Lan could hear every word. She closed her eyes again.

"You sure you're not mad at me?" said Marlow.

"Why in Sol would I be mad? I'm thrilled! You should do it."

"But . . . we haven't been apart for five years."

"So what? You think I can't manage without you?"

"No, quite the opposite."

"Oh, Marlow," said Annabelle. There was a rustling noise. When she spoke again, Annabelle's voice sounded muffled, as if her face was buried. "I always knew you wouldn't follow me around forever. You're far too handsome for that."

"Be serious, Belle."

"*You're* telling *me* to be serious? Well, this is a change. I could get used to it."

"I'll miss you."

"I will too, but it's not like I didn't catch your longing stares back at the woods along the Paver's Road. I'm glad you're finding your own way."

A loud rap on the door made Lan start. She pretended to rise as if she hadn't been eavesdropping, rubbing the sleep from her eyes.

"Is it time?" she said.

Annabelle went to the door. "I think so."

Mira entered but sent them straight back to wash and change into the clothes she'd laid out on the armchairs. Lan had not noticed them before. Nebulo had left her a red cloak with gold trim, draped over black pants, laced boots, and a white shirt. Lan donned the outfit, and Annabelle did her braid. She twirled before the mirror. It felt like she'd been meant to wear this all along.

"You look so good," Marlow said as Lan stepped out. Annabelle, dressed in blue, had gone ahead. She waited with Mira outside the door. Marlow caught Lan's hand when she moved toward them. "Wait."

His eyes gleamed, inches from her own. Pushed back, his hair was wet from the shower, just as it had been when they'd met on the river. Lan's heart began to pound.

"What I said about Annabelle back in the clearing in the woods," he said, his voice low by her ear, "I meant it about you too. If you could stay, I'd follow you."

"Luckily for you, you get to explore on your own now," said Lan with a sad smile. "You should go back to the forest, Marlow. Make your home there. I know you want to."

"Our last night in the Hollow, I wandered off for a moment when no one noticed, just to get a feel of what it might be like all on my own."

"I noticed."

"The forest's never short on good company, you know that. The nymphs couldn't be more welcoming, and there's so much to learn, but it didn't feel the same knowing I couldn't come back to us. If I never see you again—"

"Don't think about that," said Lan sharply.

"Okay," Marlow said, understanding. He smiled reassuringly. "Then we'll talk more when you're back."

He released her hand, but his words from earlier still echoed in her head. *Silva is as much your home as it is mine.* She had felt certain about so little lately, but she knew at once that Marlow was right—that it would be home as long as he and Annabelle were present. Imagining their lives continuing without her stung deeply, and suddenly, Lan felt as though she had grown much older in her short time with them.

Together, they strode down the hall to the map room. Calm purpose came over Lan the closer they drew. The black door opened at Mira's touch, and Nebulo stood inside, surrounded by cuttings from a dozen orchard plants. The air was so thick with incense smoke that it was impossible to see the bookshelves all around. Lan squinted at the portion of the map overlooking Sol. The mist had been cleared. It wasn't perfect, but the scarred coast was visible underneath the thin fog. The ground was an unhealthy yellow-brown. Annabelle's eyes widened. She approached the spot, staring intently.

"I need your word before we proceed," Nebulo said in greeting. He gestured at an open book on the edge of the map. "Your signatures."

"What for?" said Annabelle, looking up.

"I am willing to help you, but you must not breathe a word to anyone. Sol has always lived independently. I expect that to continue. We can't have people storming the capital from all over demanding favours."

"We're only here in the first place because—"

Marlow elbowed her, and Annabelle shut up, glowering. Lan looked at Nebulo's imperious expression and realized suddenly that he did not understand, had not uttered a word of apology. His reasoning for undertaking the spell reversal was selfish—likely for the gain of Annabelle returning home and singing the praises of his skill in Sol. It irked her, but at least they were getting what they needed. Lan added her signature beside Marlow's and Annabelle's, wondering if it would mean anything if she never returned.

"Miss Annabelle—" said Nebulo.

"Just Annabelle."

"A token of goodwill, before we begin," said Nebulo. He plunged a hand into the depths of the western ocean on the map and pulled out a sand dollar. He tossed it to her.

"What is this?"

"No matter the outcome, I hope you enjoy your time in Asta, Annabelle of Sol. When you are ready to return home, break the token. It'll take you as far as Silva's borders reach, to the grounds of the Academy. You'll find your way back from there."

Annabelle nodded, clutching the spell tightly. Her mouth was set, as though she could not bring herself to say *thank you*.

"As for you," said Nebulo to Lan. He drew her arrowhead pendant from his cloak. "I was told you wanted this back. You'll need your courage for the task ahead."

"I did, I meant to ask," said Lan. She fastened it safely around her neck. "But it isn't *my* courage. It's my friends'."

"Often, they are one and the same. I find courage among the most contagious of substances. That's why I favour it greatly in my spells."

"What do you want them for anyway, the items in your price of admission?"

"I seek only to return their power to those I serve. Heart, courage, and stories fuel the strongest magic, but there is only so much a single person can provide," said Nebulo. He waved a hand at the jars lining the wall, and Lan saw through the smoke dozens of items: braided string, dried flowers of all colours, unidentifiable liquids, and crumpled pages of text. They were neatly labelled with date and time, along with names Lan couldn't quite read, and organized under shelves that read PROOF OF A HEART, COURAGE IN LARGE SUPPLY, and GOOD STORIES. Lan stepped closer and saw a jar of red poppies preserved behind shiny glass, right at the front. They were distilled into a shadowy essence, but Lan recognized them as her own. It made her feel icky to see them kept in that way, ready to be used at a wizard's whim for a spell she'd never know. She wanted to say something, but Nebulo cut in.

"If you're ready to begin," he said, "I'll need you to focus. Come by my side. What are your strengths as a witch?"

"I don't suppose growing potatoes helps us now?" said Lan, pulling herself away from the jars. "I brought down a snowstorm once, and I can summon wind well enough."

She felt the air around her fingertips and was surprised to find the residue still restricted. Nebulo did not trust them enough to give her full rein of her powers.

"Seems like you have some talent as a summoner," he said.

"A summoner?"

"A broad generalization. Some witches are more inclined toward certain modes of magic—potions, transport, healing . . . If you've gravitated toward summoning plants and even the air itself, I'll have you work on my amplifiers. Mira, guard the door from outside, please. The rest of you, stay back."

Lan approached and followed Nebulo's lead. A lavender-like residue coursed through her fingers, sticky like honey. She focused on the energy and drew a stream of power from the array of cactus and desert flowers levitating above Sol on the map. Before she could truly feel the weight of their magic in her hands, the residue flowed through her straight to Nebulo, who lifted his arms over the charred desert landscape and sent a blast of cold blue mist rolling over the dunes. Thunder cracked, and rain began to pour over the replica valley. Lan heard Annabelle draw a sharp breath. She struggled to concentrate and contain the magic from seeping into the room, drenching them all.

"Keep those amplifiers running," Nebulo said tersely.

"I've got it," said Lan through gritted teeth.

Nebulo began to whisper a spell. Lan tried to hear the words, but it soon took every ounce of her energy to hold the residue from the plants around them. They shrivelled up bit by bit, the more power she drew. The air was thick with colour and so muggy that sweat streamed down her face. She could see the land on the map heal as if in fast-forward. The rains drenched the valley and the coast. Then, around the stone villages that marked Sol, green began to blossom from the sands.

"It's working," Lan gasped. She could not make sense of the way Nebulo's hands moved over the map. The gestures were so different from her summoning.

After what felt like hours, the gold of the sands faded and gave way to pastel-coloured fields. Lan did not realize she was shaking until Nebulo lowered his arms, breathing hard. Annabelle rushed forward and stared at her home, tall grass dancing on the ocean breeze. Her hands pressed over her mouth. Lan wanted to go to her but felt like she might be sick.

"Are you okay?" Marlow said. He came over and wrapped his arm around Lan. Her limbs felt like jelly. The second she'd let go of the magic, all of it disappeared.

"I feel weak," she said. "My hands—I can't feel the residue on them anymore. Not even a spark. There was so much of it in this room before."

"You may yet recover with time," said Nebulo.

"You drew all of my power," said Lan. "I can't feel a thing."

"I warned you. It worked, didn't it?"

Lan bit back a retort. Though the spell had cost an unnatural amount of magic to reverse, she'd had the strength in her to pay—in the hopes no one ever would again. Lan looked to Annabelle. Her face was alive with wonder.

It was over.

Lan had not caught her breath when the ground below her shook. A whisper of a breeze lifted in the closed room. It whistled almost cheerily in Lan's ears. Her stomach sunk. Marlow and Annabelle rushed to her side as a storm began to rise.

HOMEWARD

"Get them out of the chamber!" Nebulo shouted to Mira. He gripped the side of the table tightly. His form flickered out of focus. "Go before her storm destroys it all!"

The heavy black door flew open. Mira grasped Lan's arms, the plume on her helmet whipping wildly in the wind.

"Hold onto me," she said. "I'm lifting you out."

"Not a word to anyone," shouted Nebulo in parting.

Mira swept her cloak around Lan, Marlow, and Annabelle. They clutched each other tightly, and the stone floor dropped from under their feet. Lan felt the familiar swooping sensation of teleporting, and her eyes opened to the empty castle courtyard. Silva's constellations stretched high above the turrets. The smell of magnolia overcame the darkening night. Mira promptly disappeared in a flash of red hair before the rising winds made leaving impossible. Lan did not let go of Marlow and Annabelle beside her.

"Thank you," Annabelle whispered. "I'll never get to repay you."

"I wouldn't count on that," said Lan. "I might have to call on you yet."

"You know where to find me."

Lan smiled, shocked that her eyes remained dry. The gales were so strong now she could barely hear her own breath. Marlow bent close and whispered something in her ear, but she could not make it out. A bolt of electricity shot through the air. Lan's hands squeezed theirs with all of her might. Her eyes closed.

The next gust hit Lan directly in the gut. She buckled over and felt a pull and thud, like someone had grabbed her and shoved her backwards. The world tilted, and she landed on something soft. For a moment, she did not move, unwilling to open her eyes. When she finally did, she saw the white plaster of her basement ceiling.

Lan lay on her bed staring up, as she'd done a thousand times before in the little house on Langdon. Someone was moving about in the kitchen. She pushed herself up on her elbows. Everything was as she had left it. From the sunlight streaming through her narrow window, it must have been noon. Lan realized with a jolt that she was back in her snowflake pyjamas. Gone were Nebulo's fine robes. Her outfit was damp and stained with dirt. She reached for her arrowhead necklace and gasped to find it there, as solid as it had ever been.

She was unhurt—not even a bit of magic sickness or a scratch on her—but she felt more disoriented than ever. How could everything be unchanged around her but quite the opposite within?

I've eaten the storm, she thought drily.

Lan got out of bed and placed her feet on the floor. It was cold and creaked as she stood—then she stopped dead. Her book lay innocently at her feet. She picked it up and stifled a laugh. Above the golden dandelion on the cover, a thin script read *Operation No-More-Desert, etc.* Annabelle's name had stuck after all.

The chocolate stain remained, and no author name appeared... But the book felt hot to touch like the lamppost portal system in

Asta right after someone teleported. Without the teeming residue that she had grown used to, Lan could tell she would not be getting to Silva the same way again. The energy of the book was different.

Lan flipped through the first chapters to the lines describing Marlow and Annabelle. They didn't do them justice, she thought. Marlow wasn't just a good shot who only cared about Annabelle; his instinct was to braid flower crowns for a strange girl to help her feel needed. Annabelle was certainly tough, but the beauty of her sweet side, which emerged by the fire at the end of a long day, was entirely downplayed. Then Lan turned to the novel's last page and saw a sketch of a towering russet crab. Above it read the line: *Daisy coasted toward her on an air wave, and Annabelle knew she was home.*

Lan smiled. She remembered the comment she had made in the castle chambers before they had begun work on the spell, when Marlow had noted that Annabelle didn't take shortcuts. *Maybe that's the secret, taking care.* She'd barely understood what she was saying in the moment, but it suddenly made sense. Her mind drifted to Marlow, soon returning to the forest for a fresh start—hopefully a place of his own. They couldn't make their new homes together, but they might still get to side by side, a world or two apart.

Lan slid into her indoor slippers, holding her breath. Steeling herself, she opened the door and paused in the hall. Had her father truly not noticed she'd been away? So much had changed that the thought of it seemed impossible. The bustling from the kitchen stopped. Bình appeared around the corner, a pair of wooden chopsticks in hand—

"Bố vừa định gọi con. It's time you're up," he said before she could speak. It was as though nothing had changed.

"I—um, what day is it?" said Lan, taken aback. "Is it Saturday?"

"What's wrong with you?" her father squinted at her, concerned. "You sick? Didn't I say we could go to IKEA on Saturday? Hurry up. Get ready. You slept so late. I already made noodles. Didn't want to wake you."

He vanished into the kitchen again. Lan drew closer and stared at him turned to the stove, his hair speckled grey. The sound of the kitchen fan roared in her ears. Suddenly, she was so overcome with relief that tears leapt to her eyes. She wanted to run in for a hug and tell her father how far she'd come from, but she stopped herself. Not just yet. For the moment, it was enough that Lan had kept her word to Annabelle and could keep her promise to Manav next Monday as well. It wasn't too late. After the journey she'd had, running a hundred metres felt like child's play.

"Don't just stand," said her dad. "Come eat. Mì is ready."

Lan pushed back the familiar rickety chair and sat, her fingers tracing the scoopy plastic spoon, chopsticks, and chipped rim of the ceramic bowl her dad set in front of her. She breathed in the smell of non-instant instant noodles, her stomach growling.

Then a sudden spark on her fingertips made her start—was it plain static or faint traces of magical residue? Lan reached through the air, searching the room as closely as she had in the western valley. Details jumped out the moment she paid attention: the stains on the checkered tablecloth, the sticky mousetrap in the corner, the crooked angle of the pantry door. A quiet hum began to vibrate in her hands. She smiled. Maybe Zephyr had been right about finding the magic in her world after all.

"I wanted to talk to you about something" said Lan's father abruptly. "That running club you mentioned."

"You mean the track-and-field team?"

"Yes, that thing. I've been thinking, it's not fair for you to be cooped up all alone. Not good for child development. If you make the team, Manav's parents will make sure you get to practices and back safely. I ran into them this morning in the yard. It's settled."

Lan choked up. She squeaked in excitement. "Are you sure it won't be too much?"

"You talk to your coaches and see. We will make it work."

Thank you did not cover it, but it was all Lan could manage. Her father smiled.

"One more thing," he said in Vietnamese. "Your mother's project is almost done. She said this morning she can see the end. If all goes well, she will join us this July with your brother. We can start looking at a different place to live than this basement."

"Are you serious?" whispered Lan in disbelief.

"We told you, right?" said her dad. He smiled. "Rôi sẽ qua nhanh."

Full of the best noodles she could remember tasting, Lan rinsed her bowl in the sink. She folded her pyjamas neatly and changed into shorts and a red Chinatown shirt, her thick hair pulled back in a braid. Her face looked clear, ready for anything. She felt stronger. It was time to picture a new home.

ONE-HUNDRED METRES

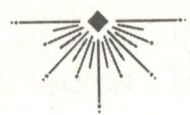

You're up next, Lan," said Manav, panting from his run. He punched her lightly on the arm. "Feeling good?"

"You bet."

"Let's save the betting till after we seal this deal," said Manav. "Speaking of which . . ."

He fumbled around in his bag and shoved a chocolate bar into Lan's hands.

"That's my end settled," he said. Then he leaned in closer and lowered his voice. "I asked my parents to give you a ride to any meets far away. I think they talked to your dad already. Hope that's okay."

Lan glanced up, surprised, hands wrapped around the chocolate. She'd assumed her father had arranged the rides when running into Manav's parents in the garden on Saturday. Manav's consideration caught her off guard.

"Oh, one more thing," Manav continued. He cleared his throat, staring uncomfortably at the ground then looking up to meet her eyes. "About what I said last week, I didn't mean to be rude. I know your dad works hard too."

"He sure does."

"Anyway, I'm sorry."

"Thank you," said Lan. She managed a small smile, unsure how to react to this not-so-bad version of Manav. To her relief, his face broke into a familiar teasing grin.

"I know how fast you are," he said. "Don't fail me."

"Don't worry about me," said Lan. "Worry about your record being beat."

"That's what I want to hear! It's so boring at the top. I'd welcome a challenge."

"Well, today's your lucky day."

Manav had run a 12.2 second tryout in the one-hundred-metre, seconds ahead of most of the kids lined up to take a shot. Segen, Lan's seatmate, came in at a respectable time of 13.1. Most members of last year's team were trying out again, with their friends watching from the benches. Lan ignored their curious gazes whenever they caught sight of her. She did not wear any of the sports gear her fellow athletes donned, rather an oversized T-shirt, tights, and beat-up sneakers. But Lan was not nervous. She'd faced worse.

The coach waved her forward to the starting line. Lan could feel the anticipation building not only in her but also in her classmates watching. A few people shouted, "Good luck!" Lan took a deep breath, her mind as clear as it was before performing a big spell. She saw the coach's hand rise, pause a second, then drop. She ran.

Lan's feet pounded on the track. She registered the crowd shouting, a few whoops and whistles, her heart thudding. All at once, the scent of ocean breeze hit her so strongly she could've been racing toward the beaches of Việt Nam, or perhaps to the sun-soaked coast of Sol—

Then it was over. The finish line was behind her, the cheers rushing back. The beep of the timer sounded to signal her tryout done.

She had held up her end of the deal with Manav. No matter the result, Lan told herself, she'd done it.

"How'd I do?" Lan asked their coach, heaving.

Wide eyes stared back at her from every direction. The coach cleared his throat, then looked down at his timer again to double-check.

"11.9 seconds," he said. He held up the clock, its digital numbers blinking. "That's a new school record."

"Yes! What did I tell you?" said Manav, jumping in the air. He patted Lan on the back. "Congrats, and welcome aboard the track team!"

Lan could scarcely believe it. Adrenalin pumped through her body, filling her with the same thrill as doing magic, practising with Phoenix and Marlow, or riding with Zephyr. People began to offer their congratulations as Lan walked off the track. She smiled back, eager to tell her parents later that night. Manav hovered over her proudly, claiming that he'd spotted her talent all along.

"So what do you think?" he asked. "Was the deal worth it?"

"You don't even know the half of it," said Lan.

"Fill me in sometime?"

"How about Monday morning at practice?"

"Sounds like a plan."

Amid the cheers of their classmates, Lan collapsed onto the school's grassy field, catching her breath from the race. The sky was a clear blue, and salty air lingered on the edges of her awareness. Her fingers brushed the grass and stems of dandelions dotting the green. Some were blooming golden with life. Others were silver and soft, ripe for wishing.

ACKNOWLEDGEMENTS

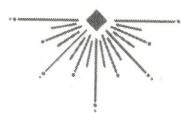

The heart of this story lives in eleven-year-old me, a new immigrant to Toronto, who began to write with the support of my grade six teacher, Nicky Ruetter. My first acknowledgement goes to her and all the public-school teachers who provided me with indispensable encouragement throughout my tumultuous teen years. I would not be a writer without you.

To the Ontario Arts Council, who generously funded my book; my agent, Emmy; and the team at HCC, who saw potential in this story when it was a second-draft manuscript—I'm so grateful. Yash, it has been such fun to work on this book with you. Thank you for your time, your feedback, and your constant reassurance and belief.

Most of all, I feel fortunate to be loved by those who stood by, long before my dreams had any guarantees: my close friends, fellow artists, and family. My parents are immigrants. They not only gave me a strong start but also agency to choose the life I want. I could not be more thrilled to be living eleven-year-old me's wildest dreams.